INTO THE FIRE

A DCI Jack Callum Mystery

Len Maynard

First published in Great Britain by LMP in 2019

www.lmp-lenmaynardpublishing.com

ISBN 978-1-9996878-5 - 4

www.lenmaynard.co.uk

Cover artwork and design by

Iain Maynard

DEDICATION

To Adrian Street, Bret Hart and the late Jackie Pallo
whose books proved invaluable to the writing of this one,
and to Roy Hudd, for the same reason.

ACKNOWLEDGEMENT

With thanks to Shara Maynard for all her technical
help in preparing this series of books

AUTHOR'S NOTE

Certain liberties have been taken with the geography of Hertfordshire for the benefit of the story. Hopefully the residents of that beautiful county, home for many years, will be forgiving.

1 SATURDAY October 15TH 1960

The MC, immaculate in his evening suit, climbed onto the apron, ducked through the ropes, and entered the ring, pulling the lead of his microphone behind him. Crossing to the centre of the ring, he stood, watching the crowd patiently, waiting for the inter-bout chatter to abate.

He waited for thirty seconds, the overhead spotlights reflecting on the pomaded hair brushed thinly across his balding head, and making the frilled ruff of his dress shirt dazzle. He gave them a few seconds more, and then raised the microphone to his lips.

"Ladies and gentlemen. The next contest tonight is a heavyweight bout, over six, five-minute rounds, with the best of two falls, two submissions, or a knockout to decide the winner." He paused for dramatic effect. "To my right, and in the red corner, weighing in at fifteen stone, three pounds, and standing six feet, two inches, from Lancashire, the Accrington Assassin, George McClusky!"

McClusky, a broad-shouldered, ugly man, with little muscle definition, and wearing black woollen trunks pulled up high to disguise his pot-belly, launched himself out of the corner, arms raised, and soaked up the applause and cheers of the excitable audience.

The MC waited for the swell of appreciation to die down, and brought the microphone to his lips again. "And in the blue corner, weighing sixteen stone, standing six feet three inches, and hailing from parts unknown, the Black Phantom!"

The level of noise in the *Stevenage Astoria* rose alarmingly, and Jack Callum settled back in his seat, a smile on his face as he waited for the booing and catcalling to calm down. *You're not a popular boy, Frank*, he thought, as he watched his sergeant, Frank Lesser, whose identity was hidden beneath a black wrestling mask, turn disdainfully from the audience, and present his outstretched hands to the referee who gave them a cursory glance as if checking for any foreign objects or sharp fingernails. The referee then took a step backwards, and allowed the Black Phantom to raise one leg at a time so the soles of his boots could be examined.

The MC watched dispassionately, as the pantomime was acted out in both corners, before lifting the microphone. "And your referee for this match tonight is Mr Teddy Bond."

There were a few jeers as the MC clambered out through the ropes, and allowed Teddy Bond to call the wrestlers to the centre of the ring to deliver his pre-match lecture.

"…and when I say break, you break the hold cleanly and fairly," Bond said, in a voice loud enough to be heard by the punters in the ringside seats. He then retreated to a neutral corner, and waited until the timekeeper bellowed, "Seconds out! Round one!" and rang the bell.

The bout never made it to the sixth round. In the third, after two rounds of nefarious tactics and blatant rule breaking, the Black Phantom delivered a flying head butt that appeared to hit the Accrington Assassin squarely in the chest, and sent the Lancashire wrestler sailing through the ropes, and out of the ring, to be counted out by Teddy Bond.

Without waiting for the MC's official announcement of his win, and ignoring the crowd baying for his blood, the Phantom made a swift exit from the ring, and trotted back to the dressing room.

Jack rose from his seat and headed to the backstage area. In one of the dingy corridors an usher stepped out in front of him and raised his hand.

"Sorry, sir. The public aren't allowed in this part the building."

Jack took out his warrant card, and waved it under the usher's nose. "I'm not *the public*," he said, and the usher moved out of the way.

Jack turned into yet another dimly lit corridor, and eventually found the dressing room. He tapped lightly on the door and pushed it open.

The room was quite brightly lit. A voice from the back called, "Queens!", and a group of wrestlers in various stages of changing in or out of their costumes fell silent, and turned to look at him with undisguised hostility.

Jack spotted Frank Lesser, sitting on a bench at the back of the dressing room, a towel draped around his neck, his mask rolled up to reveal his chin and mouth. He took a swig of water and set the bottle down beside him.

"Good bout, Frank," Jack said, walking across to him.

Lesser shook his head. "No, I was bleedin' rubbish tonight."

"I'll second that," George McClusky said, emerging, dripping wet and stark naked, from the shower. "You were miles off with that head butt. Never came close."

"You sold it well though," Lesser said. "Thanks for that."

"All part of the service," McClusky said. "You'll be back to normal once the ring rust has worn off."

Lesser reached behind his head, untied the laces of his mask and pulled it off, using it to wipe the sweat from under his arms. He looked up at Jack. "Anyway, what are you doing here, sir? If you really wanted to come and see one of my bouts you could have at least waited until I was back on form."

"Sheer chance," Jack said. "I saw the poster for tonight, and wondered how your recuperation was going."

"As you saw, I've still got a way to go. I was thinking about coming back to work on Monday though. Tonight was a try out to see if I was ready for it."

"Are you?"

"Maybe not for the ring, but I could probably do some policing."

"I'm not going to pretend you're not missed, Frank, because you are. The team are suffering for being a man down, as well as trying to break in a new chief super."

"So, they've replaced Mr Lane, have they?"

Jack nodded.

"Who with?"

"Watkins, your old governor."

Lesser rolled his eyes. "Heaven spare me. Wally Watkins was the main reason I put in for a transfer from Barnet."

"Well, no one at Welwyn nick is cheering the appointment, believe me," Jack said. "The general feeling is that Watkins sees it as an easy billet; a way of marking time until his retirement."

"Old Wally always was a lazy sod," Lesser said

"Careful, Sergeant. I'm still your DCI."

"Have you seen any evidence that says otherwise, sir?"

Jack shook his head. "Alas, no. So you see why we need the squad back to full strength."

"I'll be back in on Monday. Definitely," Lesser said, rising from the bench. "You'll have to excuse me. I need to take a shower. I'm starting to ferment."

"What did they mean when I walked in? *Queens?*"

Lesser grinned. "That's wrestlers for you. We like to keep our secrets."

"But *Queens?*"

"Queens Park Rangers – strangers," Lesser said.

"Ah. Enjoy your weekend, Frank. I'll see you Monday."

"See you, guv."

The Astoria was emptying by the time Jack returned to the main entrance, and he joined the throng of satisfied punters as they made their way across the carpeted foyer, and out through the double doors.

He walked back to the car park, but gradually he became aware of the clacking sound of high heels on the pavement behind him, matching him step for step. At a street lamp he paused under its orange glow, and looked back along the road.

The young woman following him was caught by surprise, and tried to duck into a shop doorway, but realised she was too late, and that he'd seen her.

"Can I help you?" Jack called.

The lights from the shop window illuminated her white gabardine raincoat, pale face, and black beehive hairdo. She stepped back out onto the pavement. "You're Jack Callum," she said hesitantly.

"I know," Jack said. "How may I help you?" He started walking towards her.

She opened her handbag, and rummaged inside, taking out a packet of cigarettes. She took one from the pack, and popped it between her lips. "Do you have a light?"

As he approached her, he fished in the pocket of his coat for a box of matches. He struck one, and held it in a cupped hand, allowing her to duck her head and light the cigarette.

She drew in the smoke and expelled it again, blowing it upwards for the chill evening breeze to whisk it away into the night.

"I was watching you, in the Astoria," she said. She was a pretty girl, probably in her early twenties, with heavily made up doe eyes, and full lips painted a garish shade of red.

"Why?" Jack said.

"I wanted to speak to you…but there were too many people for me to get close."

"What did you want to speak with me about? There's nobody within earshot now, so here's your chance."

The young woman glanced behind her, checking to see if there was anyone who might overhear what she was about to say.

Satisfied, she took another long pull on her cigarette, and said, "I used to go to school with Joan, your daughter."

"Really?"

"We weren't good friends or anything, but I knew who she was, and I knew who you were too, because you'd sometimes pick her up at the school gates."

"What's your name? I'll give her your regards."

"It's Dawn, Dawn Peterson, but she probably won't remember me. We only took a couple of classes together."

Jack glanced at his watch. It was pushing eleven o'clock and he'd promised Annie he wouldn't be late home tonight.

"Well, I'll be sure to mention you to her. See if I can't jog her memory. Good night, Miss Peterson." He turned to continue his walk back to his car.

She reached out and grabbed the sleeve of his overcoat. "No." she said. "There's more."

Suppressing a sigh, he turned back to her, a question in his eyes.

She took another hurried puff on her cigarette, and dropped it onto the ground, crushing it under the toe of her sling-backs. "I think someone's going to kill me," she said, the words coming in a rush.

Jack's eyes widened.

"Really," she continued. "I'm not making it up."

"I'm sure you're not," he said indulgently. "Who's going to kill you?"

"Danny. Danny Hutchence. He's my boyfriend."

"And what makes you think he's going to kill you?"

"He's going to kill me because of what I know," she said, and gave a small gasp as a black car pulled into the kerb beside them.

The driver wound down his window. "Hey, Dawn. What are you doing out so late? Hop in and I'll drive you home."

The driver was a young man with bad skin, flinty eyes, and a blond DA haircut.

"It's all right. Mr Callum here's offered me a lift." She turned to Jack, her eyes imploring him to back her up.

"Danny?" he mouthed at her. She nodded briefly.

"Don't trouble yourself, granddad," Danny said. "I can take her from here."

"It's no trouble, son," Jack said.

Danny ignored him. "Come on, Dawnie. Stop bothering the nice gentleman, and just get in the car."

Dawn looked back and forth at the two men, with panic flaring in her eyes.

Jack laid a hand on her arm. "Come on. Let's get you home." He closed his fingers, and gently steered her towards the car park.

Danny revved the car. "Dawn! I know what dirty old sods like him are like. He's only after one thing."

Jack ignored him, and hurried them along.

"Pervert!" Danny called. "She's young enough to be your daughter!"

They reached Jack's, Morris Oxford, and he unlocked the passenger door, holding it open for her to enter. "Go on. Hop in. Where do you live?"

"Graveley. Do you know it?"

"I know it."

She climbed into the car, and slammed the door behind her.

Jack got in beside her and turned the key in the ignition.

Out on the street, Danny gunned the engine of his Triumph Herald and roared off into the night.

"He's a real charmer, isn't he?"

Dawn Peterson nodded and burst into tears.

Jack rolled his eyes, found a clean handkerchief in his pocket and passed it across to her.

She accepted it without comment, and sobbed all the way back to her house.

Twenty-four hours later Dawn Peterson was dead.

2 MONDAY October 17TH 1960

The Wolseley crawled into the service road, and pulled to a halt outside the abandoned factory.

Jack looked out through the rain-spotted window. "What was this place, Sergeant?"

"No idea, sir," Frank Lesser said, shrugging his shoulders.

"I believe it used to be a print works, sir," PC Robert Meadows said from behind the wheel. "But nothing's rolled off the presses since it closed down five years ago."

Jack looked up at the dour, red brick building with sheets of exterior plywood covering the windows, and a rusting panel of corrugated iron half blocking the door. "Grim," Jack muttered, pushed open the door, and stepped out into the rain, pulling up the collar of his overcoat, and ramming his hat down more tightly on his head.

A uniformed constable stood guard at the doorway, and he saluted as Jack and Lesser approached.

"What have we got, Constable?" Jack said.

"Body of a young woman, sir. She was found this morning."

"Who found her?" Lesser said.

"Him, sir," the constable said, pointing to an old man wearing tatty clothes, his face grimy, chin covered in grey stubble, who was leaning against a low wall, smoking a roll up, and ignoring the steady rain that was slowly plastering his dirty grey hair to his equally filthy scalp.

"Vagrant, sir," the young policeman said, as Lesser wrinkled his nose in distaste. "Dosses here when the weather's bad. He phoned it in when he first arrived here this morning. Called from the phone box down there." He waved his hand airily in the direction of the public call box on the main road.

"Are you ready for this, Frank?" Jack asked.

Lesser grinned. "Nothing like jumping in at the deep end on my first day back."

"Come on then," Jack said, pushing the corrugated iron aside, and opening up the doorway. "Let's take a look."

It was dark inside the factory, and Jack switched on his torch, sweeping the beam in an arc across the floor. "Watch your step," he said, as the light illuminated the sites where the printing presses had once stood, and the bolts that had once secured the presses to the floor, but now poked out of the concrete like rotting teeth.

Lesser switched on his torch, and illuminated a tableau in the far corner of the factory: a old, dirty and blood stained mattress surrounded by four people, one of them taking photographs with a large camera mounted with an equally large flashgun.

The other figures were Inspector Eddie Fuller, DC Myra Banks and the police doctor Barry Fenwick.

Jack approached the scene, and added his torchlight to that of the others. "Do we know who she is yet, Eddie?"

It was Myra who answered. "I found her handbag, sir, but there was nothing to identify her, just her purse with three-bob in change and no notes, a twenty pack of Piccadilly cigarettes with three left in it, and no matches or lighter."

"Is that all?" Jack said.

"And a sanitary towel," Myra said, colouring slightly.

"Not a lot to go on. Did either of you speak with the tramp who found her?"

"I tried, sir," Myra said. "But I couldn't get much sense out of him. He reeks of methylated spirit and he's pretty shaken up."

"So he's got no idea who she is?"

Myra shook her head. "He says he found her like this when he first arrived here this morning, looking for a place to shelter from the rain, and that was the first time he ever set eyes on her."

"Do you believe him?"

"Yes, I do," she said. "If he'd killed her, he would have been covered in her blood. He may be filthy but there wasn't a speck of it on him that I could see."

Fuller pushed himself upright. "I think she could have been on the game?"

"What make you say that, Eddie?"

"From what she's wearing, and the amount of makeup plastered on her face."

"Anything to add, Doc?"

Fenwick looked round, swinging his torch up to shine on Jack's face.

Jack squinted, and shielded his eyes.

Fenwick lowered the beam quickly. "Sorry, Chief Inspector. I didn't mean to blind you."

"That's all right. How did she die?"

"Strangulation would be my best guess. Some sort of wire, sharp and pulled tight, like a garrotte."

"Any sign of it?"

Fenwick shook his head. "No. He must have taken it with him once he'd killed her."

Jack shuddered. "How long has she been dead?"

"Her temperature would suggest that she was killed between the hours of ten pm and two am, but we need to get her to the lab to confirm those findings. At the moment it's all speculation." Fenwick got to his feet, and turned away from the body on the mattress. "You take a look," he said.

Jack and Lesser stepped forward, and together they squatted down, and shone their lights on the victim.

"I see what you mean about the clothes, Eddie. That skirt is much too short for decency, and the blouse leaves little to the imagination. Was this all she was wearing?" Jack said.

"No sign of a coat, sir," Myra said. "She must have been chilled to the bone."

"That's what I was thinking. Even if she was on the game, what on earth would entice her to come to a dump like this to do the deed? It's hardly five-star luxury is it?"

"Did you notice that both the carotid artery and the jugular vein have been severed," Fenwick said.

Jack focused the beam of his torch on the wound to the girl's neck. "You're right. The wire's done such a good job it's virtually decapitated her."

"Which explains the amount of blood on the mattress," Lesser said. "Not much doubt about where she was killed, is there?"

"Welcome back, Frank, by the way," Fuller said. "Feeling better?"

"Much better, thanks, Inspector," Lesser said.

Jack swung the beam of the torch up to the victim's face, bent forward and pushed a curtain of jet-black hair away from her brow.

They heard him suck in his breath.

"Something wrong, sir?" Fuller said.

Jack pushed himself to his feet. "I know her, Eddie. She used to go to my Joanie's school. They're the same age."

"I'm sorry, sir. I didn't realize she was a friend of the family."

Jack shook his head. "No, it's nothing like that. According to her they barely knew each other. Shared a couple of classes with her, that's all."

"But you knew her, sir?" Myra said.

Jack nodded, "I gave her a lift home from Stevenage to Graveley on Saturday night."

Myra and Fuller exchanged puzzled looks.

"I recognise her too," Lesser said, peering intently into the young woman's lifeless eyes.

Jack looked at him. "How come?"

Lesser shrugged. "She's a ring rat; one of the many who follow us around. The boys call her 'Delicious Dawn'."

"Well, her real name is Dawn Peterson," Jack said, "and, as I said, she went to school with Joanie, so that would make her twenty-one or twenty-two. What did you call her?"

"Delicious Dawn."

"No. You called her something else."

"Ah," Lesser said, catching on. "I called her a ring rat. There's quite a posse of them. They come to all the shows, hoping to catch a fighter's eye, wanting him to buy them drinks and, if they're lucky, bestow other favours."

"Such as?"

"A knee trembler in the car park, or an empty dressing room."

Jack winced at the graphic description. "And I suppose you lot are only too happy to oblige."

"Not me, guv. I like to know who's handled my sandwich before I eat it, but the others, yes, of course. Don't look a gift horse...and all that."

Jack shook his head despairingly. "Tell me more about the ring rats. You said there is a posse of them. How many would you say?"

"In this area I'd say about eight or ten."

"Do they all know each other?"

Lesser smiled. "At a guess I'd say yes, and they're very ladylike."

"They don't sound very ladylike to me."

"What, 'cause they drop their knickers for a gin and tonic, you mean?"

"Something like that."

"I take your point," Lesser said. "But what *I* mean is, they don't encroach on each other's turf. If one of them likes a certain wrestler, she tells the others and they stay clear of him. It's a matter of honour. Like I said, ladylike."

"I might question your definition when we're not up to our necks in a murder investigation but for now, where can we find these ring rats? We'll need to speak with them."

"There's a show over at the *Hertford Corn Exchange* tonight. You'll find a bunch of them there, as sure as eggs is eggs."

"Then it looks like we're going out on a date tonight, Sergeant," Jack said.

They turned as more people entered the building.

"It looks like the forensic team have arrived at last," Fuller said, staring pointedly at his wristwatch.

"Fine, then let's leave them to get on with it. We'll go back to the station, and I'll fill you in on what transpired on Saturday night, as I can see from your faces that you're all eager to know."

There was a general murmur of agreement as they headed towards the door.

"Let's see your report as soon as you have it," Jack said to the Inspector leading the forensic team.

As they walked out into the rain, an ambulance pulled into the service road.

"I'm to accompany her to North Herts," Fenwick said. "Once the boffins have done their job."

"You don't mind hanging around that long?" Jack said.

"No, not this time," Fenwick said. "I'd hate to leave the poor girl to make the journey alone."

"An unusual show of sentiment, Barry," Jack said.

"It's my age, Jack. The older I get the more precious life becomes...and to see a beautiful young life like this one snuffed out before it has really begun breaks my heart."

"What was wrong with the doc?" Lesser said, as he climbed into the Wolseley beside Jack.

"Age, Frank. Age. I suppose it comes to us all in the end."

"Tell me about it, sir. I used to bounce back from injuries like a bleedin' rubber ball, but this chest wound has really buggered me up."

"I dare say you've never picked up a gunshot wound in a wrestling ring."

Lesser smiled wryly, and shook his head. "No. I've been attacked with hatpins and knitting needles, and even been hit on the side of the head with the heel of a stiletto shoe – Christ!

That hurt – and that's just the audience. I'm not counting the broken bones, bruises and sprains inflicted by my opponents. Usually a day's bed rest and I'm back, fighting fit again, but this…" he tapped his chest with his finger, "…this is different somehow. Sometimes it feels like I'll never fully recover from it."

"You seemed to be doing all right on Saturday night," Jack said.

"I was lucky, I was facing a pro like McClusky. Although he's billed as the Accrington Assassin, he actually comes from Wigan, and they breed them hard up there. As a young man, he trained at Billy Riley's gym. *The Snake Pit* they call it, and for good reason. Anyone who survives long enough to come though that shithole, comes out a true hooker, and with enough catch-as-catch-can wrestling knowledge to really hurt you. If he'd had a mind to on Saturday, he could have really messed me up, but like I said, he's a pro, and a good one at that. He knows there's no percentage in injuring someone so badly they can't work, because if he gets a reputation for doing that then it's only a matter of time before someone does it to him, and no matter how good you think you are, there's always someone better."

"Let's head back to the station," Jack said, and tapped Meadows on the shoulder. "Back to the nick, Bob. In your own time," he said.

3 MONDAY

They were gathered in Jack's office.

"So, she tells you she thinks her boyfriend's going to kill her for something she knows," Fuller said, "but she doesn't tell you what it is that she knows, and here we are two days later, and she's found lying on a mouldy mattress, in an abandoned factory, with her head barely hanging on by a thread."

"That's about the size of it," Jack said.

"Didn't you push her to tell you what her great secret was?"

"The journey was only ten minutes, and she was sobbing her heart out for most of them." Jack pushed himself back in his chair. It sounded inept and inadequate, even to him, and he could see from the expressions on their faces that they were less than impressed.

"Why was she crying so much?" Myra said.

"I think Hutchence just turning up on the street like that spooked her. It probably made her think he was watching her all the time."

"I can see that," Myra said. "It would probably unsettle me as well."

"What was he like, this Hutchence bod?" Lesser said.

"A pimply youth. A bit of a tearaway, but not a psychotic killer."

"Can we tell the difference these days?" Fuller said.

"I can understand you thinking that, but no, he didn't seem the type," Jack said. "I've arrested my fair share of them in my time. I have a bit of a nose for them."

"Do you think he lives in the Stevenage area?" Myra said.

"Most likely. You can run the name, Hutchence, through your system, Myra. See if you can get an address for him."

"What happens if she can't?" Fuller said.

"Then we pass his name to Uniform, and let them track him down. Let them canvass the area, the places kids like him gather. Coffee bars, and the like."

"You're not giving them much to work with, sir," Lesser said.

Jack sighed. "He has a duck's arse haircut, so that probably rules him out of the places where the beatniks and college types go. With the DA, and from the way Dawn was dressed on Saturday, and her beehive, I think it's safe to assume they were rock and roll fans. Are there any places in the area that play that kind of music? He drives a black Triumph Herald, and there can't be many of those around, they only came out last year." He was clutching at straws, and knew it.

The sight of Dawn Peterson lying dead in the print works had shaken him, and he felt a wave of guilt sweep through him. If only he hadn't been in such a rush to get home on Saturday night, he may have taken her claim more seriously.

He shook himself. "Right, let's get on with finding him, shall we? I'll go and report what we have to the chief super."

Chief Superintendent Walter Watkins reminded Jack of a corgi he'd had as a child. The dog would greet him enthusiastically, tail wagging, panting to be stroked and made a fuss of, and would then, as you tried to walk out of the room, snap at your ankles, and try to savage them. He treated Watkins with as much caution as he had shown the dog.

Watkins smiled at him from behind Henry Lane's old desk. "So, let's see if I've got this right," he said affably, rising from the desk and walking to the window to watch the rain bounce off the tarmac of the car park. "You met this young woman on the way home from a wrestling exhibition in Stevenage. She tells you that her boyfriend is trying to kill her, and you then, what? Offer her a lift home?"

"Yes, sir."

Watkins glanced back at him and frowned, the look making his forehead fold into lines, hooding his eyes, while his mouth wavered between a pout and a sneer, as if it couldn't make its mind up which form of displeasure it wanted to express.

"Did she, at any time, tell you why her boyfriend was going to kill her?"

"No, sir."

"And this morning you find the same girl, murdered in a rundown factory?"

"Yes, sir."

Watkins started to pace the floor, slowly, deliberately, repeating the entire conversation *soto voce* to himself. After circling the room, he finally returned to his chair, and settled his slight frame back down behind the desk. He folded his hands in front of him and leaned forward. "Not a very edifying tale, as I'm sure you'll agree. Not quite the apex of good policing, not to say, good detecting."

"No, sir."

"Yes, sir, no, sir. Don't you have anything intelligent to say?"

Jack flushed. "No, s…" he stopped himself. "There was a Jaguar parked on the drive at her house. A car way above her expectations, so I suspect she lived with her parents."

Watkins eyes travelled upward to meet the crinkles of his frown. "Well, they'll need to be informed. Sooner, rather than later." It was Watkins turn to pause, and then he fixed Jack with an icy glare. "You're not expecting me to break the bad news to them, I hope?"

"No, sir. I'm going to drive over there now, to tell them."

"Quite right too." Watkins adjusted the cuffs of his immaculate uniform, and smoothed his neatly cut sandy hair. "And after you've told them, you can take them to North Herts Hospital to make a formal identification."

"That was my intention, sir."

"Right," Watkins said. "It's good to see at least part of your brain is thinking like an actual policeman."

"Yes, sir."

"Well, don't just stand there like a recalcitrant schoolboy waiting to be caned. Get on over to Graveley and break the crushing news to the poor parents."

Jack saluted, spun on his heel and strode from the office.

Watkins stopped him as he walked out through the door. "Chief Inspector."

Jack turned back to him.

"ACC Hennessy warned me about you and your casual disregard for rules and regulations. I read through your file before I accepted this posting, and it read very well, so I ignored the ACC's warning." He paused and fixed Jack with another icy stare. "I realise now that was a premature action on my part."

Just like the bloody corgi – savaging my ankles at the exit, Jack thought, and made his way back to his office to get his coat.

The mortuary attendant folded the sheet down to below Dawn Peterson's chin, just enough to reveal her face, and to keep the horrific injury to her throat hidden from her parents.

"That's her," Millicent Peterson said dispassionately, staring down at her dead daughter. She was a small woman, with a pinched face, who made small bird-like flutterings with her hands as she spoke. Her husband was taller and wider than her, and his face was set in a rigid unemotional mask. He, like his wife, was staring down, but his eyes were glassy, not really focussing on what he was looking at.

Jack nodded to the attendant, who smoothly covered Dawn's face.

It was then that Wilfred Peterson cracked. With a sound that could have been from a wounded animal, the man sank to his knees, and started to sob.

"I'll give you a moment," Jack said solicitously, and stepped out of the small viewing room.

He gave them ten minutes.

The door finally opened, and Millicent Peterson led her husband back out into the corridor. "We'll go home now," she said.

"Will you be all right to drive?" Jack said to Mr Peterson. They had followed Jack here in the Jaguar and, from what he had just witnessed, he doubted that Wilfred Peterson would be in a fit state to get them home.

"I'll drive," the woman said.

"As you wish."

She reached out and grabbed Jack's sleeve. "You *will* catch the swine who took Dawn from him?"

"We'll certainly do our best," Jack said. "May I ask you one question before you go?"

Millicent nodded her head sharply.

"Did you ever meet any of Dawn's boyfriends?"

"She didn't have any boyfriends." It was Mr Peterson who answered.

"Only I spoke with your daughter on Saturday night," Jack continued, ignoring him, "and she gave me the impression that she was in a relationship with Danny Hutchence"

Millicent Peterson snorted. "Dawn? In a relationship with Dopey Danny Hutchence? Ridiculous."

"Eh?" Wilfred Peterson looked confused.

"Dopey Danny, Wilf. Irma Hutchence's lad."

"Oh."

"As I said. Ridiculous. They went to school together. Dawn would always be there for him when the other children picked on him. He was always a skinny, scrawny little kid. Dawn was his protector. Nothing more, nothing less."

"I don't suppose you know where Danny Hutchence is living now?"

She snorted again. "Of course I do. Same place he's lived for the past twenty-one years – with his mother. Three doors away from us."

It was Jack's turn to do the following.

Millicent Peterson was a very capable driver, and she handled the Jaguar smoothly, moving in and out of traffic, and obeying the Highway Code to the letter.

Jack pulled into the kerb, as the Peterson's glided onto their drive. He got out of his car, and waited until they had climbed from theirs.

"That house there," Millicent said, pointing at a house, three doors away to the left. "The one with the awful concrete bird bath, that's where you'll find Irma Hutchence, and her idiot son."

"Thank you," Jack said.

"You'll let us know when you catch whoever did this?"

"I promise I will."

"Well, good day to you, Mr Callum. It can't be easy doing the job you do."

"Days like this are difficult," he said.

"I'm sure," Millicent said, and, taking her husband by the hand, disappeared into their house.

Jack stared at the Hutchence house for a long moment, before reaching a decision, and returned to his car. He opened the door and picked up the radio, calling through to Dispatch. "It's DCI Callum. Patch me through to DI Fuller."

A few seconds later, Eddie Fuller's voice crackled from the speaker.

"Fuller here."

"Eddie, it's Jack. I've located Danny Hutchence."

"Really?" Fuller sounded excited. "Where?"

Jack told him. "Where are you at present?"

"About five miles from where you are now."

"How fast can you get here?"

"About ten minutes if I use the bell."

"Do so," Jack said. "But turn it off when you're a couple of streets away. I don't want to advertise our arrival."

He disconnected, and walked slowly back along the street. From a vantage point directly across the road, and from behind a conveniently planted lime tree, Jack surveyed the house. It all looked perfectly respectable, from the crisp net curtains, to the unblemished paintwork on the white-framed sash windows, to the immaculately painted blue front door.

He saw Fuller's Wolseley turn the corner at the end of the street, and roll slowly towards him, coming to a stop a yard away from his own car.

Fuller stepped out, and joined him behind the tree. "How do you want to handle this?" he said.

"We'll have to try the direct approach," Jack said. "There doesn't appear to be access to the rear of the house, so if he does a runner he'll have to go climbing over the neighbours' fences, and into their gardens to get away, so we should have no trouble heading him off."

"Right," Fuller said. "Let's go and pick him up."

Jack pushed open the wrought iron front gate, and they walked along the crazy-paved path to the front door. There was a garage to the right of the house, its door partially open.

"There's the Herald."

"Looks like it's just come out of the showroom. Hardly a tearaway's car," Fuller said.

"Maybe not, but its presence in the garage indicates that chummy's probably in."

The door had a gleaming, stainless steel letterbox, with an attached knocker. Jack lifted the knocker and let it drop. The door was opened seconds later by a middle-aged woman wearing a beige cardigan over a lemon coloured blouse. Her woollen skirt was a black and white hound's tooth, and her feet were encased in smart, black suede high-heeled shoes. Her black bouffant was neat, and lacquered, and her glasses were a stylish peach colour, upswept and slightly tinted. "Yes?" she said.

"Mrs Hutchence?" Jack said. "We're with the police. Chief Inspector Callum, and this is Inspector Fuller." He showed her his warrant card. Fuller did the same. "We understand Daniel Hutchence lives here. It's him we'd like to see."

"Why would you want to see Danny?"

Jack ignored her question. "Is he in?"

"You're lucky to catch him because usually he's at college, but he got a bit of a chest, so I'm keeping him off. He was very bronchial as a child."

"May we come in?"

"Of course." She stood aside to let them enter, and then squeezed past them into the freshly decorated hall. "This way." She led them along the hall.

There was a wooden barometer hanging on the wall. As he passed it Jack tapped the circular glass of the case, and watched the needle drop from *Overcast* to *Stormy*. He hoped that wouldn't be the case.

"In here." Irma Hutchence stopped at a door and opened it.

They walked into a neat and tidy living room, where a young man was sitting in an armchair in front of an electric fire with all three bars glowing red.

He was conservatively dressed in grey slacks, a colourful Fair Isle jumper, and on his feet were a pair of brown leather carpet slippers. His freshly washed, blond hair hung down in a fringe that touched the frame of his horn-rimmed spectacles. As they entered, he looked up from the book he was reading.

"Danny," Irma Hutchence said. "These gentlemen are from the police and would like to talk to you."

4 MONDAY

Fuller caught Jack's eye, a questioning look on his face.

Jack shrugged, and stared at the young man in the armchair, looking for something to connect this clean-cut youngster with the loud-mouthed lout from Saturday night.

"Do you own a black Triumph Herald?" he said.

Before Danny Hutchence could answer, his mother said, "That's *my* car."

Jack didn't respond, but saw the young man glance at Irma. "Do you sometimes drive the Herald?" Jack again addressed the question to the young man.

Danny looked at Jack uncertainly, peering at him over the top of his horn rims, and then switched his gaze to his mother.

"Would you please leave us, Mrs Hutchence?" Jack said. "The questions we have are for your son. Not for you."

Irma Hutchence bristled. "Pardon me, I'm sure," she said, and moved to the door. "After all, it's only *my* house."

Jack watched her steadily as she left the room, pulling the door shut behind her.

He turned back to Danny. "Right, lad, stop messing us about. Were you or were you not driving the black Triumph Herald that we've just seen in your garage, on Saturday night, in the Stevenage area?"

There it was, flicking across the young man's face for an instant, the same arrogant sneer he'd seen on the driver of the car the other night.

Hutchence mouthed an obscenity.

Fuller took a threatening step toward him. "Watch it."

"Or you'll do what?" Hutchence responded aggressively, but didn't attempt to rise from his armchair

"What's this, your *daytime* look?" Jack said, defusing the moment. "Where's the *Brylcreem*, the flashy clothes? Or do you keep them hidden from your mum in case she realises you're not the sweet innocent college student, but a just a nasty little yob?"

"You want to be careful how you talk to me. My dad's on the Council."

"What does he do?" Fuller said. "Pest control?"

The sneer came back with a vengeance. Danny took off his glasses, swept the blond fringe from his face, and the reversion to the yob was complete

"Do you know Dawn Peterson?" Jack said, taking back control of the questioning.

The sneer was replaced with a surly look, that was equally unattractive. "What if I do?"

"Just answer the question."

"I know her."

"Where were you yesterday evening?"

"Here, watching *Sunday Night at the London Palladium* with my dear old mum."

"Who was top of the bill?" Fuller asked.

"Do I get a *Crackerjack* pencil if I get this right?" Hutchence said.

"Just answer the question."

Hutchence looked from Jack to Fuller.

"Adam Faith."

"What song did he sing?"

"He did a stupid duet with that mug Bruce Forsyth. *Poor Me*. Poor *us* more like."

"Anything else?"

"*What Do You Want?* That was the name of the song. I'm not asking you."

"Is he right?" Jack asked.

Fuller nodded.

"So you were in all evening?"

"Ask mum. She'll tell you."

"We will," Jack said.

"Why were you asking about Dawn?"

"Because she was killed, yesterday evening."

Hutchence flinched. "Really? Stone me." Suddenly all the bluster vanished, and he shrank back into his seat. "How was she killed?"

"That doesn't concern you at the moment," Jack said. "When I spoke with her on Saturday she was very distressed, and scared."

"Why?"

"She told me you were going to kill her."

Hutchence's jaw dropped open.

"Well, what do you say to that?"

Hutchence's mouth worked, as if he was trying to find the right words. "But that's stupid," he managed at last.

"Is that all you've got to say about it? *It's stupid?*"

Hutchence nodded his head. "I'd never hurt Dawnie. I like her."

"You didn't appear to like her much on Saturday night. In fact I'd describe your attitude as positively aggressive," Jack said.

The light of recognition flashed in the young man's eyes. "You're that bloke," he said. "The one who offered her a lift?"

"That's right."

"The bloody pervert."

Fuller moved towards him again. "I've told you once. Watch your lip."

Hutchence moved further back in his chair, as if wishing it would swallow him whole.

"All right, Danny. Let's start again." Jack said. "Dawn told me on Saturday that you were going to kill her, because of something she knew. Do you have any idea what that something was?"

"Search me," he said, and then retreated still further, in case Fuller took him at his word.

"So, Dawn had no reason to think you were going to kill her?" Jack said.

Hutchence shook his head vigorously.

"Yet here we are, two days later, and Dawn Peterson's lying dead, strangled with a wire that nearly took her head off," Fuller said.

The colour drained from the young man's face, as if he was the one that had suffered the injury.

"This isn't fair," he said weakly. "You're asking me about something I know nothing about."

"How would you describe your relationship with Dawn?" Jack said, lowering his weight onto the arm of another chair.

"What do you mean?"

"Would you describe yourself as her boyfriend?"

The young man looked slightly bemused. "What do you mean?" he said again.

"As in boyfriend and girlfriend," Fuller said patiently. "Love's young dream? Romeo and Juliet?"

Hutchence shook his head. "No, nothing like that. We were mates. That's all."

"That's not how she saw it," Jack said.

"Dawnie was a bit confused about it," the young man said.

"I wonder why."

"Look. We've known each other since we were kids. We used to play together. One of her favourite games was Mummies and Daddies."

Fuller raised his eyebrows.

Hutchence shook his head. "No, no nothing like that," he said quickly. "We used to play at being grown-ups, living together, her cooking me dinner, me pretending to eat it…that sort of thing. Just stupid kid's stuff." Tears were pressing out of the corners of his eyes, as if the memories were almost too much to bear. "She would always be talking about weddings and honeymoons; showing me pictures of brides in magazines that she'd collected. Mum was no help. I caught them once or twice, sitting at the kitchen table, gushing over the photos.

'Ooh, you'd look nice in that one, Dawn,' or 'That one would really suit you, Dawn.' It used to drive me nuts."

"But you had no romantic leanings in that direction."

"I'm not a poof, if that's what you're saying," Hutchence said hotly.

"I wasn't for one moment suggesting that you were," Jack said.

"Well, you wouldn't be the first. I used to get teased something rotten. No one would believe I could be friends with a smashing looking girl like Dawnie and not be giving her one."

"You weren't sleeping together then?" Fuller said.

"Like I said, we were just mates, that's all. If she thought there was something more to it, then it was all in her head." His voice was rising in volume the more agitated he became.

"Okay," Jack said in an effort to calm him down. "We'll take your word for it. Your mum didn't know you were using her car on Saturday night, did she?"

"She works nights on Saturday, and the factory lays on a coach for their shift workers. She gets it every week, so the car's always free. I just make sure the petrol's topped up. That way she never knows I use it."

"Ingenious," Jack said. "What courses are you taking at college?"

"Bricklaying and joinery."

"No academic courses then?"

"Eh?"

"The college teaches you practical skills, not book learning."

"I can't be doing with books."

"You're reading one at the moment," Jack said, nodding to the one lying open on the side table next to the armchair.

Hutchence picked it up, and handed it to him.

"*Plumbing For Beginners*," Jack said, reading the spine.

"I'm going to build my own house one day. I only read about stuff I'm interested in."

Fuller smiled. "Building a love nest for you and Dawn perhaps?"

"Leave it out. Stop with all the Dawn and me stuff. I told you, we were just mates. If you want to know about her love life, go and talk to the grunt and groan boys she really fancies."

Fuller look blank.

"He means wrestlers," Jack enlightened him. "Dawn was a ring rat, isn't that right, Danny?"

"It's all she ever went on about. Who was fighting next week, how she was going to blow all her money following certain wrestlers from town to town. She was obsessed." The sneer on his lips was one of disgust this time. "It's how I knew she'd be at the Astoria Saturday night. Last year she was following Joe Cornelius. *The Dazzler* she called him. Went to every match of his that she could get to. Christ, she even hitchhiked down to Brighton once just to see him fight, and slept on the beach. That's how bloody potty she was for him, if you know Brighton beach – it's all pebbles and stones."

"He wasn't fighting on Saturday," Jack said.

Hutchence shook his head. "Like I said, that was last year. She went off the *Dazzler* after she saw him on the telly, and he got disqualified. I don't know who her latest obsession was."

"Okay, Danny. I think we're finished…for the moment. Just make sure you're available if we need to question you again."

Hutchence nodded. "Sorry about what I called you on Saturday," he said as they walked to the door. "I didn't know you were a copper, and I was just steamed up. She did that to me. Bloody wrestlers! What chance did I stand?"

"I thought you said you were just mates," Fuller said.

"Not from choice," the young man said gloomily, picked up his plumber's instruction manual, and started flicking through it morosely.

"Well, what did you think of him?" Jack said as they returned to their cars.

"An inadequate little squirt," Fuller said, slipping the key into the lock of the Wolseley.

"I agree. A bit sad really, but not our killer."

"I wouldn't count him out just yet," Fuller said. "Jealousy is a great motive for murder."

"Yes, but look at the way she was killed. Do you know what kind of strength it takes to garrotte someone as efficiently as she was?"

Fuller shook his head

"A lot, I assure you. Trust me, I know. Hutchence hasn't got the physique for it."

"But a wrestler might have? Is that what you're saying?"

"Let's just say I'm not ruling it out."

"We need to investigate Dawn, and her life style," Fuller said.

"I totally agree. What she told me on Saturday could all be invention. She seems like a person who invented scenarios in her head, and then tried to act them out to make them real. Her fantasies about marriage, her practice runs by playing house with Danny, the crushes she developed on the wrestlers, all these things speak of someone who had a very active imagination."

"And had difficulty separating fantasy from reality."

"Precisely. No, we start with Dawn and her dreams, and see where it takes us," Jack said.

"How do you suggest we do that?"

"I'm starting tonight. There's a wrestling match over at the *Hertford Corn Exchange*. I'm going along there to see if I can talk to the girls who share Dawns delusions – other ring rats."

Fuller looked at him questioningly. "I don't fancy your chances. Why on earth would they talk to you?"

"Because I'm not going on my own. Frank Lesser's coming with me."

"He's only just come back to work. Chucking him in at the deep end, isn't it?"

Jack smiled. "He's ready, believe me. He can recognise the ring rats, and tell me the right things to say to get them talking."

Fuller scratched his head. "I can't believe we're investigating something that's a fraud from start to finish. Have you ever watched it on TV? Everything about it screams 'fake' to me."

"When you watch John Wayne in a western, you don't really believe he shoots the bad guys do you?"

"That's different."

"No, Eddie, it's exactly the same. It's entertainment. It's the willing suspension of disbelief. That's all these guys are doing. For the people who watch these spectacles they can identify with the good guys, and they can boo and jeer the villains who, for them, represent their boss, the bank manager, the bully they had to deal with at school. You're talking about a very basic human response. White hats and black hats. It gives people a clear side to root for. That's the reason it's so popular."

"I still don't get it," Fuller said.

"Then come along tonight and see for yourself, if you're free that is."

Fuller thought about the offer for a few seconds. "Sod it! All right. I'll come along. You never know, I might learn something."

"There's always a chance," Jack said "I need to have another word with the Petersons. I'll see you back at the nick."

5 MONDAY

Jack rang the doorbell, and after a few moments, Millicent Peterson opened the door. "I thought you'd gone."

"Yes, I apologise. A couple of questions occurred to me, and it seemed foolish to go all the way back to the station only to have to come and see you tomorrow. May I come in?"

"I suppose so." She led him into the house, and through to a comfortably furnished sitting room.

Wilfred Peterson was standing at the window, staring out at the garden. He didn't turn as they entered, and gave no indication that he was even aware they were there.

"Is your husband all right?" Jack said quietly.

"He will be." She stared across at Peterson, her expression unreadable.

"I'm sorry," Jack said. "What I'm about to ask you is a little...er...delicate."

"It can't be any worse than telling us our daughter's dead." Millicent Peterson was stony faced.

"No, of course not. The thing is, when I told you this morning, both you and your husband reacted with shock."

"How would you expect us to react?"

"You must have known that your daughter didn't come home last night."

Millicent shook her head. "She never came home on Sunday nights."

"Why would that be?"

"Because she worked the night shift at Boswell House on Sunday, and on a couple of nights during the week."

"I see," Jack said. "What exactly *is* Boswell House?"

"A residential home for the elderly, in Stevenage. Dawn was a night carer there."

"So, she was a nurse?"

"Not a nurse. A carer."

"I'm sorry I don't think I know what you mean."

"Nurses are trained. They have qualifications. Dawn just used to help out with the practical needs of the residents – make their tea, sit with them to keep them company, organise games to keep them amused. That sort of thing."

"She was a saint." Wilfred Peterson spoke at last. "Nothing was too much trouble for her." He continued to stare out of the window.

"Well, that clears that up," Jack said. "I don't suppose you have a recent photograph of her I could take? I'll see it's returned to you."

Millicent crossed to the sideboard, and pulled open the top drawer. She returned seconds later, holding a silver picture frame. She unclipped the back and took out the photograph and handed it to him. "This was taken last year in a booth on the front at Bournemouth."

"Thank you. That will do fine. Right," he said. "I think I've taken enough of you time, and again, may I offer my deepest condolences. Good day." He tipped the brim of his hat.

Once in the car he put the photograph down onto the passenger seat, and sat staring at it. "A saint?" he mused. "I wonder if you were."

He started the engine, and pulled away from the kerb.

He dropped the photograph onto Myra Banks' desk. "Get me a few copies of that," he said. "And start an incident board."

Myra picked up the photo, "Pretty girl," she said.

"She was."

"Apart from the eyes."

"She had beautiful eyes," Jack said.

"But there's nothing behind them. No spark."

Jack took the photo from her and studied it hard for the first time. "I see what you mean," he conceded. "They're a bit blank."

"I see a lot of sadness there," Myra said. "She wasn't a happy girl."

"Well, she certainly wasn't the last time I saw her alive. She spent most of the time sobbing her heart out." He passed the photograph back to her. "Three copies and one for the board."

"Do you have anyone else to join her on the board?"

He shook his head. "Early days, Myra. Early days."

"Very good, sir," she said, and started to rise from her seat.

"Not so fast. I haven't finished yet. What do you know of Boswell House in Stevenage?"

Myra settled back into her seat. "It's a retirement home for old theatricals."

"Old theatricals?"

"Yes, sir, people who once trod the boards – entertainers, music hall comics and clowns, singers and dancers. It's a bit like Brinsworth House in Twickenham, or Denville Hall in Hillingdon, only cheaper."

Jack looked at her open mouthed. "How do you know all this?" he said, shaking his head.

"My dad, sir. Old-time music hall and variety theatre are a bit of a passion of his. I think he harboured ambitions of going on the stage himself when he was younger, until he met my mother anyway, and she soon knocked any fanciful notions like that out of him, but he watches *The Good Old Days* religiously every week, and sings along with all the songs. He's quite a good tenor."

The Good Old Days, broadcast weekly from the City Variety Theatre in Leeds, was one of the television programs Jack had managed to avoid watching so far, but he'd seen a snatch of it, with a woman on a stage, trying to give an impression of Marie Lloyd to an audience dressed in period garb representing Victorian and Edwardian England. He remembered being unimpressed and switched it off.

"I can give pretty good renditions of *My Old Man* and *Daisy, Daisy* myself actually, and have done when I've had a few drinks."

"Then remind me to avoid you when you're drunk," Jack said with a smile. "As you know so much about the place, pop on over there later, and ask them how well they knew Dawn Peterson, and whether she was there on Sunday evening. Apparently, she was one of their occasional care workers. Copy the photograph first though."

"Will do."

Boswell House stood in its own grounds on the northern outskirts of Stevenage. Set in a few acres of rolling lawns and coppices, it was an attractive Edwardian building with a number of wings. There was nothing at all oppressive about the place. Quite the reverse in fact. Even the journey up to the front of the house was pleasant and picturesque, with neat, well-tended flowerbeds lining the drive, and an ornamental pond at the end of it, complete with a fountain featuring stone sculptures of woodland nymphs spouting sprays of water with carefree abandon.

She passed a large, dark blue sign with gold lettering.

Boswell House Retirement Home.
Bringing sunshine to your later years.
Proprietor: Elise Gerard.

Myra could see the attraction of the place for those in their twilight years.

She parked her car, and made her way up the steps to the red-painted front door. There was another sign. This one had simple black lettering on a white card. PLEASE ENTER. She pushed open the door, and stepped inside.

A bell tinkled, and a second later a comfortable-looking woman wearing a beaming smile appeared behind the reception desk. "Hello, dear. May I help you?"

"I'm looking for Elise Gerard," Myra said, returning the smile.

"Well, you've found her." The woman clasped her hands together delightedly.

"My name is Myra Banks. I'm a detective constable with the Welwyn and Hatfield police."

The smile was unshakeable. "Are you indeed? That sounds like an awful lot of responsibility for a young woman like yourself."

"I manage," Myra said.

"I'm sure you do. You look very capable. Now, how can I help you?"

"It's about one of the people you have working here. Dawn Peterson."

"Dawn? Why on earth are you asking about her?"

"I'm afraid Miss Peterson was found dead this morning."

If Myra had punched the woman in the stomach the effect would have been just as dramatic. She staggered, and clutched the desk for support. "How shocking," Elise Gerard breathed.

"I was wondering when you last saw her."

Elise made an effort to gather herself. "I think you'd better come along to my office." She came out from behind the desk. "This way." She led Myra though the foyer and down a brightly lit corridor, with doors leading from it on either side. One of the doors was open, and Myra peered in as they passed. There was a group of a dozen or so elderly people sitting in a semi-circle around a piano, while another aged resident played a tune Myra didn't recognise, but that didn't stop the others singing along with gusto.

They reached Elise's office, and the woman unlocked the door, and pushed it open for them to enter. Once they were both inside she closed it behind them, and locked it again. "So that we're not disturbed," she said. "Please take a seat."

While Elise sat behind a small functional desk, Myra found a chair pushed up against the wall. She pulled it out, and dragged it across the floor to the desk, sitting down so she was facing the woman.

"So, when was it?"

"Eh?"

"That you last saw Dawn?"

Elise seemed distracted. She was picking at her bitten nails, and staring at them as if they offended her in some way. "Thursday," she said. "I said goodnight to her when I left here on Thursday evening. She was due in yesterday, but she didn't show up for work. I assumed she was ill."

"What can you tell me about her?"

"What would you like to know?"

"What was she like? Was she good at her job? Did the other members of staff get on with her? Did the residents like her?"

Elise Gerard focussed. "What was she like? I would describe her as charming and eager to please. Was she good at her job? Yes, extremely. Some of our guests can be difficult and quite trying. Some of them have peculiar little ways, probably habits they picked up when they were working the halls, but Dawn never showed them anything but kindness and patience." From her desk drawer she took out a packet of cigarettes, took one out and lit it, blowing smoke up at the ceiling. "I shouldn't smoke," she said. "It's not something I encourage with our guests. If they have to, I ask them to smoke in their rooms, or out in the garden, and not to inflict it on other guests. Where was I?"

"Did the other members of staff get on with her?"

"Because she worked evenings and nights, she didn't come into contact with many of them, but I never had any complaints from those who did."

"And the residents?"

"Well, of course, many of them were asleep when she was on duty, but if you really want to know whether she was liked or not, you'd be better off speaking with Leo Keating. He's one of our longest serving guests, and I know that he and Dawn spent hours in conversation, sometimes up until one o'clock in the morning."

"Where can I find Mr Keating?"

"I'll take you along to his room. He won't be with the others in the morning room. Sing-songs aren't really his cup of tea." She ground the cigarette out in a glass ashtray, and got to her feet. "Come along." She led Myra from the office, down the length of the corridor, and turned right at the end, into another passageway. At a door about halfway along she stopped, and knocked politely with her knuckles. "Leo? Are you there?"

She took a step back as the door was wrenched open, and a small man with grizzled white hair, and a heavily lined face stuck his head out of the room. "What do you want?"

"I have someone here who would like to speak with you."

"Go away." The grizzled head withdrew, and the door started to close.

"It's about Dawn, Leo. This young woman would like to speak with you about Dawn."

The door opened again, and Keating stepped out, looking Myra up and down approvingly. "Why didn't you say so," he said to Elise gruffly.

"I'll only take a few moments of your time, Mr Keating. It's very important."

"You'd better come in," Keating said to Myra. "And you can take as long as you like. They cancelled my luncheon appointment at the Palace. Seems that the Queen has the sniffles." He gave her a gap-toothed grin. He held the door open for her to enter, closing it quickly in the face of Elise, who had made a move to follow Myra inside.

6 MONDAY

Leo Keating's room was surprisingly large, bright and comfortable. As well as the single divan, there was a small wardrobe, a chest of drawers, a table and two chairs. French windows gave onto the garden, and there were smooth-fronted radiators affixed to two of the walls, making sure the temperature in the room was comfortably pleasant. There was no television, but a wooden wireless sat on the chest of drawers, a copy of the *Radio Times* lying open next to it.

Two of the walls were covered in colourful theatre playbills, and above the bed was a small gallery of photographs, some of people who bore a striking resemblance to Keating, and other older snaps, some signed and inscribed, some not, including one of Max Miller, the comedian, in his gaudy suit and hat, the only face familiar to Myra in a sea of strangers.

On the playbills, Keating's name was writ large, indicating that he was often top of the bill.

The old man noticed Myra's interest in the memorabilia. "I was a *siffleur*," he said proudly.

"A what?"

"*A siffleur*. A whistler. Not many of us made the top spot. Me and Ronnie Ronalde had it pretty much sewn up between us. That Eva Kane would never have got a look in today if we were still around, but then most people go to hear her sing, not to whistle. No one would pay to hear me sing. Like a donkey with laryngitis, that's me. But to hear me whistle…even song birds listen and take notes."

Myra smiled indulgently.

"Leo Keating – 'Whistle a Happy Tune'. That was my bill matter. Of course, Oscar Hammerstein nicked it in the fifties, and used it for a song title in the *King and I*, but I was using it forty years ago!" he said, feigning outrage, but giving her the gappy grin again. "Now, Dawn. My little ray of sunshine, I call her. What do you want to know about her?"

"You'd better take a seat, Mr Keating. I'm afraid I have some very bad news."

"Dead? I don't believe it. I was only talking to her in this very room on Thursday."

"I'm afraid it's true," Myra said.

Keating pulled a large handkerchief from his pocket, and used it to dab the tears from his eyes. "It's not fair," he said. "I'm eighty-two! Why didn't He take me instead of her? She was just a child, with the rest of her life in front of her. He should have taken me!" He slapped his hand on his knee angrily. "How did she die? No, don't tell me! I want to remember her just as she was. Bright, funny, so quick to laugh at an old man's jokes."

"You two had quite a bond?" Myra said, reaching out and covering Keating's liver-spotted hand with her own.

"Oh, I know she was only doing her job – getting paid to humour an old man and his waffle – but I felt that we really connected, that she sat with me way into the small hours, not because the rules of her job demanded it, but because she was *enjoying* spending her time with me, as much as I was enjoying her company."

"What kind of things did you talk about?"

Keating had sunk down onto the edge of the bed. Myra pulled a chair across from the table and sat opposite him, so that their knees were almost touching.

"All this," he said, waving his hand at the wall of playbills. "I'd tell her about my years in the halls; the people I worked with, all the characters I knew through the years. Funny stories mostly. Especially about that bugger there." He pointed to the photograph of Max Miller. "Pardon my French. But Max and me, we had some rare old times. He was a lot younger than me, of course, but that didn't matter."

"What did Dawn talk about?" interrupting the old man before he could launch into a monologue of reminiscences.

"Wrestling, mostly."

"Wrestling?" Myra said.

"Professional wrestling. Not so different from my world, if you think about it. Larger than life characters, speciality acts; she told me about one of them who calls himself the Wildman of somewhere or other – I can't remember where now. Lots of mad hair covering his face, and animal grunts…but still wears woolly maroon swimming trunks and wrestling boots." Keating chuckled. "As I say, not a million miles away from my world."

"Did she ever talk about her love life? Boyfriends, that kind of thing?"

The smile slipped from the old man's face to be replaced by a darker expression. "No, she didn't, and if she had, I certainly won't be repeating anything she told me. That was in confidence, and I won't betray her trust."

"Even if it means we catch the man who killed her?"

"Dawn was killed? As in murdered?" Keating blanched his voice incredulous.

"I'm afraid so."

He put the handkerchief to his eyes again, and rocked back and forth on the bed. Myra tentatively put her hand on his knee. "I'm sorry," she said. "I didn't mean to give you such a shock."

Keating took the handkerchief away from his eyes and stared at her, anger in his eyes. "If you find who did it, just leave him in a room with me for five minutes. I'll tear *his* heart out, just like he's torn mine from me." He swore, with no apology this time, for French, or for something more Anglo Saxon.

"I'd better go. I'm sorry again," Myra said, getting to her feet and walking to the door. Keating followed.

She had her hand on the doorknob when Keating said, "There *was* one chap she told me about."

Myra returned to the bed, and sat down again.

"Over the past few weeks Dawn talked about him a lot. So much so that when she didn't come in on Sunday, I assumed she was seeing him."

"Did she tell you his name?"

The old man shook his head wearily. "No names, but I think he was connected in some way to her passion, the wrestling."

"He was a wrestler?"

"Or just a spectator, a fan like herself. She was never clear about that. Is that of some help?"

"It could be," Myra said. "Thank you, Leo."

Keating looked at her bleakly, and took her arm, squeezing tightly with gnarled fingers. "Catch him for me, and for Dawn. She was such a lovely girl. She shouldn't have died like that."

Myra leaned forward and pecked the old man on the cheek. "We'll certainly try, Leo. You have my word," she said.

"You're home early," Annie said as Jack walked into the living room.

"I'm not stopping," Jack said. "I'm afraid I have to work this evening. I hope I'm not spoiling dinner."

"It's only leftovers. I was going to use up the rest of the beef."

"Sorry."

"Don't worry. I haven't even peeled the potatoes yet. What is it you're working on?"

"A case," Jack said with a smile. "Have you seen my binoculars?"

"Why? Does this case involve bird watching?"

"Something like that. Do you know where they are?"

With a sigh Annie dropped her paperback to the floor, and got to her feet, crossing to the sideboard. She squatted down and opened the bottom drawer, taking out a brown leather case. "Here," she said, handing it to him.

He took it and flipped open the lid, taking out the binoculars and hanging them around his neck by the leather strap.

"Come on," Annie said. "You've got to tell me where you're going."

"I'm going to the *Hertford Corn Exchange*."

"What's on?"

"Wrestling."

"Again? You only went on Saturday. You're not becoming a *fan* are you?"

Jack laughed. "No, nothing like that."

"Only I don't want you glued to the television every Saturday afternoon, watching semi-clad men hurl each other around a boxing ring."

"Saturday night was different," he said. "I was watching Frank Lesser, and checking to see if he was fit enough to return to work."

"And tonight?"

"Like I said. Work."

She wrapped her arms about his waist. "A girl could feel neglected, you know?"

"Tell me her name and I'll make sure she isn't."

"Beast!" she said, and gave him a playful slap. "What time will you be in?"

"About eleven if it's anything like Saturday. So don't wait up."

"Long gone are the days where I sit up waiting for you to grace me with your presence."

"Not too long gone, I hope."

"You'll just have to wait and see," Annie said, and then something flared in her eyes. "You *will* be home on time tomorrow, won't you?"

"I should be. Why?"

"Rosie's coming to dinner."

A smile split Jack's face. "Really?"

"Yes, really."

It was three months since their youngest daughter got back in touch with them after running away from home. Although it was lovely that she had, and a lot of their heartache had been assuaged, it was still early days. Contact with her was sporadic, and bridges were still being built. Her coming to dinner, and spending some time with them was a huge leap forward.

"Paul is driving them over. They'll be here about seven."

Jack's face darkened. "Paul's bringing her?"

"How else is she going to get here from Harrow? Of course he's bringing her."

Jack's sudden dark mood deepened as he thought about the young man whom he held responsible for Rosie absconding in the first place.

"You *will* be nice to him, won't you?"

"I'll make no promises."

"Please, Jack." Annie stared up at him, her eyes beseeching him.

He let the anger go and relaxed. "Okay. For your sake, I promise." He smiled at her reassuringly. "What will *you* have to eat tonight?"

"The leftovers of course. Eric will home soon and the beef wants finishing up. What about you?"

"Don't worry about me. We'll pick up fish and chips on the way to the *Corn Exchange*."

"*We'll* pick up fish and chips? Who else is going?"

"Eddie and Frank."

Annie rolled her eyes. "I see. So really it's a boy's night out. You'll probably end up in a pub somewhere, if I know Eddie Fuller."

"I promise you, Annie, my love, my pet. Not a drop of alcohol will pass my lips."

"You know I'll smell it on you if you're lying, so you'd better not be."

"Cross my heart," Jack said.

She shook her head. "Go on, get out of here, before I change my mind and kick up a stink."

"You wouldn't," he said.

Her eyes narrowed. "Do you really want to test that theory?" She reached up, and gave him a brief peck on the lips before pushing him towards the door. "Go on, scram."

"See you later," he said, blew her a kiss and left the house.

7 MONDAY

The first bout had already started by the time they arrived at the *Corn Exchange*. A large SOLD OUT board was attached to the door and when Jack pushed it open, a burly usher rushed across from the ticket booth to block his entrance. "Can't you read?" he said menacingly.

"Yes, I can read. Can you?" He pulled out his warrant card, and held it under the usher's nose.

The man stepped back. "All the seats have gone. You'll have to stand at the back."

"Suits us," Jack said, and led the others through the double doors into the auditorium.

There was already a line of people standing at the back of the hall, so the three men edged a few of them along, and stood against the low wall.

A wrestling ring had been erected on the stage, and was lit by harsh overhead spotlights. Microphones had obviously been fitted to the ring floor because, as the wrestlers moved around, their feet thudding on the canvas-covered boards boomed out into the arena.

Jack watched the action. The wrestlers were both young men, small and lithe, and they threw each other around, ran back and forth across the ring, running and hurling themselves off the ropes, and missing each other by inches as they crossed in the centre.

The audience's apathy was almost palpable. Most of them were chatting amongst themselves and, for the most part, ignored the valiant efforts of the wresters to entertain them.

Lesser shook his head. "They're wasting their time. Two blue-eyes. No heat. They may as well call it a day."

After another five minutes of lacklustre action, one of them caught the other in some kind of leg hold. The striped shirted referee hurriedly slid to the mat and asked the boy in the leg hold if he wanted to submit. The boy nodded his head furiously. The ref pointed at the timekeeper who rang the bell, ushering in the Master of Ceremonies, a thin, weedy-looking man wearing an evening suit and glasses, who put a microphone to his lips and announced the winner to a smattering of polite applause.

"Like I said," Fuller sneered. "A load of bollocks."

"That was just the warm up. Wait for the next bout," Lesser said.

The next match certainly promised better.

First out of the wings was a tall, dark-haired man with a thin goatee beard. He was dressed entirely in black – boots, leotard and tights – and appeared to a chorus of jeering and booing. He entered the ring, and scowled at the audience.

The next to arrive was a good-looking youngster with blond, wavy hair and a toned physique, who sprang impressively over the top rope, and climbed onto the ropes attached to the corner post, raising his arms and letting the crowd's cheers of adoration wash over him.

The MC made the announcement, pointing to the preening young man and introducing him as "the local hero, from Hertfordshire, Bobby Lee."

The ecstatic audience cheered even louder.

"Now watch," Lesser nudged Jack, and pointed to movement in the first two rows of the audience.

Within moments a small group of women had left their seats and gathered at the wall of the boarded-over orchestra pit, slapping their hands on the boards and yelling out to Bobby Lee.

"See?" Lesser said. "Ring rats."

To make sure that the crowd knew who to cheer, as if they needed any more confirmation, the MC announced, "And his opponent tonight, from Dagenham, 'Nasty' Norman Lane!"

The black-clad wrestler punched the air, and gave the crowd a bigger scowl.

The cacophony of derisory whistles and shouted obscenities made Jack flinch.

The match started and Jack put the binoculars to his eyes, but he wasn't watching the wrestlers. Instead he focussed on the rats. There were seven of them, ranging in age from sixteen to sixty. He watched them closely as they screamed and shouted at the fighters, banged their fists on the boards, and tried to make themselves as conspicuous as possible, presumably to catch the eye of their adored target.

If it was the local hero they were trying to attract then they were badly out of luck, because "Nasty" Norman was pummelling their boy mercilessly, throwing him around the ring like a rag doll, using every dirty tactic in his arsenal to inflict pain and suffering, and the more Bobby Lee suffered, the louder their screams of protest became.

Jack picked out the two young women closest in age to Dawn Peterson, and pointed them out to Frank Lesser.

"They're the two we want to talk to," he shouted in Lesser's ear, trying to make himself heard over the din.

Lesser nodded. "Leave it to me." He peeled away from the wall, and made his way down the aisle to the front of the auditorium.

Through the binoculars Jack watched his progress. Using his six foot plus frame as a psychological battering ram, Lesser moved easily through the throng at the front of the stage, and approached the ring rats, separating the two Jack had selected from the others. Within moments he had engaged the young women in conversation

"As easy as that," Jack muttered, and turned his attention back to the fight.

The match was about to enter the fourth round, and all seemed lost for Bobby Lee. For fifteen minutes he had absorbed the most terrible battering, and was now panting, sagging against the ropes in the corner while his second gave him water, and tried to revive him by flapping a towel in his face.

The second stepped out through the ropes, leaving his charge still hanging in the corner, looking as if he was at death's door.

The bell sounded to signal the start of round four, and "Nasty" Norman flew out of his corner, charging across the ring like a belligerent rhino. With a split second to spare Bobby Lee spun out of the way of Lane who crashed into the padded turnbuckle and rebounded back towards the centre of the ring. Lee, quick to capitalise on his opponent's badly timed misfortune, ducked down behind him, and let the bigger man topple over him, and land flat on his back. Moving like greased lightning, Lee threw himself on top of him, and pinned his shoulders to the floor. The referee, who was proving himself to be as agile as the wrestlers, threw himself to the mat and delivered the three count.

The winner, by the only fall required, the local hero, Bobby Lee.

The audience went wild, cheering and stomping their feet, laughing as a groggy and not so nasty Norman Lane sat up with a bewildered expression on his face.

Fuller was laughing as well. "Total bollocks!" he said. "What a bloody charade!"

Jack glanced round as Lesser appeared next to him, his mission an apparent success.

"We're meeting them in the bar during the interval," he said. "They're willing to talk to you."

"How did you manage that?"

Lesser grinned. "I promised them I'd introduce them to Bobby Lee after the show, and they went for it."

"Do you think you can keep that promise?" Jack said.

"Without breaking a sweat," Lesser said. "I know Bob. We train at the same gym, and he owes me a favour or two."

Jack chuckled. "This world of wrestling never ceases to surprise me."

The MC was entering the ring to announce the next contest.

"Come on, let's go to the bar, and see if we can get a table before the break comes, and we find they're all taken."

"Good idea," Lesser said over the sound of the MC making the introductions. "We're missing nothing here. It's a tag match. Mick McManus and Steve Logan against the White Eagles, and the Eagles are going to lose."

"How do you know?" Fuller said.

"Because McManus wields the pen in the office. He's the bloody matchmaker. He's not going to let himself get beaten and ruin his reputation."

Fuller shook his head and opened his mouth to speak.

"I know, Eddie." Jack stopped him. "Total bollocks."

Frank Lesser went to the bar, whilst Fuller and Jack found a table in the corner. There were four seats at the table, and Fuller pulled one across from the table next to theirs. Moments later Lesser appeared carrying a tray containing three halves of bitter, and two port and lemons.

"The girls should be here in a moment. The match has just finished."

As his words died there was a hubbub from outside. The doors were pushed open, and a crowd of excited wrestling fans poured into the room and jostled their way to the bar.

Lesser stood up and scanned the doorway, spotted the rats and beckoned them over.

"Ladies," he said, as the women made themselves comfortable in their seats and picked up their drinks "These are the two gentlemen from the police who would like a word with you. Jack, Eddie, this is Candice and this is Joyce. Have I got that the right way around?" he asked the women.

They nodded, and giggled.

Close to, they were both older than Jack had guessed from viewing them through the binoculars. Candice was the youngest, but whereas he had estimated her to be in her early twenties, under the harsh barroom lights, the faint lines and wrinkles around her eyes made her look a decade older. Joyce suffered more from the harsh lighting. She was forty if she was a day, and even her hands were showing signs of age, especially the third finger of her left hand, which bore the tell-tale marks of wedding and engagement rings recently removed.

Jack took the photograph of Dawn from his pocket and laid it on the table.

Candice leaned forward to look at it, giving Fuller a flash of the ample cleavage beneath the cream blouse she wore. "That looks like Dee-Dee. What do you think, Joy?"

Joyce stared down at the photograph. "Yeah, that's Dee-Dee."

"Dee-Dee, for Delicious Dawn," Fuller said.

Joyce scowled. "She hates that nickname. She calls herself Dee-Dee because she says it stands for Dawn Delivers."

"Well, it stands for Dawn's Dead now," Fuller said bluntly.

Both women recoiled in shock.

"You're kidding," Candice said. "When?"

"When did she die? Sunday evening or Sunday night, or it's even possible it was the early hours of Monday morning," Jack said. "When did you last see her?"

"Saturday, at the Stevenage Astoria. She seemed fine then."

Jack nodded. "Yes, she was. I saw her there as well, but something happened between then and Sunday evening that led to her being killed."

"So, it wasn't an accident," Joyce said, her face serious.

"I'm afraid Dawn, sorry, Dee-Dee was murdered."

"Oh, good God!" Joyce said, and crossed herself.

Candice looked as if she might be sick. She was shaking her head slowly. "I knew it," she said softly. "I knew it."

"What did you know, Candice?"

"That it would end badly. I warned her that she was jumping out of the frying pan…"

"And into the fire," Joyce finished for her.

"Okay," Jack said. "Let's start from the beginning, shall we? How long have you known Dee-Dee?"

"She started hanging around with us just over a year ago," Joyce said. "She was following Joe Cornelius then. Potty about him she was, though Lord knows why."

"He's very good looking," Candice said.

"I suppose, if you like them swarthy. Looks too much like a gypsy to me…and he's a bit old."

"He's not old," Candice said.

"Well, he is for me."

"Just because you prefer them with bum fluff and nappy rash."

"Bitch!"

"If we can try to stay on track," Jack said.

"Well, pardon me for breathing," Joyce snapped.

"More drinks, ladies?" Lesser said smoothly, reaching out and picking up their empty glasses. They had finished their port and lemons with the speed of professional drinkers.

"So," Jack said, "You knew her for over a year. Did anything about her change recently? Candice, you said that you warned her about jumping out of the frying pan."

Candice nodded her head. "Yes. I warned her to stay away from him, but she didn't listen, just told me to mind my own business."

"Come on, love," Fuller said, losing patience. "Give us a name."

Candice paused, leaning towards her friend and starting a whispered conversation.

Eventually they parted, and Candice looked at them directly. "Dougie. Dougie Marshall."

"Is Marshall another wrestler?"

"Well, if he is, I've never heard of him," Lesser said, as he returned to the table with the drinks.

"No," Joyce said. "That's the funny thing. He wasn't a wrestler, never had been. I couldn't see what she saw in him myself."

"Oh, come off it, Joy. You know full well what the attraction was," Candice said.

"There was never any proof that Dee-Dee was using."

"Using?" Jack said. "Was Dawn taking drugs?"

"Well, I never saw…"

"Ignore Joyce," Candice said. "She has her head buried in the sand most of the time."

"I do not."

"Yes," Candice said, cutting across her friend's protest. "Dee-Dee wasn't only taking drugs she was swallowing them like *Smarties*. It's why she was always in a funny mood. One minute she'd be up, manic like, the next she'd be in tears, threatening to end it all. You're not trying to tell me, Joy, that she was right in the head?"

"I suppose you've got a point," Joyce said grudgingly.

"Do you know what drugs she was taking?"

"I saw them in her hand once. Little blue pills. Triangle shaped."

"*Purple Hearts*," Lesser said.

"When did she start using them?" Jack said.

"About six months ago, just after Tommy Apollo gave her the heave-ho, and told her he didn't want her hanging around him anymore."

"Is Tommy Apollo a wrestler?"

"Yes, and a bloody good one," Candice said.

Frank Lesser confirmed it with a nod of his head.

"Okay," Jack said. "She got the brush off from Apollo and what, fell into the arms of Dougie Marshall?"

"Not at first," Candice said. "She carried on going to Tommy's matches, just hanging around, making herself obvious. In the end it all got too much for him so he belted her one."

"He struck her."

Candice nodded. "Tommy isn't what you'd call a gentle, caring type of bloke."

"He's a brute," Joyce said. "He doesn't mind hitting women. He probably kicks cats for fun as well."

"He can be a bit violent," Candice agreed. "I know when he hit Dee-Dee it wasn't the first time it had happened. That's why, when she finally accepted that Tommy didn't want her, and she hooked up with Dougie, I tried to warn her off. Tommy's violent, and a bit of a sod, but he isn't a criminal. Dougie, on the other hand, has been in and out of remand homes, borstals and prisons since he was a kid."

A bell rung loudly in the bar, telling patrons that the interval was over, and the second half was about to begin.

The women gulped down the remainder of their drinks.

"Thank you, ladies. It's been informative," Jack said.

Candice looked at Lesser. "Did we do all right?"

"You did fine. Yes."

"You'll still introduce us to Bobby?" Joyce said.

"I promised, didn't I?"

Smiling broadly the young women nodded their goodbyes, and bustled back to the auditorium.

"I'd say that the mission was successful," Jack said to Fuller.

"We'll have Dougie Marshall on file somewhere."

"Do you want to stay for the second half?"

"What do you think?"

"What about you, Frank?"

Lesser shrugged. "Promises to keep," he said. "Don't worry, I'll get a lift back with Bobby. He only lives half a mile away from me. So it's not out of his way."

"See you tomorrow, then."

"Yeah, see you, guv, Eddie."

"Inspector please, Sergeant, or Sir," Fuller said.

Lesser stared at him for a long moment before he realised that Eddie Fuller was joking, and then he smiled. "Yes, sir," he said, and gave a mock salute.

8 TUESDAY October 17TH 1960

It was standing room only in the squad room as Jack gave his report on the events of the previous evening.

The mood was generally light-hearted, and there were even a couple of off-colour jokes at Frank Lesser's expense. Lesser took the ribald cracks with good humour, and threw a rolled-up piece of paper at one of the perpetrators, bouncing the paper ball off the man's shiny forehead.

"Here, watch it!"

"Okay. Okay. Settle down," Jack said, restoring order. "Myra, how did you get on at Boswell House?"

Myra was seated at a desk. She leaned back in her chair and folded her arms. "Well, sir, listening to your report about Dawn Peterson was odd. It's as if you were talking about a completely different person to the girl who worked at the home. Phrases like, sweet, kind, conscientious and, in one case, a little ray of sunshine, don't match with the picture you've just painted of a promiscuous, drug-addled depressive who thought only of her own pleasure and personal gratification."

Jack stared at her, nodding thoughtfully. "Right," he said. "So, what does that tell us about Miss Peterson?"

"Split personality," someone called from the back

Jack rubbed his chin thoughtfully. "That's a possibility," he said. "Or are we just dealing with a fragile, young women, so uncertain of who she is that she can mould herself to suit whatever company she's keeping. The Dawn Peterson I met on Saturday night did not strike me as a drug-addled hedonist, but then neither did she appear to be a 'little ray of sunshine'. All I saw was a frightened young woman, desperately reaching out to whoever she thought could help her and, as far as that's concerned, I failed her miserably, because twenty-four hours after spilling her heart out to me, she was lying dead in an abandoned factory, killed in the most gruesome way imaginable. So now we have to do something to prove to her that her death wasn't in vain, that it meant something, and that she's not just another statistic in the monthly crime figures," He caught Myra's eye. She was nodding in enthusiastic agreement.

"So," he continued, "Where do we start?"

"We pull in Dougie Marshall for starters," Eddie Fuller said.

"And Tommy Apollo," Lesser said.

"Well, that's very much your department, Frank. I'll leave you to deal with it."

"Eddie, go and have a word with Bob Lock, and see if he can provide Marshall's criminal record which, according to Candice, is pretty extensive."

"And me, sir?" Myra said.

"Dig up what you can about Boswell House. There are drugs involved in this case, and I should imagine the home has its own dispensary. They must have, to be able to cater for the elderly residents' medical requirements. Find out who had access to it, and whether or not Dawn was ever left in charge of it. She must have got her supply of drugs from somewhere. Boswell House seems the most obvious place to start. Oh, and Frank, isn't there a monthly wrestling magazine?"

"There are a couple, sir."

"Well, get on to them, and see if they can't conjure up a decent photo of Tommy Apollo. Our incident board is looking rather sparse. We need to populate it."

"And you, sir?" Fuller said.

"Although I said I wouldn't, I'm going back to have a word with Dawn's parents, and while I'm at it, I'll have another chat with Danny Hutchence and his mother. They saw Dawn on a regular basis. If she was taking drugs, they might have noticed something. Any other questions?"

Amid much shaking of heads, the squad dispersed, and went back to their on-going cases.

"Sir," Myra said, as the room emptied.

"Yes, Myra?"

"How deep do you want me to dig into Boswell House? I think some of the residents there are in a delicate state."

"I want a full excavation, Myra. How is it funded? Who is the medical supervisor? Get them to provide a list of all the staff working there. I know the residents are a bit fragile, so be discreet – discreet but thorough. Just try not to cause any coronaries or strokes."

"I'll get on it right away, sir."

"Yes," Jack said. "I thought you might."

"Morning, Bob," Eddie Fuller said, as he walked into Collator Bob Lock's basement office.

Lock put his bacon roll down on the plate and wiped his lips with a handkerchief. "Good day, Inspector. How may I help you this morning?"

Fuller sank his weight into a chair on the opposite side of the desk. "Does the name Dougie Marshall mean anything to you?"

A gleam appeared in Lock's eyes. "Do you know how long I've been waiting for one of you lot to come down here and ask me that?"

"You've heard of him then."

"Dougie's been on my radar since he was ten years old. I've watched his criminal career develop since they first pulled him in for stealing other kids' bikes and selling them on. He was sent to a remand home for that. Westdene in Bishops Stortford, do you know it?"

Fuller shook his head.

"Not surprising. The place burnt to the ground about three months after Dougie arrived there."

"You're not suggesting that he had something to do with it, are you?"

"Well, here's the funny thing," Lock said, taking a bite out of his rapidly cooling breakfast roll. "When it happened, the fire was put down to an accident, faulty electric wiring or some such. It was only as the years went by, and Dougie's name started dropping onto my desk with alarming regularity, I began to suspect that he might have had a hand it. Do you know, he was arrested and charged with arson on no fewer than four occasions."

"Did the charges stick?"

Lock shook his head. "No, the slippery sod managed to avoid conviction every time – a combination of a slick lawyer, and an inept prosecution case each time. I started to wonder if he was ever going to be brought down."

"And was he?"

"Oh, yes. Back in '53, he got done for a handful of car thefts. Your old governor at Stevenage, Charlie Somers, cracked that one. Got Dougie sent to borstal for a year. Since then he's been in and out of prison like a yoyo.

"Either his brief got tired of his continual offending and stopped trying to get him off, or maybe it was a case that Dougie's run of luck just ran out on him. Whichever it was, he's spent over half his life in one institution or another."

"Has there been anything in the last year?"

"Only one that I heard of. He was arrested outside the gates of St John's Primary School in Knebworth on suspicion of selling pep pills to the pupils, but they turned out to be nothing more than sulphur tablets, and he was conning the kids, so he was let off with a warning, and told to keep away from every school in the area."

"Do you have his file?"

Lock swallowed the last mouthful of bacon roll, and got up from his desk, going across to one of the filing cabinets lined up against the far wall of the office. He pulled open a drawer, and rummaged through its contents,

"Here we are," he said, returning to his desk. He handed Fuller a brown folder about two inches thick.

Fuller hefted it in his hands. "He *has* been a busy boy," he said. "Is there an up to date photograph in here?"

Lock grinned. "There are photos taken after every conviction. He can't have changed much since the last one. That was two years ago, when he got six months for receiving stolen property."

"He only got six months for that? With a record like this?"

"Read the trial report, and notice who was on the bench. Judge Manners."

Fuller rolled his eyes. "*Milky* Manners? If Jack the Ripper came up when he was presiding, he'd let him off with a slapped wrist and probation."

"Or a stiff talking to."

"Beaks like him make our lives that much more difficult," Fuller said bitterly.

Lock nodded in agreement. "And the lives of criminals like Marshall that much easier."

"You said it, Bob."

"Don't you realise that you're just prolonging the agony," Millicent," Peterson said.

"Yes, and for that I sincerely apologise, but I'm afraid that in investigating Dawn's death, some things have come to light that require me to ask you some more questions," Jack said.

"Then you had better come in," Millicent said, with a look of patient resignation. "I'm afraid Wilf's still in bed. There's no rousing him this morning. Come through to the kitchen, and I'll make us a cup of tea."

Jack followed her through the neatly decorated house to the rear, and entered the kitchen. Millicent crossed to the gas cooker, and lit the ring under the kettle. Jack sat down at the Formica-topped table.

"What questions do you have?" she asked, as she busied herself spooning tea leaves into the pot, and lining up cups and saucers.

"Did you notice any change in Dawn's behaviour in the past year?"

Millicent pulled a cigarette from a pack lying on the counter, and lit it with the cooker's gas wand. "Apart from her being a pain in the neck, no, nothing in particular." She drew in a lungful of smoke, and let it dribble out through her nose.

"Did you and your daughter get on?" Jack said, catching the edge in Millicent's voice.

"Dawn was my step-daughter, and no, relations between us have never been what you would call rosy since Wilf and I first got together. I think she resented me for replacing her real mother, and was never shy about making me aware of it."

"I see," Jack said, as he watched her pour boiling water into the pot.

"I'll just let that brew for a while," she said, and set the steaming kettle down on the cooker.

"What happened to Dawn's real mother?"

"She ran away with the insurance man when Dawn was seven, and left Wilf to bring her up, which he did, to his credit, as well as any man could. But it was when Dawn hit her teens that the trouble started...of course that coincided with me appearing on the scene."

"Where did you and Wilf meet?"

Millicent took a long pull on her cigarette, and flicked the ash into the sink. "I was working at the greengrocer's in town, and Wilf would come in once or twice a week, and then one day we just happened to start chatting. I think it was a bit of a slow day, and he seemed in no hurry to get going. Our eyes met over a pound of runner beans, and the rest, as they say, is history." She stubbed the cigarette out in a saucer, and immediately lit another one. "I knew Dawn. I'd served her a few times, but I'd never really paid her much attention. Boy, was that about to change!" She gave a harsh laugh, and poured the tea, setting the cups down on the table in front of him.

"Teenage girls can be difficult sometimes," Jack said.

"Do you have any kids yourself?"

"I have two daughters, and a son."

"My sympathies," Millicent said. "Milk and sugar?"

"Just milk."

"I tried to love her, for Wilf's sake if nothing else. But I think she had too much of her real mother in her, and we clashed on almost a daily basis."

"I see," Jack said. "So, when she got the job at Boswell House I suppose it was a relief."

Millicent shook her head. "It didn't make much difference to me. She insisted on working nights, so I still had to put up with her during the day. In the end I got my old job back at the greengrocer's, just to get me out of the house, letting her have the run of the place, so Lord knows what she used to get up to when I wasn't here. Nothing good, I'm sure."

Jack sipped his tea. "You're not painting a very flattering picture of her," he said.

"I'm not going to lie to you, Mr Callum. I'll leave that to Wilf. He only ever saw his daughter through very rose-tinted glasses. All that nonsense about her never having a boyfriend... She had boys. Of course, she had boys. Had them here during the day when I was at work, and they had her too I suspect."

Jack ignored the loaded comment. "How did she get to work?" he said. "It's a fair distance from Graveley to Boswell House. Did Wilf take her in the Jag?"

"At first, but then she started getting the bus. There's a stop at the end of the road, and the number eighty-three takes you to the gates of Boswell House. She started catching that because I think she saw it as a way to get her independence."

"Did she get the bus to work on Sunday?"

Millicent nodded. "Well, she left the house at a quarter past six in time to get it, so I can only assume so. It's the only service on Sunday evenings, and she couldn't be late for it, so she was in a bit of a rush."

"Do you remember if she was wearing a coat?"

"Her raincoat, yes."

"Was that the white gabardine mac she was wearing on Saturday?"

"That's right."

"Yes," he said. "I remember it."

"I thought it made her look like a Parisian streetwalker," Millicent said unkindly.

9 TUESDAY

Myra spent a productive morning on the telephone, making calls to the County Council, and to national organizations and charities, slowly building up a comprehensive picture of the infrastructure of Boswell House. Her final call was to Elise Gerard at the House itself.

"Mrs Gerard, this is Detective Constable Banks. I came along to see you yesterday concerning Dawn Peterson."

"I remember," Elise Gerard said. "I don't think Leo Keating has quite recovered yet." There was a note of criticism in her voice.

"Is Leo all right? He was pretty cut up at the news."

"He'll get over it, I'm sure," she said dismissively

"I need something from *you* now," Myra said.

"Oh?"

"Yes. I need you to compile a list of all the staff who work at Boswell House."

"*All* the staff? Why ever would you need that?"

"Just procedure," Myra said lightly. "Could you have it ready for me if I call by in, say, half an hour?"

"I'm very busy," Elise said. "Tuesday mornings are a very hectic time for us."

"It *is* very important."

There was a pause on the other end of the line. Eventually the woman came back. "I'll need a bit longer than that."

"An hour?"

"I suppose I can arrange it by then. Is that all?"

"No," Myra said. "I've been looking into Boswell House and, although you're listed as the proprietor, you actually co-own the place with a Mr Duncan Farlowe. Is that correct?" She could almost hear Elise Gerard bristling.

"Duncan's my business partner, yes. Why is that of any concern?"

"Will he be there when I come in an hour? I'd like to speak with him."

"Why on earth would you want to talk to him? As I said, he's my business partner. He has nothing to do with the day to day running of Boswell House. That's down to my staff and myself."

"Like I say," Myra said. "It's just procedure. I's dotted, tee's crossed."

"Sounds like a funny business to me."

"But necessary. Will he be there?"

"No, he won't." There was almost outrage in her voice.

"Then can you add his address to the list you're compiling for me? As I said, it's very necessary."

"Well, I can't see why, but yes, I'll add his address to the list."

"Splendid," Myra said. "I'll be with you in an hour."

Elise Gerard rang off without a goodbye.

"And a good day to you," Myra muttered, and replaced the receiver in its cradle.

"Did you find out anything interesting?" Eddie Fuller said, as Myra hung up.

"It could be something, or nothing," Myra said, stretching her arms wide. She had been sitting in the same position for over an hour and there was cramp in her elbows, and a crick in her neck. She told Fuller what she had discovered. "That in itself is nothing spectacular, but Elise Gerard's reaction to my questions about this Farlowe chap was quite interesting. She didn't want him involved in this at all, and didn't seem keen on giving me his address, which is a bit suspicious, don't you think?"

"It could be. What do we know about him?"

"Apart from his name, absolutely nothing, but, after hearing her reaction, I certainly want to find out more. She's piqued my curiosity."

"Fair enough," Fuller said. "I've known you long enough to trust your instincts."

"Thank you. Any luck tracking down Dougie Marshall?"

Fuller pointed to the thick file on the desk in front of him. "I'm still working through this lot. I called one number we had for him but it's been disconnected. If I don't have any joy with the others we have, I'll take Harry Grant and go and pay a visit to his last known address."

"That's a big file," Myra said. "What is he, some kind of criminal mastermind?"

"If he is, then he's a pretty inept one. He can't seem to drop a piece of litter without being arrested for it."

"Maybe he's just unlucky."

"Maybe," Fuller said. "Or maybe he's just useless. Some people just aren't cut out for life as a career criminal."

"We'll go into my office," Elise Gerard said, as Myra walked through the door at Boswell House, "and we'll keep this as brief as possible. I have a lot to do."

"Do you have the list?" Myra said, as she sat at the office desk.

Elise pulled open a drawer, took out a sheet of paper, and slid it across to Myra.

Myra picked it up and scanned down the list, "Ah, good. You added Duncan Farlowe's name."

"It's what you asked for, isn't it? But as I told you over the phone, Duncan has nothing to do with the running of the House. Will that be all?" She started to rise from the desk.

"Do you have a dispensary here at Boswell House?" Myra said, stopping Elise mid-rise. The woman flopped back into her seat. "Yes, we do."

"And who supervises the treatment, and prescribes the medication?"

"Dr Maitland in Walkern."

"I'll need his contact details as well," Myra said, sliding the paper back across the desk.

"I can't see what any of this has to do with Dawn's death." Elise scribbled down the doctor's details.

"Investigations are continuing," Myra said blandly.

"Well, Dr Maitland prescribes the medication for the residents, but I take overall control, making sure there are no mistakes."

"Who has keys to the dispensary?"

"Only me."

"What happens if you're not here?"

"I'm always here."

"But what if you're suddenly called away, perhaps a family emergency, or an important engagement that you have to attend?"

"Then I see to it that a senior member of staff has access to the keys should they need them."

"And did Dawn ever have access to them?"

"No," Elise said, her voice rising. "What an absurd suggestion. Dawn Peterson was a junior member of staff…a very junior member of staff. To suggest that she would have access to a room filled with potentially lethal drugs is frankly ridiculous, and I'm surprised that you could even suspect such a thing. I monitor every pill that leaves the dispensary, and the doses are stringently monitored. Now, is there anything else?"

"I don't think so."

"Then I'll bid you good day, I've had quite enough of this meaningless twaddle."

"Mrs Gerard, a young woman has been murdered when she should have been here working for you. I wonder if you would tell her parents that her death was meaningless twaddle."

Elise Gerard coloured, but said nothing. Instead she stared at Myra, as if willing her to leave.

Myra got to her feet. "Well, that will be all…for now," she said, and walked from the office.

As she crossed the foyer to the front door, Leo Keating caught her eye. He was standing just inside a corridor, peering out and watching the proceedings but making sure he was unobserved. He made a quick beckoning motion.

Myra hurried across to him. "What is it, Leo? Is there something you wish to tell me?"

He put his finger to his lips. "Not here. Come along to my room."

Intrigued, Myra followed him along one corridor and, like before, down the passageway where his room was situated. "Come inside," he said opening his door. She stepped into the room, and he turned and locked the door behind them. "I heard you asking the old dragon about Farlowe."

"That's right. Were you eavesdropping, Leo?"

He shook his head. "No, I was earwigging."

"Okay," she said, wondering what the difference was.

"She made it sound as if Farlowe has nothing to do with this place."

"She did."

"Poppycock. He's as involved here as she is. It was mostly his money that got this place started. He has a vested interest, and he comes here regularly to see that his investment is being looked after. Why she felt she had to lie about that is anybody's guess."

"Did he know Dawn?"

"He was here on Thursday evening at the same time as she was, so yes, he knew her. He's got an eye for the ladies, that one. And let's face it, Dawn was a very pretty girl, just the type he goes for really."

"What else can you tell me about him?"

Keating's eyes lit up. "I'll go one better. See that case?" He pointed to an old brown suitcase perched on top of the wardrobe. "Help me get it down."

Myra pulled a chair across the room and placed it at the side of the wardrobe. Using his shoulder to balance herself, she climbed and reached up for the suitcase. It was heavy, and it took all her strength to lift it down.

She dropped it onto the bed. "What on earth have you got in here, Leo?" she said, breathlessly.

"A life," he replied. "*My* life." He slid back the catches, and the locks flipped open.

Myra sat down on one of his chairs and watched as he rummaged through the contents of the case, taking out random objects and depositing them on the bed. Eventually he exclaimed. "Got you!" and lifted out a large, bulging book, with paper covers.

He laid it on the bed, and sat, opening it and flicking through the pages. From where Myra sat, she could see it was some kind of scrapbook, with pieces clipped from newspapers, more playbills, and a collection of photographs.

After a few moments he called her over to him. "Here, look at this."

Myra sat next to him on the bed.

He had opened the book on a browning, press cutting, showing a young couple; him with saturnine good looks, dark polished hair, a thin moustache, and wearing an evening suit. Her, astonishingly pretty, with fine cheekbones, spun gold hair, and dressed in a diaphanous gown.

Underneath the image was a line of text. *Duncan Farlowe and Elise Gerard, headlining at the Palace Theatre, June 1934.* Myra looked closer, and realised that this young beauty, and the motherly woman running Boswell House, were one and the same. "How extraordinary," she said.

Keating was nodding sagely. "I thought you'd be surprised. Farlowe and Gerard. He was a tenor, and she a soprano. They were no Anne Ziegler and Webster Booth, but I reckon they ran them a close second."

"What happened? When did they stop performing?"

Keating's good-humoured eyes narrowed into slits. "Some would say that they never did, but in reality, they packed up a few years after this was taken. They disappeared for ages, amidst rumours of breakdowns and alcohol problems, and then they resurfaced five years ago, when this place opened its doors.

"I gave up the stage – or I should say – it gave me up, in '55, and I booked myself in here, to live out my remaining time in relative comfort. Imagine my shock when I realised that the woman running the show was none other than the same Elise Gerard of the beautiful voice, and even more beautiful face. It took me some time to even recognise her. Of course, I knew her from her publicity photos, but we'd never played on the same bills, and the image I had of her in my head was of a sweet natured beauty, who looked like an angel, not a fat old harridan, who was as sweet natured as Mussolini."

"Quite a shock," Myra agreed.

"She'd like me out of here, I'm sure, but, as long as my cheques keep being cashed, I think she'll tolerate me for a little while longer."

"Are they married?" Myra asked.

"If they are, she didn't take his name. She remains Elise Gerard, but then that's not so unusual in our game. People are rarely who they say they are. My real name, for instance is Leopold Kozlowski. My father was a Polish tailor who settled in England in the last year of the nineteenth century. He was the one who taught me to whistle. When I was a kid, I used to watch him sewing the buttons on suits, whistling Polish folk songs as he did so."

"And you're sure Farlowe is a regular visitor here?"

"At least three times a week. He takes community singing on Wednesday afternoons. I don't attend for obvious reasons." He closed the scrapbook, and dropped it back into the suitcase, shutting the lid and snapping the locks. He looked up at Myra. "If you could…"

"Of course," she said, and lifted the case from the bed.

"The other thing she lied about was the pills."

Myra expelled air through clenched teeth as she hefted the case back on top of the wardrobe. "What do you mean?"

"All that guff about carefully monitoring the residents' medication. Look." He pulled open the drawer of his bedside cabinet. He took out an Old Holborn tobacco tin and opened it. Inside were thirty or forty small white tablets."

"What are they?" Myra said.

"They're supposed to help with my indigestion. I get heartburn something shocking."

"But you don't take them?"

"I used to. I was taking them for months, and was feeling pretty awful, really listless and tired, so I stopped. I didn't let her know of course. She would give me my dose, and I would palm the buggers, and slip them into my tin when she wasn't looking.

"Let me see."

He handed her the tin.

"Was it only you who got the tablets?"

Keating chuckled. "No. Everyone gets them. She hands them out like sweets, and the poor blighters here swallow them down, as if she's doing them a huge favour."

"But instead she's drugging them. Why?"

"To keep us docile, so no one can make demands on her and ruin her peaceful existence. It works too. Living here is like living with the undead. 'Yes, Mrs Gerard, no, Mrs Gerard, excuse me while I shuffle off this mortal coil, Mrs Gerard'."

"Why don't you leave, Leo?"

"To go where?" He shook his head. "Anyway, I'm not the only one. There are a few of us who know what the old cow's game is, and one day, sooner rather than later, we're going to scupper her, and Duncan-mister-ever-so-posh-Farlowe."

"Did you tell Dawn any of this?"

"Oh yes. Dawn knew what was going on."

She closed the lid of the tobacco tin and handed it back to him. "I'd better go, Leo," Myra said. "I'll try to sneak out without being seen, so she doesn't know I've been to see you."

"Probably a good idea." He smiled. "It's all a bit *Bulldog Drummond,* isn't it?"

Myra smiled, and kissed his cheek. "Thanks, Leo."

"Do please call again," he said, and winked at her.

"I will." she said. "Don't worry."

10 TUESDAY

Myra sat in her car on the drive outside Boswell house, a notebook on her knee, into which she was scribbling furiously.

There was a sharp rap on the window. She wound it down.

"I thought you left twenty minutes ago," Elise Gerard said accusingly.

"Just using the time to write up my notes," Myra lied.

Elise harrumphed, turned and stalked back into the home.

Myra switched on the engine and eased out of the drive.

Danny Hutchence opened the door, saw it was Jack on the doorstep, and immediately tried to shut it again.

Jack put his boot in the way. "Don't be like that, Danny. Anyone would think you don't want to see me."

"I don't."

"Hard luck." Jack pushed the door, sending Hutchence staggering backwards,

"I'll come in then, shall I?"

Hutchence moved away from the telephone table that had saved him from falling on his backside, and nodded his head,

"Good. I'll take that as an invitation," Jack said, and stepped into the house, making his way to the living room. "Is your mum not in today?"

"She's shopping."

"Getting you something tasty for lunch, I suspect. Something to build you up, and get you over your cold. Only you don't have a cold, do you, Danny? You're swinging the lead."

Panic flared in Hutchence's eyes.

"I thought so. The question I have to ask myself is, why?" Jack sat down on a hard seat. "There you are, taking college courses in bricklaying and joinery and reading a book on plumbing, for the sole purpose of building your dream house, yet here you are, squandering your opportunity to make life better for yourself by faking a cold, and getting your mum to write a sick note for you."

"She didn't write a note."

"But I'll bet she phoned the college to tell them you wouldn't be in because you were sick."

Hutchence avoided his eyes.

Jack shook his head. "You really are pathetic, you know?"

Hutchence curled up in his armchair, using it again as some kind of protection.

"Okay. Tell me why are you dodging college?"

"He said he'd kick my head in if I didn't stop seeing Dawn."

"Who did, Danny?"

"This bloke. He was waiting for me outside college on Friday. Cornered me behind the bike sheds."

"Does 'this bloke' have a name?"

"Doug or Dougie, something like that."

"What do you know about him?"

"He's a hard nut," Hutchence said.

"Anything else?"

"He does drugs, and sells them to the other students."

"Is this Dougie a student himself?"

Hutchence shook his head. "But he hangs around the college a lot."

"And Dougie threatened you because you were seeing Dawn?"

"How many more times have I got to tell you? We were..."

"Just mates. Yes, I got that. But Dougie didn't believe you?"

"He just slapped me round the face, and told me to keep away from her."

"We have it on good authority that Dawn was on drugs. Was she getting them from Dougie?"

"No," he said. "You got that wrong. *He* was getting them from *her*."

Jack stared at him open mouthed. "Are you sure about that?"

"Positive. It's why I was waiting for her outside the Astoria on Saturday night. I wanted to tell her what had happened at the college on Friday. I thought she had some kind of hold over him because of the drugs, and figured if I told her what happened on Friday she could..." His voice faded away.

"Protect you? Like she used to do at school?"

Hutchence nodded, avoiding Jack's gaze.

Jack scratched his head. This case seemed to spring a new surprise every hour. He stood, and walked to the window to stretch his legs. "Did Dawn ever tell you where she was getting the drugs from?"

"No, but she seemed to have a ready supply of them. Enough to keep Dougie's business going, and a supply for herself."

"Okay, Danny. I'll leave you in peace," Jack said. "You've been very helpful."

Hutchence shrugged.

Jack let himself out of the house and drove back to the station.

"What have you got there, Frank?" he said, as he walked into the squad room.

"A magazine," Lesser said, raising it for Jack to see. "*Wrestlers World*. I phoned them up about the photo of Tommy Apollo, and they said they were running a feature of him in this month's issue, so I popped into town and picked up a copy."

"Let's have a look at him then."

Lesser flicked through the magazine to the article, and laid it open on the desk.

Jack picked it up and started to read through.

"It says here that Tommy Apollo's the son of a Greek shipping magnate, and Apollo's the name he uses to avoid the glare of publicity falling on his family."

Lesser laughed. "Yes, I read that too. In reality his dad's a porter at Billingsgate fish market. He's not even Greek. He's Cypriot, and his family live in Streatham."

"Then why the lies?"

"Never let the truth stand in the way of a good gimmick," Lesser said. "I'm billed 'from parts unknown,' but I was born in the Old Kent Road. It's the same thing. They say that if you put a group of wrestlers in a room together, all they do is sit around and lie to each other."

"It's all ballyhoo."

"Then it's true what my old whistler from Boswell House said: wrestling and music hall are very much the same kind of beast," Myra said.

"Old whistler?" Jack said.

"Leo, Leo Keating. Whistling is what he used to do on stage. He called it a funny name though."

"He was a *siffleur*," Lesser said. "I think it's French."

Everyone turned to look at him in astonishment.

"What?" Lesser said. "Because I'm a wrestler, I'm thick? Is that it?"

No one answered.

"Thanks a bunch," Lesser said.

Everyone laughed. Except Jack, who had finished the article, and was staring at the photograph that accompanied it. Apollo was a good-looking young man with thick, wavy,

Brilliantined hair, a slim waist and a fine, well-muscled physique. "How tall is he, Frank?"

"Six one, six two."

"With all those muscles, yet he still felt it was all right to strike Dawn Peterson who was five-feet four, and seven stone soaking wet. Let's pull him in, and make him sweat for a while. Let him know what it feels like to be bullied." Contempt dripped from his words, and they subdued the squad.

"I'll get on it," Lesser said. "Trevor, you come with me."

Trevor Welsh jumped to his feet, dragged his jacket from the back of his seat. "Do you know where to find him?"

"As I said, he was born in Streatham. He may not live there anymore but I'm pretty sure his relatives still do. The family name is Constantinides. There can't be many of those in the phone book, or on the electoral roll for that matter. We'll find out where he is, or find someone who knows how to find him."

"Or you could simply go to the town hall in Hitchin tonight," Jack said.

Lesser turned to him. "Sir?"

Jack raised the magazine. "You should have read to the end of the article, Frank. It gives a list of his forthcoming fights, and tonight he's wrestling Tiger Ali Singh at *Hitchin Town Hall.*"

"Well, I'll be…"

Trevor Welsh sighed, returned his jacket to the back of the chair, pulled a file from his IN tray, and muttered, "Back to indecent exposures, and grannies caught shoplifting."

"Stop moaning, Trevor. Someone's got to do them," Lesser said.

"But why is it always me?"

"The joys of being a detective constable, lad. If you want to avoid the donkey work…" Jack said.

"Stop being a donkey, and take your sergeant's exams," Lesser finished for him.

Welsh rolled his eyes. "It's like working with Morecombe and Wise in this place sometimes."

The telephone rang in the squad room. Lesser picked it up. "Sir, it's for you. Professor Strong." He held out the receiver to Jack.

"He can't have the post mortem results this early," Jack said, but took the call.

"Professor Strong? Jack Callum. How may I help you?"

"*I* may be able to help you," Strong said. "We ran some tests on the young lady's blood, and had some interesting results."

"Go on," Jack said.

"There were elevated readings for *Amylbarbitone* and *Dextroamphetamine*."

"What does that mean exactly?"

"Well, *Dextroamphetamine* is an anti-depressant and the *Amylbarbitone* is added to counter the side-effects of the *Amphetamine*, which can be agitation and psychosis."

"So, one drug is added to another to make the first drug safer."

"Now you're getting it," Strong said. "That combination was first introduced in 1950 in the United States as *Dexamyl*, a combination of both words you see, but more and more recently we're seeing it used as a recreational drug under the name *Drinamyl* or..."

"*," Jack said.

Strong was taken aback. "But you knew."

"Not for certain, Professor. Your call has just confirmed it."

"So where did this young lady obtain *Purple Hearts* – a poor description really as they're neither purple nor heart-shaped. They're more..."

"Triangular and blue."

Strong gave an exasperated sound. "Is there nothing I can tell you?"

"Actually, there is," Jack said. "Could these tablets cause mood swings, erratic behaviour, paranoid delusions?"

"All of the above unfortunately, especially if the dose isn't properly regulated and administered, and from the figures I'm seeing here, no reputable doctor would prescribe *Drinamyl* in this kind of quantity, without risking their patient's mental stability. Is that useful to your investigation?"

"Yes, Professor. It explains a lot."

"You'll get the full post mortem report in the next couple of days. Possibly even as early as tomorrow."

"Thank you, Professor." Jack rang off and turned to the room. "We have confirmation. Dawn Peterson was taking *Purple Hearts* and large quantities of them, so that makes anything she said in the weeks preceding her death highly suspect."

"Including what she told you on Saturday about the boyfriend who was going to kill her?" Lesser said.

"Yes," Jack said. "For a start I don't think Danny Hutchence *was* her boyfriend, and I don't think he was going to kill her. If I'd been aware of her drug use, I may have pushed her a little bit harder, because I believe her paranoia was based in reality. I think she was terrified because she'd convinced herself that *someone* was going to kill her as a result of something, some secret, she knew about that particular person. But her wires were crossed, and she chose Danny because he had played such an important part of her rather erratic life for so long. So her killer was someone who she saw as some kind of boyfriend. The problem we have is to unpick the web of lies and half-truths she spun around herself, and find out who that person actually was." He took a pair of scissors from a desk drawer and cut the picture of Tommy Apollo from the magazine, went across to the incident board and pinned it up. "The first...of many, I suspect."

11 TUESDAY

"Myra, when are you going to see this Farlowe character?"

Myra looked up from the file she was reading. "His secretary has added me to his schedule for two o'clock this afternoon."

"What does a retired music hall singer need a secretary for?"

"That's what I asked myself, so I did some research on Mr Farlowe. Apparently, Boswell House is not the only business he has investment interests in. That's what I'm reading at the moment." She nodded to the file in front of her. "He is on the board of several companies, as well as being a director of a number of charities. He's uses his status as a name in the entertainment industry to maximum effect, and apparently it carries a lot of weight."

Jack shook his head. "I'd never heard of him before all this started. I don't even remember him when he was singing for his supper. The names Duncan Farlowe and Elise Gerard somehow completely passed me by."

"Me too, sir," Myra agreed, "But then Leo Keating had a whole gallery of entertainers on his bedroom wall, and the only one I recognised was Max Miller. Remember that most of these people made their name before the introduction of television."

"Agreed, but they were big names on the radio. Tommy Handley, Bud Flanagan, Arthur Askey, George Formby, they were like friends who came to visit every week," Jack said.

"But what did we actually know about them? Unless you saw them on stage, or in the cinema, you didn't even know what they looked like. They were just disembodied voices coming to you out of a loud speaker on your sideboard."

"I know what George Formby looks like."

"But is that because you saw him on stage, or did you catch one of his films, or see him in the *Pathé* newsreels?"

"Fair point," Jack said.

"It's possible to be a national success, and remain anonymous in your private life, should you wish to do so. Leo told me that when Farlowe and Gerard finally retired it was amidst rumours of breakdowns and alcohol problems, but I can't remember hearing, or seeing, anything about them in the papers, can you?"

Jack shook his head. "As I said before, they certainly slipped under my radar."

"So, we shouldn't be surprised that Farlowe is now a successful businessman, and yet we know nothing about him."

"Come and see me before you go to meet him. I might come along with you. He sounds like a fascinating character."

"Very good, sir. I'll come and fetch you.'

"Good girl," Jack said.

He would never admit it to her, but he wasn't going to let Myra interview Farlowe, or any of the suspects for that matter, on her own. She was a capable policewoman, and a damned good detective, but she was still a vulnerable young woman, and he'd seen first-hand what the monster that killed Dawn Peterson was capable of doing to young women, and it wasn't pretty.

"Where are we going?" Jack said, as he slid into the car beside Myra.

"Benington," she said. "Farlowe has three homes, a flat in Chelsea, a cottage in the west-country, but his main residence is in Benington, just up the road from Stevenage."

"Three homes eh? He's done all right for himself."

"And, of course, his share of Boswell House," Myra said.

"I should have taken up singing, instead of becoming a copper," Jack said.

"Can you sing, sir?"

"Not at all, Myra, not at all."

As Myra drove, Jack read through the notes she'd made about Boswell House. "That's convenient," he said.

"Sir?"

"Farlowe lives in Benington, and Terence Maitland, the doctor who takes care of the medical needs of the Boswell House residents, lives in Walkern."

"Yes, sir," Myra said. "I checked on the map. They're almost next-door neighbours."

"Well, perhaps we'll pay Dr Maitland a visit once we're finished with Farlowe."

The house in Benington sat back from the road. A low brick wall surrounded it, topped with wrought iron railings, and access onto the gravel drive was through matching iron gates. Myra swept through the gates, and crunched up the drive to the front door.

The house itself was turn of the century, red brick with a green-tiled roof.

"It looks pretty grand," Myra said.

"For some reason I expected nothing less."

They got out of the car, and climbed the red brick steps to the door, which opened before they could reach the top.

A woman stood in the doorway. She was in her twenties, attractive, but dressed severely, and elegantly, in a grey suit. Her brown hair was swept back from her face, and held in a chignon at her neck. The makeup was light, but subtle, and her kohl-lined blue eyes looked out from behind a pair of tinted metal-framed glasses.

She welcomed them with a smile that didn't reach the eyes. "Detective Constable Banks," she said. "And this is?"

"Chief Inspector Callum," Myra said.

"I'm Veronica, Duncan's secretary."

"Yes. We spoke on the phone."

"Indeed we did." She glanced at the gold watch on her wrist. "Very punctual," she said approvingly. "Won't you come in? Duncan's waiting for you in his study."

The entrance hall was large, with grey and white tiles set in a checkerboard design. A large, long-cased clock stood in the corner, ticking loudly, and chiming the hour, as Veronica led them to a large oak door, knocking sharply once, and pushing it open.

"Your two o'clock appointment, Duncan. Detective Constable Banks and Chief Inspector Callum."

"Thank you, Ronnie. That will be all." Duncan Farlowe turned away from the window to face them.

Myra recognised him immediately from the newspaper clipping Leo Keating had shown her. The hair and moustache were silver now, instead of black, but his handsome face had hardly aged at all.

He was shorter than she was expecting, probably no more than five foot nine, but he was slim and stood erect which seemed to give him extra height. He was dressed in a dark purple smoking jacket over a cream shirt and light grey slacks. A matching purple cravat at his throat completed his debonair, slightly rakish appearance, a look enhanced by the long, thin, silver holder in which a *Sobranie Black Russian* cigarette smouldered.

Myra couldn't shake the feeling that he had just stepped from the stage at a Mayfair nightspot.

"I can't stand autumn," he said, gesturing out through the window. "You end the summer filled with hope and optimism, only to have it dashed by grey skies and falling leaves. It's like the presage of death, and then in a matter of months winter comes along to prove the point. Hello," he said, extending his hand. "Duncan Farlowe."

Myra shook it uncertainly. "Hello," she said. "Myra Banks."

Farlowe smiled. "How may I help you today, Myra?" He gave Jack a cursory nod and proceeded to ignore him.

"We understand you are the co-owner of Boswell House," she said.

"Your understanding is correct."

"We're here concerning the death of one of your staff members."

"Young Dawn Peterson, yes. Elise telephoned me to tell me the distressing news. Please, take a seat. I'll get Ronnie to organise some coffee."

"Don't trouble on our account, sir," Jack said, "We'll not be staying very long."

Farlowe gave a graceful shrug. "As you wish."

He took the *Sobranie* from the holder, and ground it out in a cut glass ashtray on the desk, then opened a silver cigarette box and filled the holder again. "Can I interest you?" he said, indicating the box.

Both Myra and Jack declined.

Again the elegant shrug, and he lit the cigarette with an onyx table lighter. "Awful business", he said, puffing pungent smoke into the room. "You're no further forward with your attempts to apprehend her killer?"

"Inquiries are progressing," Myra said.

"Towards a hasty conclusion, I hope."

Jack shrugged, nowhere near as elegantly as Farlowe.

"Did you know Miss Peterson?" Myra said, perching on the edge of a Queen Anne chair, taking out her notebook, and crossing her ankles demurely.

"Not personally," Farlowe said. "But then I hardly know any of the staff personally. They are what they are: staff. When I visit Boswell House I'm there for the guests, to bring a dash of sunshine into their world." Farlowe settled himself behind the desk, in a black leather captain's chair, and observed them imperiously.

"Why, with all your other business interests, and the work you do for so many charities, did you and Miss Gerard decide to open Boswell House?" Jack said.

"Well, there you have me. How can I answer you without sounding pretentious?" Farlowe said.

"Try," Jack said.

A smile flickered on Farlowe's lips. "We brought Boswell House into existence as a way to give something back to a business that sustained us for many years, and gave us so much joy."

"And yet you charge your residents for the privilege of living there."

"A paltry sum, I assure you, compared to the charges of Brinsworth, Denville, and a few other residential homes I could name."

"I just wondered why you didn't lump Boswell in with all your other charitable interests."

Farlowe drew in a lungful of smoke, and exhaled through his nose. "I do believe you are judging me, Chief Inspector."

"Just making an observation," Jack said. "If, as you said, you were giving something back to a business that gave you such joy and sustenance, why then decide to turn it into a profit-making business?"

Farlowe spread his arms. "What can I say? The money Boswell House makes goes towards the well-being of our guests, making sure they have a comfortable place to spend their twilight years, safe in the knowledge that they will always have a place they can call home, with excellent food, and with comprehensive and top-notch medical care. It goes without saying that these things don't come cheaply."

"I can imagine," Jack said. "Do you make regular visits to the home? Only Miss Gerard led our constable here to believe that you have very little to do with the running of Boswell House."

"I do what I can," Farlowe said. "I lead the guests in community singing on Wednesdays for instance."

"Yes, we're aware of that. Other than your concert parties, you wouldn't describe yourself as a regular visitor?"

Farlowe shook his head. "I don't visit as much as I would like, but then I do have other business interests…and my charities of course."

"Of course." Jack rubbed his chin. "You see, the problem I'm having is that we've been told that you visit the home much more regularly than you say. I just wonder why you're not telling us the whole truth."

12 TUESDAY

For an instant, irritation flashed across Farlowe's urbane expression, but he said nothing.

"I was told that you're there at least three times a week," Myra said. "The same person told me that you were at the Home on Thursday evening, so it's inconceivable that you didn't know Dawn Peterson, because that was the last evening she was there, and there are only three staff members on duty on Thursday nights. Two of them nurses, Sara Clay and Rodney Barton, and the other one was Dawn."

"All right, I admit it," Farlowe said. "I *did* know Dawn."

"Then why lie?" Jack said.

"It's a trifle delicate." He looked at Jack seriously. "If we could talk in private?" He looked pointedly in Myra's direction.

Jack shook his head. "Constable Banks will continue to take notes of our conversation," Jack said.

Farlowe shifted uncomfortably in his seat. "Very well. Dawn and I had, how can I put it, an arrangement?"

"You were sleeping with her."

"Yes."

"But you're old enough to be..." Myra began, but a look from Jack silenced her.

"I know it looks bad," Farlowe said, "But she was such a wonderful girl. So full of life, so full of *Spring*."

"I take it he's talking about the season?" Myra muttered.

"I believe so," Jack whispered to her. "Go on," he said to Farlowe.

"When a man is approaching a certain time of his life, where everything is so bleak, so depressing, it's hard to fight the allure of a creature like Dawn, whose zest for life was like the fountain of youth."

"I should remind you that Miss Peterson is dead, sir." Jack said bluntly.

"And what a tragedy, that a life so young, and vital, can be so cruelly snuffed out."

"Miss Gerard was unaware of your trysts with Miss Peterson, and would have disapproved had she found out, which is why you found it necessary to keep her in the dark," Jack said.

"I have a private room at the Hall and, when I stayed there overnight, Dawn would often visit me. She did so last Thursday, once she had rid herself of that old fool, Leo Keating, who kept her talking into the early hours."

"An arrangement," Myra said. "You said you had an arrangement with Dawn? What kind of arrangement?"

Farlowe coloured. "An unfortunate choice of words."

"Were you paying her?" Jack said.

Farlowe's blush deepened. "I refuse to answer any more of your questions."

"You just have," Jack said. "Where were you on Sunday evening?"

Farlowe shot to his feet. "You surely don't suspect me of killing her?" There was outrage in his voice.

"Where were you?" Jack held the man's gaze, until he simply deflated, and sank back into his seat. He plucked the cigarette from the holder, and clamped it between his lips, sucking on it furiously. "I was with Elise, at her house. She cooked me dinner, and we sat together listening to music."

"What then?"

"We went to bed…together."

"Where you stayed until the morning. You didn't get up, and go out in the night…for maybe another tryst?"

"What kind of man do you take me for?"

"I think we've established that, sir."

Farlowe looked resigned. "Very well," he said. "I stayed there until Monday morning, and no. I didn't get up in the night. You can check with Elise. She'll confirm that I'm telling you the truth."

"Oh, don't worry, Mr Farlowe, we will."

"You won't tell her, about Dawn and me?"

"Not unless it's absolutely necessary."

"Thank you."

"Don't thank me," Jack said. "I'm not keeping your secrets out of any regard for you, but I don't deliberately spread misery. There's enough of that in the world, without me adding to it." He stood up. "That will be all for today. Please don't leave the area until we have solved this case. We might need to speak with you further. Come along, Constable."

Myra got up, and followed Jack to the door.

Veronica was standing just outside the door, from where she had probably listened to the entire interview.

"I'd keep your hand on your tuppence if I were you," Myra said, as she walked past her, "working for that one,"

The secretary said nothing, but blushed furiously.

"I feel like I need a long hot bath after that," Myra said, as she started the car. "What a horrible man, and I didn't have Dawn pegged as a prostitute either."

"I don't think she was, Myra, not really. What I do think is that she was a vulnerable young woman, ripe for the picking by the Duncan Farlowes of this world. If she had a drug habit, which seems very probable, then Farlowe exploited her need to make the money to pay for it."

"She could have got the drugs from the dispensary at the home?"

"But according to Miss Gerard she didn't have access to it."

"And I suppose there's no guarantee that they even keep *Purple Hearts* at the home," Myra said.

"Well, there's one way to find out. Let's pay a visit to Dr Maitland."

Terence Maitland lived in an eighteenth-century cottage, separated from the road by a meagre strip of garden, bordered by a wooden fence with creosoted palings. The walls of the cottage were painted duck-egg blue, and the roof was tired, and badly in need of re-thatching.

Myra tugged on an antique bell pull, and waited for the door to be opened.

"Hello," the small, elderly woman who answered the door said, peering at them myopically through a pair of the thickest glasses Myra could remember seeing.

She made the introductions.

"Do you have an appointment?" the woman asked querulously.

"We're not expected, but if you tell Dr Maitland it concerns Boswell House, I'm confident he'll want to see us."

"I'll ask him," the old woman said sharply. "Wait here." She shut the door.

"I think you're losing your charm, Myra," Jack said.

"Cantankerous old bat," Myra said. "I would have shown her my warrant card, but I doubt she could have read it. Did you see the thickness of those glasses?"

A very tall man, who looked to be in his forties, wearing a tweed suit with a rumpled shirt, and stained red tie, opened the door. "You'll have to forgive Miss Cavendish. She's my housekeeper, but seems to see her role more as a guard dog, keeping unwanted visitors and timewasters away. Do come in."

They followed him into the cottage. The ceilings were low, and the doorways even lower, and Jack had to duck his head to enter the living room. He imagined Maitland must have a permanent crick in the neck.

Maitland noticed his discomfort. "Take a seat. It's less of a strain sitting down."

"How do you manage? The ceilings are very low."

Maitland smiled. "I was born here, and as I got older I developed a kind of sixth sense about low doorways and ceilings. I haven't cracked my head in a long while, but it still gives Mrs Cavendish the advantage over me. She scurries about the place like a dormouse whereas I have to take my time." He sat down in a comfortable-looking armchair, and crossed his long legs. "Doris tells me you want to speak with me about Boswell House?"

"How long have you been associated with the place?" Myra asked without preamble.

"Since it opened in '53," Maitland said. "Duncan Farlowe looked me up when he first came to the area, with a view to buying the old place and turning it into a residential home. I suppose it was a matter of convenience. I'm one of the few doctors living in the area, and I'm only a stone's throw away from his house in Benington. I flatter myself to think that I was his first choice."

"Are you aware that a young member of staff, Dawn Peterson, died at the weekend."

A shadow fell across the doctor's face. "Yes. Duncan came here and told me about it in person. Dreadful business. He told me she'd been killed – murdered. Is that the case?"

"I'm afraid so."

Maitland shook his head. "Dreadful," he said again. "Sometimes I don't know what this world's coming to. How can I help you?"

Jack came straight to the point. "The post mortem revealed that Miss Peterson had a large amount of *Drinamyl* in her bloodstream, and we've become aware that she was taking *Purple Hearts* for recreational purposes."

Maitland grimaced. "A scourge of modern society. I'm seeing it more and more in general practice these days. All recreational drugs seem to go through periods when they're in vogue. *Drinamyl* was first introduced in 1950, and when it arrived on the scene it was hailed, like so many of modern science's discoveries, as the new *wonder* drug. The prime minister at the time, Anthony Eden, was prescribed it to combat the abdominal pains he was suffering, but no one took into account the side effects, and it's widely thought now that it was those that impaired his judgement during the Suez crisis, and we all know the catastrophic results of that.

"But it's those same side effects that today's thrill seekers are after. It gives its users a *high,* but continued use can lead to complete psychosis. Like all these fashionable drugs, the *highs* come with a cost, sometimes a tragic cost."

"We were wondering," Myra said, "if anyone at Boswell House was being prescribed *Drinamyl,* and if the dispensary there could be Dawn Peterson's source."

Maitland nodded thoughtfully. "I see your thinking, but let me reassure you that I have no patients at the home who need to be on anything as strong as *Drinamyl.* I hate to disillusion you, but the dispensary at Boswell House is pretty basic – paracetamol or aspirin for general aches and pains, laxatives, of course, and antacids for minor digestive problems, but the most popular item the dispensary has by far is Epsom Salts." He smiled. "Sorry, not the most iniquitous pharmacopeia is it?"

Jack returned the smile. "What you're saying is, if Dawn Peterson was getting a regular supply of *Purple Hearts,* she wasn't getting them from Boswell House."

"In a nut shell, yes."

Jack stood. "You've been very helpful, Doctor."

Myra remained in her seat. "What are your views on the over-prescription of drugs?"

Maitland looked at her appraisingly. "I hope you're not suggesting what I think you're suggesting, Constable."

Myra looked at him steadily. "Could sedatives be used, to keep patients docile, easier to control?"

Jack was looking at Myra closely, wondering where on earth she was going with this line of questioning. He said nothing out of curiosity. Instead he was watching Maitland's reaction to it.

"Theoretically, yes they could, but I don't prescribe sedatives to any Boswell House residents."

"And you wouldn't sanction such a practice?"

"Certainly not. I deplore the misuse of any drugs."

Myra closed her notebook, and stowed it in her handbag. "Thank you, Doctor. I think we've taken enough of your time."

Maitland relaxed visibly, and got to his feet, "I'll see you out," he said.

"What was all that about?" Jack asked her as they climbed into the car.

"Leo Keating told me that the residents are being given regular doses of some kind of sedative, to keep them manageable."

"That's a pretty outrageous accusation to make."

"He had proof – an old tobacco tin containing twenty or thirty tablets that he'd managed to squirrel away without the nurse noticing. I just wondered if Dr Maitland was over-prescribing in order to make Elise Gerard's life easier."

"You should have told me about this first, before steaming in and mentioning it to Maitland," Jack said.

Myra flushed. "I'm sorry, sir. I just wanted to see his reaction."

"What do you think now you've seen it?"

"Unless he's a bloody good actor, I'd say that he hadn't got a clue what I was talking about."

Jack nodded. "That was the impression I got as well, but next time you play a hunch, run it by me first, okay?"

"Yes, sir."

"It's a pity you didn't squirrel away one of the tablets yourself," Jack said. "We could have had it analysed."

Myra took out a handkerchief from her pocket, and unfolded it on her lap. In the centre of the cloth was a small white pill. "I did, sir."

Jack shook his head. "Sometimes, Myra, you surprise me."

"In a good way, I hope."

"Sometimes." He smiled. "The Stevenage lab is only a couple of miles away. Let's go and get it tested."

Myra was a popular figure in the squad room these days, in part because she was spending less time in the office she shared with Eddie Fuller, and more at a desk with the other detectives. She had also given up the onerous, and often demanding role as Fuller's bagman, passing that dubious honour to Constable Brian Peck, a recent recruit to Welwyn and Hatfield police station, having arrived fresh out of Hendon with a slew of distinctions and favourable comments from his tutors.

Myra's desk in the squad room was in the corner. Along with two telephones and a Rolodex, it also boasted an electric typewriter, and Myra ingratiated herself to many of the detectives by offering to type up their reports on the new, much faster machine.

So, when she announced to the room that she was investigating a case concerning the abuse of illegal substances at a residential care home for the elderly, pens were laid down, telephone conversations were cut short, and every eye in the squad room focussed on her.

She stood at the incident board, and outlined her suspicions concisely. Even Eddie Fuller had abandoned his office, and was standing at the back of the room listening with rapt attention.

"Do you have any evidence to support this?" DC Harry Grant called.

It was Jack's turn to speak. So far he'd been sitting quietly in the corner, listening to Myra outline her case; now he got to his feet. He cleared his throat to attract attention. "I believe we have compelling evidence to suggest that the residents at Boswell House are being fed a constant supply of drugs to keep them passive and malleable." He turned to Myra. "Tell them about Leo Keating," he said.

As Myra finished her account of her conversation with Leo, a general susurration of disgust rippled around the squad room.

"I agree with all of you," Jack said. "But there is another element in all this, and one that links indirectly to the murder of Dawn Peterson."

The room fell silent as they waited for him to enlighten them.

"The lab confirmed that the pill Myra took away from Leo Keating's room was *Nitrazepam – Mogadon*."

"But surely, sir," Fuller said, "If the doctor was over-prescribing on that kind of scale, alarm bells would be clanging at the chemist's where they get their prescriptions filled."

"Agreed, Eddie, but we met with Terence Maitland this afternoon, and the more I think about it, the more I'm convinced that he isn't the source of the tablets. I think it's possible that Gerard and Farlowe are getting the drugs they need elsewhere."

"An illegal source then?"

Jack nodded. "Someone who wouldn't raise an eyebrow at the amounts of drugs they're getting through at the home."

"Whoever it is could also be the source of the *Purple Hearts*," Lesser said.

"That thought crossed my mind too, Frank," Jack said. "So, we'll start with known drug dealers, and see if we can connect them to Boswell House. In the meantime, we need a fuller picture. I'm going to call Elise Gerard tomorrow morning, and tell her that I need to speak to Leo Keating here at the station concerning the Dawn Peterson case. Myra, you can pop along there, pick him up, and bring him back here. It will save all the ducking and diving you did this morning."

"Shouldn't we be concentrating on the murder, sir?" Grant said. "Instead of wasting time on Constable Banks' *Don Quixote* impressions?"

"No, Constable. You're being a little short-sighted." Jack said. "I think we have to take a two-pronged approach – use the one case as a blind, while we investigate the other at the same time. Farlowe and Gerard know we're looking into Dawn Peterson's death, but, as far as the other matter is concerned, they are unaware that we suspect anything about the doping of their patients, and Frank could be right. Whoever is supplying them with *Mogadon* could also be providing them with *Drinamyl* and, if that is the case, I think we'll be a step closer to finding Dawn's killer." He walked to the door. "Frank, when are you picking up Tommy Apollo?"

"I phoned the hall and asked the time of Apollo's match, and they told me he had the match before the interval, so he should be finished about eight forty-five."

"Then pick him up when the fight's finished, bring him back here, and throw him in a cell. I'll interview him in the morning. I'm off home."

13 TUESDAY

"Roast chicken and stuffing?" Jack said as he walked into the kitchen. "It's not Christmas is it?"

"Stop it," Annie said, flicking him with a tea towel. "I wanted to make this evening special. Barbara gave me the afternoon off so I could come home and prepare it all."

"It smells delicious. Where is everyone?"

"In the front room. Eric is gracing us with his presence tonight, and he's brought Gerry with him. Joanie's here, and Rosie and Paul arrived ten minutes ago, so it's a proper family dinner, and I can't remember when we last had one of those. Take your coat off, go in and say hello to everyone."

"After a kiss for the cook," he said, and pecked Annie on her lips.

"This is stupid," she said grabbing hold of his hand. "I feel so nervous.It doesn't make sense. I've cooked dinner hundreds of times before."

"You'll be fine," he said.

"I wish I had your confidence," Annie said.

Joan appeared in the doorway. "Anything I can do, Mum? Oh, hello, Dad."

Jack blew her a kiss and Annie shook her head. "No, love. Thanks, but it's all in hand. Why don't you go back and keep them entertained?"

"They don't need me," Joan said. "They're talking music, and that stuff goes straight over my head."

"I suppose you could make a start on the gravy. The meat juices are in that jug on the side, and there's *Bisto* in the cupboard."

"Consider it done," Joan said, crouching down and opening a cupboard to find a saucepan.

"I'll leave you to it," Jack said, and went to hang his coat on the hallstand.

He hesitated outside the door to the front room, listening to the thrum of conversation from within, the butterflies beating their wings in his stomach just as franticly as the ones in Annie's. "Calm down, you silly sod," he told himself quietly. "It's just your daughter."

He took a breath and pushed open the door.

"I tell you, Gerry, Floyd Cramer is about the best session pianist out there. When you were playing in the Vikings, backing Rosie on all those Brenda Lee songs, you were probably playing all his licks without even realising it." Paul Bolton was speaking, gesticulating wildly, his fingers miming imaginary keyboard runs.

Eric was sitting cross-legged on the rug. He looked up as Jack entered. "Oh, hello, Dad. I thought I heard you come in."

"Hello, son. Gerry, it's good to see you."

Gerry Turner got up from her armchair and smiled. "Hello, Mr C. It's kind of you to invite me."

"Not a bit of it," he said, marvelling again at how Gerry had grown from the shy, gawky thirteen-year old he first met just two short years ago, to the confident, attractive young woman who now stood before him. "It's lovely to see you. How are your grandparents?"

"They're good. They send their regards," she said.

"Send mine back." His gaze travelled across the room to his youngest daughter, Rosie, who was sitting on the settee, legs curled beneath her in her usual pose. She was smiling at him.

"Come and say hello to your old man properly," he said gruffly, opening his arms.

She uncurled herself, crossed the floor in a heartbeat, and hugged him warmly.

He wrapped his arms around her, and rested his chin on the top of her head, closing his eyes to stem the tears that were stinging and threatening to escape. "It's so good to see you," he said, the words muffled by her dark hair.

"Not so tight," she said breathlessly. "You're crushing the life out of me."

He relaxed the hug, and held her at arm's length. "Let me look at you," he said. "You've lost weight."

"I've just shed the puppy fat," Rosie said.

"Are you keeping her well fed, Paul?" he said to the tall, blond young man who was watching the display of familial affection with a mixture of envy and embarrassment. "I'm not, sir, but my mum sees that she has three square meals a day."

Jack disengaged himself from Rosie, went across to Paul and shook his hand. "Well, thank her for me."

"I will, sir."

"Call me Jack. You're making me feel like I'm still at work."

Paul coloured. "Yes, sir…er…Jack."

Jack went back to Rosie, took her hand, and led her back to the settee, flopping onto a plumped-up cushion, and pulling her down onto his lap. "Right, young lady, tell me all your news."

"I've got a job," she said.

"You *had* a job, and mum says that Barbara Painter is still missing you."

"Yeah," Rosie said. "I feel bad about that. I'll call into the shop and see her in the morning to apologise."

Jack looked at her sharply.

"In the morning? Are you planning to stay the night?"

"Mum said it would be all right. Is it?"

Jack chuckled. "Of course. Your bedroom is still where it was." He shot a glance across the room at Paul, who was still standing there, looking slightly lost.

"That's all right, Dad," Eric said, reading Jack's expression. "Paul can sleep in my room tonight. I'm going back with Gerry, and staying at hers."

"Hang on a minute. Have you…"

"It's okay, Jack." Annie said, as she entered the room. "It's all arranged. Laurence and Jean are fine with it. They'll take Eric back with them when they come to pick Gerry up later. Anyway, I'm ready to dish up. Can you come and carve?"

The conversation around the dinner table was lively and animated as they caught up with what had been happening in their lives since they were last together. During a lull, Jack turned to Rosie, who was sitting to his right. "So what's this job you have?"

"I'm working at *Saville's* in Harrow. It's a music shop that sells record players and radios, sheet music and records."

"And guitars, Eric," Paul butted in. "They've got a lovely cherry red *Hofner* semi acoustic. Just come on the market – a *Verithin* I think it's called. I'd buy it myself…if I could play guitar that is."

"So this job," Jack continued. "Does it pay enough to allow you give Paul's mother some rent money? I don't like the thought of one of mine relying on someone else's charity."

Rosie smiled. "Don't worry, Dad. I'm earning enough, what with my pay from *Saville's*, and from what I earn from sessions."

"Sessions?" Joan said. "What kind of sessions?"

"Singing of course. What did you think I meant?" Rosie said. "Arnie Schuster uses me from time to time to sing the background vocals on some of the records he's making."

"Am I missing something here?" Jack said. "Who's Arnie Schuster?"

"He's a record producer we know," Paul said. "He produces records for some top people. Dickie Valentine, Michael Holliday…he's got a record on the hit parade at the moment. *Endless Dreams* by Sonia Carmichael."

"Ooh, I know that one," Annie said. "They play it all the time on the radio."

"Well, listen closely to it next time you hear it, because the oohing and the aahing in the background is your Rosie."

"Is this true, pet?" Jack said, squeezing Rosie's arm.

Rosie blushed and nodded.

"Well that's fantastic. My Rosie, on the radio," he said.

"I can go one better," Rosie said. "Eric, can you fetch me my bag?"

"Where is it?" Eric said.

"In the other room. Down by the side of the settee."

"Two ticks," Eric said, and rushed from the room.

He returned quickly and handed the leather handbag to his sister. She opened it quickly, produced a seven-inch disc in a white cardboard sleeve, and handed it to Jack.

He took it, and turned it over in his hands, reading the words, handwritten in pencil, on the white label in the centre of the record. "What am I looking at here?" he asked his daughter.

"It's what they call a Demonstration Record."

"Or, Demo for short," Paul added.

"It's sent out to various record companies to try to generate some interest. Arnie recorded it for me."

"How much did it cost?" Jack asked.

"Nothing," Rosie said. "Not a bean. Arnie paid for it all, hiring the studio, getting the musicians together, having the record cut, everything."

"He's even paying to send them out," Paul cut in again.

"Very generous," Jack said. "What does this Arnie get in return?"

"Exclusive rights to produce Rosie's first five records should she get picked up," Paul said.

"How likely is that?"

"So far, he's sent it to *Pye*, *Phillips*, *Regal Zonophone*, *Parlophone* and a few others." Paul said.

"Any interest so far?" Jack said.

"*Pye* could be interested, and *Decca*. Arnie is still weighing up the options?"

"Can we hear it, Jack?" Annie said.

"Of course…that is if Rosie doesn't mind."

"No," she said. "That's why I brought it with me. I want you all to hear it."

"Do you mind if we finish dinner first?" Jack said. "Then we can all go in the other room, and play it on the radiogram."

"I've finished," Eric said.

"Me too," said Gerry.

Everyone else around the dining table laid down their knives and forks and looked at Jack expectantly.

He stared down ruefully at his last roast potato and sighed. "All right," he said, dropping his napkin on the table next to his plate. "Let's play it now."

"Play it again," Annie said. "Please play it again, both sides."

Jack crossed to the radiogram, flipped the record over, and lowered the arm onto the vinyl disc.

As the instrumental introduction began, Eric said, "Nice guitar work. Who is it?"

"Big Jim Sullivan," Paul said. "And that's Bobby Graham on drums."

"Nice," Eric said again.

"Sshh!" Annie said, as Rose's voice broke from the speaker.

The song was up-tempo, and Jack soon found his foot tapping along to the beat.

"Who wrote it?" Annie said, as the song faded to a close.

"Aaron Cole," Rosie said. "He's Arnie's protégé. He's only a few years older than me."

"Marvellous," Annie said, getting up to turn the record. As the simple piano intro heralded in a soft, poignant ballad, she said, "And this one?"

"Rosie did," Paul said proudly.

"Hush," Rosie said. "I just did the words. Aaron wrote the music."

"Yeah, but even so…" Paul said.

"Aaron thinks I've got potential," Rosie said, blushing.

Jack watched the tears trickle down Annie's cheeks as she listened to the words. He reached out and wrapped her hand in his.

"That was beautiful," Annie said as the song finished. "Play it again."

Jack felt someone tugging at his sleeve. He glanced around.

"Washing up, dad?" Joan hissed at him. "Let's save mum the work."

Jack smiled as the ballad started again. "Good idea," he whispered. "It looks like we've lost her for the rest of the evening anyway."

"Do you remember a girl from school?" Jack said. "Dawn Peterson. I think she was in your year."

Joan was filling the sink with hot water, and pulling on a pair of pink rubber gloves. "The name doesn't ring a bell."

"Black hair, soulful eyes, slim; a pretty girl."

Joan squirted some washing-up liquid into the water and glanced around at him. "It sounds like you're talking about *Dodgy Dawn*," she said

"*Dodgy Dawn?*"

Joan laughed. "It's what me and a few of the other girls used to call her."

"That's rather unkind."

"You wouldn't say that if you ever met her."

"I did meet her actually. Last Saturday night."

"Bad luck," Joan said, as she dunked some dirty plates into the piping hot water.

"She was killed on Sunday night," Jack said.

Joan swore and turned to gape at him. "You're kidding?"

"I'm afraid not. What can you tell me about her?"

Joan picked up a dishcloth, and started to clean the plates. "Well, the nickname says it all really."

Jack shook his head, and handed her another couple of plates. "No, the nickname tells me nothing. Dodgy how? Be specific."

"If I told you that she used to spend the lunch hours behind the bike sheds with some boy or other, and would usually emerge reeking of fags, with the hem of her skirt tucked into her knickers, would that be specific enough for you?"

Jack cleared his throat. "I think I get the picture." He reached for a tea towel, and started to dry the wet crockery. "Anything else."

"She'd sit in the playground drawing fake tattoos on her arms in Biro."

"What kind of tattoos?"

"Names mostly, from what I remember."

"Whose names."

"Boys of course. Oh, and she had a pet, some scrawny, specky boy who was always following her around, but she mostly always ignored him, unless she wanted something from the tuck shop, then it would be, 'Oh, Danny, darling, fetch me a *Wagon Wheel*,' or, 'Danny, darling, I need some crisps,' and off he'd trot to the tuck shop, and buy them for her. I never once saw her pay him back."

"What did Danny get out of the transaction?"

"Nothing, the sap, apart from being allowed to bask in her glory for another break time. As I say. He was a bit of an idiot."

"He hasn't changed," Jack said.

"You've met *him* as well? Hand me the knives and forks."

"Yes, I met him on Saturday as well, driving his mum's car, and playing the big 'I am'. I've interviewed him since, and he isn't the big 'anything'. Just a rather sad, insignificant figure, really."

"Yes, that sounds like him." Joan washed the cutlery, and shook her head as the sound of Rosie's ballad floated into the kitchen again. "There won't be any grooves left on that record by the time they've finished with it."

"You're right," he said, "But it *is* rather good, isn't it?"

"Yes, it is," Joan agreed. "Bless her."

14 WEDNESDAY October 19TH 1960

"Well that was some evening," Jack said, as he crawled into bed beside Annie. He glanced at the alarm clock, and saw it was a little after one in the morning.

"Rosie seems really content, doesn't she?" Annie said.

He nodded. "Yes, she does."

"I'm so happy for her, Jack…and so proud. That song she wrote was beautiful."

"I think it's beautiful that she's sleeping under our roof again."

Annie laid a hand on his arm. "You really miss her, don't you?"

"I didn't realise until tonight just how much." He turned, and threaded an arm under her shoulders. "I miss them all, Annie. Rosie, making her own way in the world now, and doing it so successfully, Joanie who we rarely see these days, and as for Eric…"

"Gerry's turning into a lovely girl, isn't she?"

"I was thinking that myself earlier. She's come a long way from the fragile little mouse who approached me at the school, the day I gave the talk there. It's remarkable the difference living with Lawrence and Jean has had on her."

"It's quite simple, Jack. She's very loved…as are our three. Lord knows, it hasn't always been easy to show them that but, deep down I think they all know it. We've got three remarkable children."

"Yes, I know." He hugged Annie reassuringly. "When I think about the case I'm working on now, it makes me realise what a lucky so and so I am. It could have all worked out so differently."

"What's the case?"

Jack explained it briefly. "The same age as Joanie, can you imagine?"

Annie shuddered. "Yes, unfortunately I can. Things with Ivan could have been so much worse," she said, making a rare reference to the abusive Polish émigré their daughter had eloped with when she was just sixteen. "I feel so sorry for Dawn's parents."

"Don't waste your sympathy," Jack said. "The step-mother never gave two hoots for her, and the father was too weak to stand up for his own daughter. I think Dawn was broken at an early age, and just grew up wrong. It's tragic."

"Do you think you'll catch who killed her?"

"Eventually, yes I do. Whoever did it will trip themselves up in the end, they almost always do, and when I catch whoever it is, I'll see they hang."

Annie pulled away from him and sat up in the bed, staring at him wide eyed. "Jack, I've never heard you talk like that. I thought you were against capital punishment."

He reached up and tugged her back into his arms. "I am," he said. "At least I thought I was. It's because every time I think of Dawn Peterson lying on a slab, her life taken away from her, an image of Joanie comes into my mind. I can't shake it, and I feel all the anger and hunger for revenge that Dawn's own father should feel. Is that wrong?"

Annie reached up and stroked his cheek. "Yes, Jack, it's very wrong. I'm sorry, pet. I really feel for any parent who has their child taken from them so brutally, but I've never believed in an eye for an eye. It would make me as bad as the murderer, and I'm not saying that from any high-minded position. God knows I'm not religious in any way shape or form, but I do honestly believe that, and I know you do too."

"Yes," he said. "You're right. I'm just feeling a bit emotional tonight." He reached out and switched off the reading lamp.

"Make love to me," Annie said.

"What now?"

"No, next week! Of course now."

"But Joanie, and Rosie and Paul…"

"Are all probably tucked up in their own beds and sound asleep by now, but I'm awake, and I really need to feel your skin against mine."

"Hussy," he said, then kissed her and rolled on top of her.

The first few tendrils of grey were streaking the sky as Jack sat alone at the kitchen table, eating a bowl of porridge. Avril had picked Joan up just before dawn to take her to Buntingford, to practise the styles they would be creating at a wedding tomorrow, when they would be doing the hair of the bride, six bridesmaids, and two soon-to-be mothers-in-law. Rosie was still asleep, making the most of being in her own comfortable bed for the first time in months, and Annie was upstairs getting ready for her job at the baker's.

Paul Bolton came into the kitchen.

"There's tea in the pot," Jack said, "and if you want toast there's bread in the breadbin. Pop a couple of slices under the grill. Butter's in the fridge. Or there's Cornflakes in the cupboard if you prefer."

Paul sat down opposite him at the table and reached for the teapot. "Just tea at the moment, I think." He poured a cupful and added a dash of milk from the bottle on the table. "As I've got you on your own, I need to ask you something."

Jack paused, a spoonful of porridge hanging between the bowl and his mouth, "Go ahead, but make it quick. I need to go up, and shave, once my wife's finished in the bathroom."

"It's about Rosie," Paul began.

"I thought it might be."

"What did you think of her demo disc last night?"

Jack swallowed his mouthful. "I think I said when I heard it, it was very good."

"Yes, yes you did."

"Then get to the point, Paul," Jack said, starting to lose patience with the young man. He liked the peace and quiet of his breakfast routine, and this conversation was an unwelcome intrusion.

"I think it's very good too. In fact, I think it's excellent, and I really believe that one of the record companies is going to offer her a contract."

"That's good news isn't it?" Jack said, scraping the last of his porridge from the bowl.

"Yes, yes it is…but…"

Jack met the young man's eyes. "But?"

"If they offer her a recording contract Rosie's still only seventeen. She can't legally sign it. It would need the signature of a parent or guardian to make it binding."

"Quite right too," Jack said, dabbing at his lips with a napkin.

"Well, would you be willing to countersign?"

Jack dropped the napkin to the table and got to his feet. "Of course," he said. "You don't honestly think I'd stand in the way of my daughter's happiness, do you?"

"No," Paul said. "Not at all." He tried for a smile and failed. Jack Callum still intimidated him, despite all the *call me Jack* bonhomie the man had shown last night.

"But," Jack said, as he took his bowl to the sink, and rinsed it under the tap. "I'll want it read through thoroughly by a solicitor. I know a good man who specializes in contract law. Get the contract to me, and I'll have him go it through. I'll not have Rosie signing her life away for the sake of making a record."

Paul tried for the smile, and managed it this time, and was still smiling when Rosie wandered into the kitchen, yawning, hair dishevelled. She saw the smile. "Did he say, yes?"

Paul nodded.

She ran across to Jack, who was still standing at the sink, and hugged him. "Thanks, dad."

He kissed the top of her head. "But I mean what I say. A solicitor gets to read it first, understand?"

They nodded in unison, wearing matching grins.

He left them to it, sitting at the kitchen table, toasting their good news with cups of tea and wondered, as he walked upstairs to the bathroom, if the only reason for their visit yesterday was to get him to agree to be co-signatory. "Stop being a bloody policeman for once, Jack," he muttered to himself as he walked into the bathroom, and ran hot water into the sink.

Frank Lesser was sporting an angry red mark underneath a slightly swollen eye.

"What happened to you?" Jack said as he came into the squad room.

"Tommy Apollo," Lesser said with a rueful smile. "He was fine when we brought him in, but cut up rough when I told him he wouldn't be going home. He head-butted me."

"So what happened?"

"I slapped a sleeper hold on him, and he went out like a light. When he came to, I charged him with assaulting a police officer, and locked him in a cell. He's still down there, and giving the custody sergeant verbal hell."

"Ah, well, good work, Frank. I'll be down to see him in a little while," Jack said, and went up to his office.

He put in a call to Boswell House, and told them Myra Banks would be coming to collect Leo Keating to bring him in to answer a few more questions about Dawn Peterson.

Elise Gerard seemed most put out. "Well, that's certainly going to disrupt my day," she said tartly

"I do apologise, Miss Gerard but, I assure you, I wouldn't be calling him in if it wasn't absolutely necessary."

Grumbling about police insensitivity, Elise Gerard hung up, leaving Jack with a smile on his face as he rang through to

Myra and asked her to go and pick Leo up. "As soon as you like," he said. "Might as well give the old fellow a nice day out. Bring him back here by the scenic route if you like. I'm probably going to be tied up for a couple of hours. Sergeant Lesser's arrested Tommy Apollo, and I'm going down to interview him."

"Very good, sir," Myra said brightly.

"My office, Chief Inspector, if you please." The sound of Chief Superintendent Watkins' slightly nasal voice wiped the smile from Jack's face.

The man stood in the doorway to his office, looking immaculate in his freshly pressed uniform, not a dull crease to be seen, his sandy hair freshly cut and *Brilliantined*.

Prissy, Jack thought. *Definitely prissy*. He pushed himself out of his chair, and went along to the chief superintendent's office, that looked for all the world as if Watkins had spent most of his morning so far cleaning and dusting. There wasn't a mark on the carpet, and the desk positively gleamed. The thick smell of lavender polish hung in the air, competing with the sickly scent of Watkins' hair oil.

"Have your team got a good reason for turning my station into a rough house last night?"

"As I understand it, sir, a prisoner had to be restrained."

"And now said prisoner is in the cells wreaking havoc down there."

"He's a professional wrestler, sir, with a bit of a temper."

"This is all to do with the Peterson murder, am I right?"

"Yes, sir."

"Well, get down there and get him processed as quickly as you like. I want him either taken off to Bedford Prison or released, one or the other. Either way I want his disruptive presence neutralised. Do I make myself clear?"

"Crystal, sir. I was just about to go and question him."

"Well, what are you waiting for?" Watkins said.

"You, sir," Jack said. "You called me into your office."

Watkins slapped his hand on his thigh. "Damn your impertinence, Callum."

"Yes, sir," Jack said. "Will there be anything else?"

"That will be all," Watkins said tightly. He flipped his fingers dismissively. "I'll be keeping my eye on you, Chief Inspector."

Trying hard not to smile, Jack left the pristine office and headed to the cells, collecting Frank Lesser on the way.

"I can see why you left Barnet," he said to Lesser as they trotted down the stairs. "Watkins is a prig of the first order."

"I can think of worse things to call him, sir."

"I'm sure you can. What cell is Apollo in?" Jack said, as they entered the block.

Lesser looked puzzled as he regarded the thick steel doors. "I put him in three, sir. I can't understand why it's so quiet." He turned to the custody sergeant. Martin?"

Sergeant Martin Follett shrugged. "Search me, Frank. Up until ten minutes ago he was raving. Kicking the walls, punching the door, and then it stopped. Dead silence."

"Did you check on him?" Jack said.

"Sorry, sir," Follett said. "I value my life."

Jack frowned. "You'd better unlock him."

Follett took the keys from a hook above his desk and inserted one into the heavy door. He unlocked it and pulled it open."

Tommy Apollo was lying on his back on the floor, eyes closed, his face a mask of blood. On the wall above him was a smear of red, and droplets of blood on the plain wooden bench.

15 WEDNESDAY

"Bloody fool," Jack said. "It looks like he rammed his head into the wall and brained himself."

"Careful, sir," Lesser said, as Jack squatted down beside the prone body.

Jack reached out to lift one of Apollo's eyelids. In an instant his wrist was seized and Apollo twisted, throwing Jack across the cell to crash into the wall. The wrestler sprang to his feet and charged at the door, knocking Follett sideways in his dash for freedom. He made it as far as the doorway and was almost through when Lesser dropped to the floor and caught Apollo's ankle between his legs, pitching the man forward to crack his head against the edge of the steel doorframe. With a groan, and holding his head in his hands, Apollo sank to his knees.

"Your handcuffs, Martin," Lesser said.

Follett was hauling himself to his feet. He fished in the pocket of his tunic, found the cuffs and passed them to Lesser.

Grabbing Apollo's arm and dragging it behind his back, Lesser cuffed him, first one wrist, then the other, and then he spun Apollo around, pushing him down onto the bench. "Now sit there, Tommy and behave yourself. You don't want another sleeper, do you?"

Tommy Apollo shook his head.

Jack was on his feet. "Well done, Frank. How did he manage it?"

"Check his hairline or earlobe, sir," Lesser said. "He bladed himself. It's an old wrestling trick to produce the claret when you need it. Judging from the amount of blood, I'd guess the earlobe. They bleed like a bugger if you nick them. It's easy then to spread the blood over your face to make the injury appear far worse than it actually is."

"But what did he use to cut himself?"

"My guess is a sliver of razor blade. He was probably going to use it in the ring last night but didn't have need of it in the end. Hold on."

Lesser bent and picked up a square of sticking plaster from the floor. It had been folded in half. Lesser pulled it open. "There you are, sir." He held it out in the palm of his hand for Jack to see.

Resting in the centre of the adhesive strip was a silvery shard of metal, about half an inch long, and quarter of an inch wide. Jack could see the wickedly sharp edge. "Well, I'll be…"

"Nice try, Tommy," Lesser said to a subdued Apollo.

"Get him cleaned up, Frank and bring him along to Interview Room One."

Shaking his head, Jack walked out of the cell.

On his way to the interview room he saw Eddie Fuller hurrying down the stairs to the foyer, with DC Harry Grant at his heels, both struggling into their overcoats, Grant's hat perched on his head at an impossible angle.

"Where's the fire?" Jack said to Fuller.

"Can't stop to chat, guv. We've had a tip off. We know where we can find Dougie Marshall. If we're quick we can get there before he goes underground again."

Jack waved them past. "Don't let me stop you," he said. "Just go and nail him." He watched as Fuller and Grant ran from the building. Seconds later a Wolseley's engine roared into life, and there was a screech of rubber on tarmac as they tore out of the car park. He glanced round at Andy Brewer at the desk. "Quite a morning, so far," he said.

"Very lively, sir," Brewer said. "And it's only Wednesday. Lord knows what the rest of the week will bring?"

"Variety is the spice of life, Andy."

The doors to the station opened, and Leo Keating walked in on the arm of Myra Banks.

"Speaking of which. Good day, Mr Keating. Myra, take our guest to the canteen and get him a nice cup of tea, and have Yvonne rustle up a slice of her splendid carrot cake."

Myra grinned. "Yes, sir," she said and led the old man through the foyer and down the passage to the staff canteen.

Jack pushed open the door to the interview room. Lesser was already in there sitting across the table from Tommy Apollo, who was smoking a cigarette, flicking the ash onto the floor, ignoring the ashtray in the centre of the table, and ignoring Jack and Lesser as well. A sticking plaster was taped to his right earlobe.

Jack took off his jacket, hung it on the back of a chair, then removed some photographs from the folder he was carrying and slapped them down on the table.

The first was the holiday snap of Dawn Peterson smiling and happy, taken at Bournemouth last year. The second was a head and shoulders shot of her lying on a mortuary slab, a sheet up to her neck. The third was a photograph taken at the crime scene, showing Dawn with her throat hanging open, her head barely attached.

"Look at them, Tommy."

Resisting at first, until curiosity got the better of him, Apollo looked at each in turn, giving a lascivious grin at the first photo, his face darkening to a frown as he saw the second one. When he saw the third photo he reeled backward with a cry, vomit bursting from his clenched lips in a fine spray that spattered the table.

"Get him a glass of water, Sergeant," Jack said. "And bring a damp cloth."

"What the hell did you show me those for?" Apollo said, wiping his mouth on his sleeve.

"You recognise her?" Jack said.

"Of course I recognise her. It's Delicious Dawn. She's a ring rat. So?"

"She was a little more than that though, Tommy, wasn't she?"

Apollo shook his head. "She may have thought so, but a rat was all she ever was to me."

Jack let that one go. "When did you last see her?"

Apollo shrugged. "Can't remember."

"You must have some idea. Did you see her last Sunday?"

"No. Not Sunday."

"Then when?"

"I can't say for sure. A couple of weeks ago?"

"When you hit her?"

Apollo's gaze flicked from Jack to the murder scene photograph, and then back again. He shook his head. "Oh no. No! You're not going to pin that on me. I might have clipped her one, because she was being such a bloody pain, but that..." He pointed to the photo. "That wasn't me. I could never do something like that. It looks like someone tried to cut her head off."

"Where were you on Sunday evening?"

Panic flared for an instant in Apollo's eyes, and then it vanished and he visibly relaxed. "Gawd, you had me worried there for a moment, but on Sunday I was with Becky. She's another of the rats. Beautiful mouth, and tongue. The things she can do with that tongue," he said, grinning. "If you know what I mean?"

"I think I can imagine," Jack said.

"I bet you can't," Apollo said, the grin growing ever wider.

Lesser returned to the room with a glass of water and a dishcloth. He handed the glass to Apollo and proceeded to wipe the sick from the table.

Apollo took a long gulp of water. "Is that it then? Can I go now?"

Jack stood, gathered up the photographs, and walked to the door. "This girl Becky. I'll need her name and address."

"No problem."

"And no, you can't go. You're still under arrest for assaulting a police officer."

"That was self-defence."

"Was it, Sergeant?"

Lesser shook his head.

"Right, Frank," Jack said. "Get the name and address for this Becky girl, and take Mr Apollo back to his cell."

"Hey!" Apollo called. "That's not fair!"

"Nor is life, Mr Apollo. Nor is life." Jack walked from the interview room. Shutting the door behind him.

It seemed that half the station had gathered in the canteen.

Leo Keating was standing at the front of the room, two of his fingers stuck in his mouth, his other hand flapping in front of his lips as he produced the most melodic whistling sound imaginable.

As Jack pushed his way through the crowded room, the tune Keating was whistling ended, and his audience burst into spontaneous applause.

Jack reached the front. To Myra he said quietly, "I'm ready for him now." To the rest of the canteen he said, "That's it. Show's over. All of you get back to your duties."

Amid the general grumbling were calls of, "Spoil sport!" and "Encore!" Jack shot them a look, and gradually the room cleared.

Leo Keating was smiling happily. "As appreciative an audience as I got at the Finsbury Park Astoria back in '49," he said.

Jack looked around at the empty canteen. "I think we'll conduct our interview in here," he said to Myra. "Take a seat, Mr Keating. More tea?"

"Yes, please," Keating said and sat down at a table.

Myra pulled up a chair opposite him and Jack sat at the head of the table.

Yvonne Morrison brought over a tray of tea cups, milk jugs and sugar bowls to the table, went back behind the counter, and returned with a large stainless-steel tea pot, and a plate of chocolate digestive biscuits.

"This is better service than we get at Boswell House," Leo Keating said, picking up a biscuit and nibbling its edge.

"About Boswell House," Jack said, as Myra poured tea into their cups. "You showed Myra here a tobacco tin full of tablets. What can you tell me about them?"

"What do you want to know?" Keating said, popping the whole chocolate digestive into his mouth.

"How often were you given them?"

"Every day, without fail," Keating said as he chewed.

"Did Dr Maitland prescribe them to you?"

Keating shook his head. "Him? I hardly ever saw him. Once about a year ago when I had an attack of the *Farmers* – he gave me some cream – but I've not seen him since."

"Farmers?" Myra said.

"Farmer Giles, Myra," Jack said. "Cockney rhyming slang."

Understanding flickered in Myra's eyes, and she blushed. "Ah, right. I see."

"So you wouldn't say he was a regular visitor to Boswell House."

Keating took a sip of tea, added two heaped spoons of sugar and stirred it, "No, I didn't say that. He used to call in about once a week, but I never had call to see him."

"Right," Jack said.

"Some of the others did though. Especially Daphne Sanders – a real hypochondriac that one, she always has something or other wrong with her...or thinks she has."

"But you rarely saw him?"

"Do I look sick to you?" Keating said.

Jack shook his head. "No. I must say that you look very well."

"A picture of health," Myra agreed.

"Well, I wouldn't be looking half as good as I do if I'd carried on taking those bloody tablets – excuse my French. Took them for a couple of weeks, until I realised they were making me feel awful, so I stopped."

"Very wise," Jack said. "You told Myra that others had stopped as well."

"Yes, I did. Would you like their names, so you can check?"

"That would be very helpful, Leo," Myra said, and produced her notebook and pen.

"Well, Freddie Cotton for one. He's ninety if he's a day, but still as fit as a flea." Keating chuckled. "Ironic really because that was his act. – *Professor Cotton's Amazing Flea Circus.* But after a couple of weeks on those bloody pills – pardon my French – he could barely get out of bed in the mornings."

"Was he one of Dr Maitland's patients?" Myra asked.

Keating shook his head again, and helped himself to another biscuit. "No. He's never bothered himself much with doctors. He prefers to medicate himself." He mimed pouring a drink. "If you get my drift."

Both Myra and Jack nodded, and Keating continued to recite names.

By the time he had finished, Myra had a list of eight. "All the names here are doing what you are doing, hiding the tablets away and not taking them?"

"That's right. It must be driving old Gerard barmy. There's a small army of us who aren't stumbling around the place like the living dead, but I don't think she's rumbled us yet. It serves her right, the silly cow."

16 WEDNESDAY

"Are there any residents who see Dr Maitland regularly?" Jack said.

Keating took another sip of tea. He was enjoying himself. "Percy Campion," he said. "He's a martyr to his bunions, and Lilly Icoff, who sees him for her nerves, not surprising really considering the act she used to do."

"Which was?" Myra said.

"She was the beautiful assistant of the *Great Ronaldi*, juggler and knife thrower." Keating watched Myra's face as she listened to him intently. "Old Ron was on the sauce as well," Keating continued. "It got so bad with him that one night at the *Bradford Empire* he was so sozzled he juggled his knives, and threw his juggling clubs at Lilly. Poor dear, she copped one full in the face, and it knocked her two front teeth out – ruined her looks. They chucked in the game not long after that."

Myra's eyes widened in shock.

The perfect stooge, Jack thought as he watched the old man's eyes twinkling. "Myra, why don't you take Mr Keating for a guided tour of the station, and when he's ready you can run him back to Boswell House."

"Already?" Keating said, "I was just getting into my stride."

"That's what I'm afraid of," Jack said knowingly. He got to his feet. "Thank you, Mr Keating. You've been a most helpful witness. We'll be along at some stage to question the other names on your list."

"Righto," Keating said, tugging at his forelock. "I'll tell them. They'll be looking forward to it. Oh, and remember to bring some of those chocolate biscuits with you. We don't get anything like them at the home. A couple of *Osborne* with your cup of tea if you're lucky, or *Rich Tea* if the old dragon is feeling particularly generous."

Smiling, Jack went back to his office.

"Well?" Myra said, when she returned ninety minutes later from taking Leo Keating back to Boswell House. "What did you think?"

Jack leaned back in his chair. "I think there's something there," he said. "It's just a case of sorting the wheat from the chaff."

"I don't know what you mean, sir."

"Really, Myra? Lilly Icoff?"

"I believed him."

Jack chuckled. "Yes, I saw that. You took the bait, and he hooked you. All he had to do was reel you in."

A frown crinkled her forehead. "Don't you think he was telling the truth?"

"About the pills and Elise Gerard keeping her guests sedated, yes, I think he was right on the money, but all the other stuff was flim-flam, showbiz hokum. He's probably been telling the story of Lilly Icoff and the *Great Ronaldi* for years to any mug gullible enough to listen to it."

"And I was the mug."

"Don't feel too bad about it," Jack said. "Tommy Apollo put one over on me earlier. These people are all the same – showmen and shysters. We'll just have to be on our guard, and not take anything at face value."

"It's a shame," Myra said. "I really liked him."

"So did I. I just wouldn't let myself be drawn into his imaginary world. Once in one day is more than enough for me."

"So, where do we go next?"

Jack rubbed his chin. "I think we can totally rule out Maitland as a source for the drugs, but they're coming from somewhere. Didn't you say that Farlowe and Gerard left show business amidst rumours of alcohol problems?"

"Yes."

"I wonder which of them had the problems."

"Maybe it was both of them."

"Maybe. I'm wondering if they ever received treatment for the problem, and if so, where did they receive their treatment? I should think they both made a lot of money in the business, so they probably sought out a private clinic or something. Somewhere discreet, where they could dry out without the newspapers getting wind of it. Rumours are one thing. Stories published in the paper, are something else entirely. Yes," he said, considering the point. "A private clinic, or maybe just a private doctor who'd be willing to supply drugs on a cash-on-delivery basis."

"It's certainly a thought," Myra said.

"It's a thought that brings us squarely back to Boswell House. Pull out all the stops, Myra. Assemble a team to look into it. I want Farlowe and Gerard's lives put under a microscope. They're the key to Dawn Peterson's murder. I'm sure of it."

"Helen Carter's back from leave tomorrow. Can I have her on the team?"

"Yes, good idea, and that new chap, Constable Peck. He got top marks from Hendon, so he could be an asset."

"Inspector Fuller won't like that, sir. Brian Peck is his bagman."

"Then bring Inspector Fuller into your investigation as well. I'll see that he doesn't give you any grief."

"Okay, sir. I'll start right away."

"Good, and if you have any problems from further up the line, let me know and I'll make them go away."

"Do you mean Chief Superintendent Watkins, sir?"

"You know the form, Myra. No names, no pack-drill. Just make sure you keep me informed."

"Yes, sir."

The *Ace of Clubs* transport cafe stood on a slip road off the A1, just outside Bedfordshire.

It was a rectangular box of a building, with white-painted walls, and dark green metal windows. Alongside the colourful tin-plate signs advertising *Tizer* and *Castrol Oil* were other aged and rust-spotted ones, for *Ferodo Brake Pads,* and *Norton Motorcycles.*

As well as the three goods lorries parked in the pot-holed car park was a line of motorbikes, seven of them, leaning up against the front wall of the café.

Lesser pushed open the door to be met by the smell of frying bacon, and the sound of rock and roll music blaring from a jukebox standing against the far wall. Three leather-jacketed youths were standing at the neon-lit jukebox, drumming their fingers on the domed plastic top, while a few others were seated at the Formica-topped tables, drinking tea from large earthenware mugs. Seated in a cluster at a table, as far away from the jukebox as they could get, were three older men; the lorry drivers, tucking into greasy-looking fry ups, and trying to ignore the music and the bikers.

Behind the counter was a small, fat man, wearing a stained white apron, his thinning hair plastered to his scalp with a mixture of sweat and hair oil. He was frying eggs on a smoking hot plate, flipping them over with a metal fish slice, and watching as the yolks sizzled in the oil.

"Excuse me," Lesser said, as he approached the counter. "I'm looking for Becky Shearing? I was told she works here?"

The fat man glanced over his shoulder as he flipped the egg onto a buttered slice of bread and stuck another slice on top of it. "She's on her break. Egg sandwich!" he called, and one of the leather boys peeled away from the jukebox and went to the counter to collect the unappetising breakfast.

The fat man handed the boy a plate, and took a few coins from him, opening the cash register, and dropping them into their individual sections of the till.

"When does she finish her break?" Lesser said.

The biker set his plate down on the counter and took a step towards Lesser. "Who wants to know?" he said aggressively.

"None of your business," Lesser said dispassionately, effectively dismissing the boy. "How long will she be?" he called to the proprietor.

The biker grabbed the sleeve of his overcoat. "I said, who wants to know? Only Becky's my girl so it's *my* business."

The other bikers in the café started to take an interest in events unfolding at the counter, the two at the jukebox taking menacing steps forward, sensing the potential action.

Lesser glanced down at the silver signet ring, with its skull and cross bones motif adorning the middle finger of the tattooed hand gripping his sleeve and sighed.

Before the biker could make a move, Lesser grabbed the boy's hand and began squeezing the oil-stained fingers together, crushing the silver ring into flesh and bone. The biker yelped, his eyes widening, searching his friend's faces, appealing for some support. No one in the cafe moved, except one of the lorry drivers, who ostentatiously turned the page of his newspaper, and continued reading the racing results.

A young woman appeared behind the counter. She had a blonde beehive, and wore thick black eye makeup.

"Let him go, mister," she said. "I'm Becky Shearing. It's me you want.

"Go and eat your breakfast like a good boy," Lesser hissed into the biker's ear, and released his hand.

The boy yanked his hand away, and tucked it under his arm, blinking away the tears of pain and humiliation that had sprung to his eyes.

"You want to watch it, mate," he said when he was out of Lesser's range. "Me and the boys…"

"Leave it, Jessie!" Becky snapped at him. "Do as the man said. Go and eat your breakfast."

Lesser turned to face her and smiled. "Do you like to watch the wrestling, Becky?"

Becky looked at him uncertainly. "It's all right. Who are you?"

"I'm a policeman, and I'd like to ask you some questions."

She frowned, her forehead creasing into ridges. "What about?"

"About wrestling, or to be more precise, about a certain wrestler. Tommy Apollo?"

Panic flared in her eyes, and she rushed to the flap in the counter and lifted it. "Come through. We can talk out the back."

"Hey!" the fat proprietor protested.

"It's all right, Uncle," Becky said to him. "We'll only be few ticks."

"But I've got customers."

"Well, serve them. I'll only be a couple of minutes." She led Lesser through a door at the back of the counter, to what looked like a small storeroom, and then she opened a door at the rear of the building, and led him out onto an area of oil-stained gravel and scrubby grass.

She turned to face him, standing with her arms crossed over the top of her grease-spotted tabard, and said defiantly, "Right. Tommy Apollo. What do you want to know about him?"

"Tommy tells me you're his girlfriend."

"In his dreams."

"So you're not? Is that what you're saying?"

"I'm going steady with Jessie, in there." She jerked her thumb in the direction of the café.

"But you see Tommy Apollo as well?"

"There's no law against it, is there?" Becky said belligerently.

"I think Jessie might have different ideas," Lesser said.

Becky shrugged nonchalantly.

"Well, let's call him out here and ask him, shall we?" He took a step towards the door.

"No!" Becky said, moving herself quickly between Lesser and the café.

"So, there *is* something between you and Tommy?"

Her expression softened. "He's lovely," she said. "He calls me his little ring rat. Isn't that sweet?"

"Adorable," Lesser said. "He told me he was with you on Sunday night."

Becky's brow wrinkled again. "Why would he tell you that? They don't have wrestling matches on Sunday nights, and that's the only time I ever see him – when he's on a card in the area."

"Did you see him at all at the weekend?"

"I saw him Saturday. He was fighting at Ware. He was up against Masambula. Tommy lost of course, but it was a great fight, and he took me for a meal afterwards. Steak and chips, his favourite."

"So you didn't see him on Sunday."

She rolled her eyes. "I just told you, didn't I? They don't hold wrestling matches on Sunday nights. Something to do with keeping the Sabbath holy."

The back door of the building opened, and the fat man poked his head out. "Becky? Get your scrawny arse back in here! A coach party's just turned up, and I can't manage them on my own." He ducked back inside without waiting for Becky's response.

"Sorry, mister, I've got to go in. Uncle Tony will have my guts if I don't give him a hand, and I need this job."

"You go on, Becky. I think you've told me everything I need." Lesser waved her away, and went back to his car, circling the outside of the café rather than going through the inside.

A red and white coach had pulled up next to his car and was disgorging passengers. They looked like a group of old age pensioners out for a day trip – most of the men in their jaunty corduroy sailors' hats and shiny windcheaters, the women, a collection of matching lilac-rinsed perms – all marching determinedly to have their full-English breakfasts and cups of tea.

I wonder how they'll cope with a motorcycle gang and a rock and roll jukebox, he thought idly as he started the car. *I think I pity the bikers.*

He smiled wryly, put the car into gear, and drove back to the A1.

17 WEDNESDAY

"Becky Shearing just torpedoed Tommy Apollo's alibi," Lesser said as he walked into Jack's office. "She only ever sees him after wrestling matches, and there wasn't a card on Sunday."

"Do you know him well, Frank?" Jack said.

"I've shared bills with him in the past, but I've never fought him. Why?"

"He just doesn't seem very bright. Why give us an alibi that can be so easily trashed?"

"Well, I don't think he's the sharpest knife in the drawer," Lesser said. "His escape attempt earlier wasn't exactly well thought through. I mean, what did he hope to achieve by breaking out of the cellblock into a building holding at least thirty coppers? Not very smart, whichever way you look at it."

"Well, let's go and see what he has to say for himself," Jack said.

Apollo was sitting morosely in his cell, the lump on his brow, from where he'd smashed his head on the doorframe, had swollen to the size of a hen's egg. The custody sergeant and a constable took him from the cell to the interview room, where Jack and Lesser were waiting for him.

The sergeant sat him down on a hard chair and left his wrists cuffed. Apollo stared down at his feet.

"You don't have an alibi for Sunday night, Tommy," Lesser said.

Apollo's head jerked up. "But Becky…" he began,

"You saw Becky Shearing on Saturday, not Sunday night," Lesser said.

Apollo sagged in his seat, returning his gaze to the floor.

"How about you come clean with us, Tommy?" Jack said.

"I saw her," Apollo mumbled into his chest.

"Becky said you didn't."

"Not Becky…I saw Dawn."

Jack and Lesser exchanged looks.

"Take us through your day, Tommy. What you did on Sunday," Lesser said.

Apollo shook his head, and remained silent.

"It's in your own interests, son," Jack said. "Tell us exactly what happened."

To their astonishment Tommy Apollo burst into tears. "I don't want to hang," he said.

"Did you kill her, Tommy?" Jack said.

"No…but I know how it looks," he said through the tears.

Jack turned to the constable standing guard at the door. "Get him some water."

The constable retuned a few moments later with an enamel mug filled with water, and set it down on the table. Jack slid it across to Apollo who took it in his cuffed hands and began to sip. Gradually the tears subsided, and he started to breathe calmly.

"Did you stay the night with Becky on Saturday?" Jack said.

Apollo nodded.

"Where?"

"She has a room at her uncle's place. Like a bedsit."

"Her uncle owns the *Ace of Clubs* transport café just off the A1," Lesser said.

"Where does her uncle live?"

"He's got a house in Biggleswade. Becky's got the attic," Apollo said.

"You were fighting in Ware on Saturday," Lesser said. "How did you get from Ware to Biggleswade?"

"I drove. I drive to all the shows."

"So, you drove back to Biggleswade on Saturday night," Jack said, "and you stayed the night with Becky."

Apollo nodded.

"Then what? What did you do the next morning?"

"Becky had to go to the *Ace of Clubs* with Tony, so I drove down to Stevenage."

"Why?"

"*deMarco's Gym.* I always go there to work out when I'm in the area."

"I know *deMarco's,* sir," Lesser said. "I use it myself from time to time."

"And you stayed there all day?" Jack said.

"Mostly."

"What do you mean, *mostly*?"

"I left about four."

"To go home?"

Apollo shook his head.

"Then what?"

Apollo sat back in his chair and stared up at the ceiling.

"What, Tommy?" Jack said.

"I couldn't get her out of my mind."

"Dawn?"

"It's stupid," Apollo said. "She's nothing, just another ring rat, but she dumped me. Dumped *me* for that druggie. He wasn't even another wrestler. If he had been I would have understood it, but he was just some scumbag lowlife, and I *didn't* understand it. I don't know what she saw in him."

"So, what did you do, Tommy?" Lesser said.

"I drove to Graveley. I was going to have it out with her."

"And did you?"

Apollo shook his head. "I bottled it. I just sat outside her house until she left for work, and then I followed her."

"On foot or in the car?"

"In the car. I hung right back, but I knew she was going to catch the bus, so I drove down there, and saw her at the bus stop, and offered her a lift."

"Which she accepted?"

"Yeah."

"Did you take her to Boswell House, to her job?"

Apollo shook his head. "I was going to."

"But something happened?"

"We were getting on so well. It was just like old times, so I took a little detour."

"To where?"

"A layby on the A1. It leads to an old service road," Apollo said. "We'd used it before. I parked up and we got into the back seat."

"And you did the deed?" Lesser said.

Apollo gave a bark of laughter. "I wish! But it never got that far."

"Explain."

He shook his head. "Like I said, we got into the back seat. She took her mac off, and we were just getting down to business, and she says, 'Do you love me, Tommy?' and I said, 'Not if you're going to go off with every junkie who offers you a fix.'"

"To which she replied?"

"She went mental on me – shouting, screaming in my face. Slapping me, punching me, pulling my hair."

"Did you hit her back, Tommy?"

Apollo stared shamefacedly down at his feet. "I might have clocked her one."

"So what happened then?"

"That was it. She was out of the car and running away."

"Did you follow her?"

"I tried. There's an old disused factory out there at the back of the service road, with a fence around it. I couldn't see a sign of her, so I figured she'd slipped through the fence and gone to hide in the factory. Well, I wasn't going to piss around looking for the silly cow. It was starting to rain. So I got back in the car and drove home."

"Ever the gentleman," Jack said.

"Well, what would you have done? She was a head case – half barmy. I decided there and then to cut my losses, and get the hell out of there."

"So you never saw her again after she got out of your car?"

Apollo shook his head. "Not until you showed me that photo, and I thought, shit! They're going to blame me for it, so I told you the lie about Becky. I've probably made it worse for myself, haven't I?"

"You haven't helped your case," Jack said.

"But it's true. I swear it. She was so keen to get out of the car she didn't even stop to pick up her mac. I saw it when I dove to the show last night."

"Where is it now?"

"Still there, and my car's still in the car park at the Corn Exchange. I had to leave it there when you picked me up last night."

Jack got to his feet. "You're allowed one telephone call," he said to Apollo. "I suggest you use it to call a solicitor." He turned and walked from the room.

Outside in the corridor Lesser said, "Are you going to charge him, sir?"

"I haven't decided yet."

"He had motive, opportunity and, by his own admission, was at the scene of the crime."

"But not inside the factory itself. Only on the slip road." Jack shook his head. "Let him make his phone call, and then put him back in his cell, and get someone over to the *Hertford Corn Exchange* car park to check out his motor. See if he's telling the truth about that part of the story at least. If he is, then Dawn's coat will be on the back seat."

"This has just arrived by courier, sir," Andy Brewer said, holding out a large brown envelope to Jack as he walked past the front desk on his way back to his office.

Jack took it from him. "This must be the PM report. Thanks. Andy."

On his way back up to his office, he peeled back the flap of the envelope and removed the contents and started to read.

Ten minutes later Lesser appeared in his doorway.

Jack looked up. "Well?"

"He called his brief. He's on his way here now, and Apollo's back in his cell.

"I'm just reading through the post mortem report," Jack said.

"Anything we didn't know?"

"Barry Fenwick was way off with the time of death."

"How far off?"

"Five or six hours, but then he was only going on body temperature. Professor Strong can run far more tests. Of course, it's impossible to establish the actual time, unless you happened to be there when she was killed, but Strong has far more experience dealing with corpses."

"What are we looking at?"

"It says here that she was killed between six and twelve Sunday night."

"Which put's Tommy bang in the frame. Are you going to charge him now, guv?"

"Have we heard anything from Inspector Fuller?"

"Not that I'm aware. Why?"

"He and Harry Grant ran out of here a while back like their tails were on fire, chasing a lead to Dougie Marshall. I'll hold off on charging Tommy until I get an update on that."

"Tommy's brief is going to demand his release, guv, unless we can provide a good reason to keep him locked up."

"I'm aware of that, Frank, and all we have is circumstantial evidence, and nothing to say that he actually strangled Dawn." Jack ran his hands through his hair. "I hate days like this."

"Do you believe Apollo's story then?"
"That's the trouble, Frank. I think I do."
"Bugger!"
"My thoughts exactly."

18 WEDNESDAY

Norton Crown Park straddled the Baldock border and, despite its grand sounding name, was little more than a large field separated from a neighbouring farm, cornfields and the Royston road, by a high chain-link fence. It was home to twenty permanently sited caravans, along with three large Nissen huts that served as the toilet, shower and administration blocks, and reminded Eddie Fuller of a cross between a German POW camp and a gypsy encampment. The latter comparison was reinforced by the site of a dozen raggedy children chasing balls, hoops, mangy-looking dogs, and each other, between and around the caravans, yelling at the top of their lungs, and swearing like stevedores unloading cargo onto the docks.

"Are you sure about this, Inspector?" Harry Grant said.

"Norton Crown Park was the name we were given," Fuller said. "Who am I to argue with an anonymous tip off?"

"I think the clue is in the *anonymous* part of that last statement. How do we know it's not someone pulling our chain?"

"We don't," Fuller said. "But if it's on the level, and Dougie Marshall *is* holed up here, it's going to save us and Uniform many miles of shoe leather, and I for one am not going to turn my nose up at that."

"Fair enough."

"The caravan we're looking for is on Plot seven. Come on, and be ready, he might just cut up rough."

The road leading into the Park was pot-holed concrete, decorated with tufts of scrub grass and thistle, and it led up to a chain link gate of equal height with the fence.

"Welcome to Stalag Norton," Grant said, as he pushed through into the Park.

"I was thinking the same thing," Fuller said as they checked the plot numbers for the caravans. "This is it," Grant said, as they stopped beside a large but badly dilapidated trailer. There were holes in the fibreglass shell, and many of the cosmetic details had been worn away by age and neglect.

There was a six-inch high metal step to the front door. Fuller stepped up and rapped on the door. He waited for a full minute before knocking again and calling out, "Dougie? Dougie Marshall?"

At the side of the door was a square plastic window. He peered through but the grime on the plastic, combined with dirty net curtains inside, obscured his view.

"I'll check the window at the end," Grant said, and walked around to the rear of the caravan. Standing on tiptoe, he pressed his nose against the rectangle of glass, recoiling instantly as a ferocious-looking bull terrier threw itself against the window, barking furiously. "Jesus Christ!" Grant yelled, as he stumbled backwards. "Watch out, sir! There's a rabid dog in there."

Fuller came around and looked through the window. The dog had made short work of the curtain inside, and it was hanging in ragged strips at the window, which allowed him to look through to the caravan's interior.

His gaze met the bull terriers as it sat growling on the unmade bed just below the window. "Get a tyre iron, Harry. We're going to have to break in."

"Why's that?"

"Take a look."

Nervously Grant took a step forward and looked inside.

The first thing he saw was the dirty white bull terrier. The second was the body sprawled face up on the bed that the dog seemed to be guarding. "I'll fetch the tyre iron," he said, and ran back to the car.

When he returned it took them only seconds to jemmy the door and get it open.

Fuller entered first. "All right, boy," he said soothingly to the dog. "It's all right."

The dog growled louder.

Fuller looked beyond it to the body on the bed, which appeared to be that of a half-naked young man, with tattoos covering much of his exposed flesh. The only other remarkable thing about him was his throat, which had been opened up in much the same way as Dawn Peterson's.

"Bloody hell!" Grant gasped.

"Well, don't just stand there gawping. Go and call it in. We need Doc Fenwick, an ambulance, and a full forensic team here, sharpish, and it wouldn't do any harm to get the chief inspector down here as well."

"Right," said Grant, and hurried back to the car.

The bull terrier had stopped growling, and was watching developments in a mildly curious way, but when Fuller moved to get a closer look at the body it bared its teeth and started to growl again.

"It's okay, boy," Fuller said, trying to reassure it. "You've done your job. Good dog."

He extended his hand tentatively, all the while crooning soothing platitudes. The dog stopped growling and sniffed his fingertips. Seconds later it allowed Fuller to stroke its rather ugly head, and pet its pointed ears.

"Is that dog safe?" Jack said as he entered the caravan.

"He's fine," Fuller said, ruffling the dog's grubby-looking coat. "You're a good boy, aren't you?" The dog twisted its bullet-shaped head and licked his fingers.

"Is it Dougie Marshall?" Jack pointed at the body.

"Judging by the name in the tattoo on his forearm, I'd say yes."

As Jack stepped forward to look at the tattoo, the dog started to growl again.

"I thought you said it was safe," Jack said.

"He is – just protective of his master."

"Not protective enough to save his life though."

"He's a bit soft, once you get to know him."

"Then maybe the killer knew him as well as Dougie did."

"Yeah. I was thinking the same," Fuller said.

"See if you can find a lead and take him outside. We don't want him taking lumps out of the doctor."

There was a thick, plaited-leather dog lead hanging from the back of the door. Fuller snapped the catch onto the dog's collar and led it from the caravan.

Grant was leaning against the fibreglass shell of the caravan smoking a cigarette. He dropped it to the ground as Fuller emerged and stamped it into the grass.

"Here," Fuller said, handing him the lead.

"What do you want me to do with it?"

"Take it for a walk, Constable," Fuller said. "The poor thing's been cooped up in there for God knows how long. It probably wants to do its business."

"But why me? I don't even like dogs."

"From the way he reacted when you stuck your ugly mug against the window, he doesn't like you very much either. Treat it as an opportunity to build bridges. Go on, scoot."

Grumbling, Grant tugged on the lead, and led the dog away from the caravan.

A maroon and grey Vauxhall Victor pulled onto the site, and Barry Fenwick stepped out, reaching back into the car to retrieve his brown leather bag. "Hello, Inspector." He sketched a wave to Fuller, and trotted the hundred or so yards to the caravan. "Another one?"

"See for yourself," Fuller said, and ushered him inside.

"Ah, yes," Fenwick said, as he spotted the body. "Much like before."

As Fuller followed the doctor inside, the glint of something shining caught his eye, coming from the dog's padded bed that was pushed up against the nearest wall. Fuller squatted down, and pulled a damp and crumpled tartan blanket to one side.

Fenwick leaned over the body. "The same as last time. The wounds look identical. Still no sign of the murder weapon?"

"I wouldn't say that, Doc."

Taking a pen from his pocket he threaded it through a loop of thin silver wire. Carefully he lifted the wire away from the blanket and held it up for Jack and the doctor to see.

"My word," Barry Fenwick said. "That looks like a…"

"A garrotte," Jack said. "I had to use one during the war. It's a horrible weapon, but very effective. Let's have a look at it."

The wire was about twenty-four inches in length, and attached to each end was a small wooden dowel, each measuring three inches.

"The silent killer," Jack said. "Form a loop in the wire, drop it over the victim's head and pull it tight – simple and deadly. With a wire that thin, it would be easy enough to sever the carotid artery. When I saw the wound to Dawn Peterson's neck, I thought that's what we were dealing with."

He looked closely at the dowels. They were both blood-streaked.

"How did it end up in the dog's bed?" Fenwick said.

"The dog probably grabbed it from the killer, took it to his bed and wouldn't let him get near enough to take it back." Fuller said. "When we first got here the dog was standing guard over the body. He was very protective of Dougie. Shame he didn't act faster."

"Don't blame the dog, Eddie. From popping the loop over the head, and pulling it tight enough to inflict that kind of damage, we're talking about a few seconds. I doubt even Dougie would have had time to react. This killer is fast and utterly ruthless.'

"And strong," Fuller said. "You said the murderer would have to be very strong to inflict wounds like Dawn's."

"That was before I saw the murder weapon. With wire that thin it would only take a person of average strength to achieve that result. It would be the same amount of effort to slice through a lump of cheese."

"So, I suppose that puts Danny Hutchence back in the frame."

"That, and Professor Strong's new estimate of the time of death. I'm afraid Danny can no longer rely on Bruce Forsyth to provide him with an alibi."

Fenwick was still leaning over the body. "I don't suppose either of you two detectives noticed that this body is still warm."

"So that means he was killed..." Jack said.

"A few hours ago," Fenwick finished for him, "and I'm sure Professor Strong will agree with me, once he's had a chance to examine the body," Fenwick added pointedly.

"Get a bunch of uniformed officers down here to canvas the residents. This happened this morning, so someone must have seen or heard something," Jack said. "And make sure they question the kids. They've probably been dashing around, wreaking havoc here since first light. The joys of the half-term holidays."

"What's that, sir?" Fuller said. "By your foot."

Jack looked and stooped down to pick up a small, blue triangular tablet. "*Drinamyl* is my guess." He held it out in the palm of his hand to show Fenwick.

"Impossible to say conclusively without testing it, but on appearance alone I would say, yes."

"It's not really a surprise to find a stray *Purple Heart,*" Fuller said. "We've been told that Dawn was supplying drugs to Dougie, so he probably had a stash of them somewhere.

"Really? *She* was supplying *him?*" Fenwick looked up from the body again. "Where on earth was she getting enough pills to supply someone else as well as feeding her own habit?"

"That, Barry, is what we're doing our damnedest to find out."

The jangling sound of *Winkworth* bells split the afternoon peace, as two Wolseley police cars, and an ambulance pulled onto the site. Suddenly it was more than just a handful of scruffy children staring at the vehicles with widening eyes. Doors to the caravans were opening, and a motley collection of adults joined their offspring, to watch what was happening in their midst.

"I'll leave you to supervise. I'm going back to the station. I have a wrestler I need to release," Jack said, to Fuller. "Where's Constable Grant?"

"He's taken the dog for a walk."

Jack look at him. "You're being serious, aren't you?"

Fuller pointed to the figure of Harry Grant in the distance being dragged across a field by the gleeful bull terrier.

"Who's taking who for a walk?" Jack said.

"He's a novice, sir," Fuller said with a smile.

19 WEDNESDAY

"I've been waiting here for two hours!"

Jack had just walked through the door and was shrugging his arms out of his overcoat when an overweight man, wearing a cheap suit and scuffed shoes, stood up from the seat he was occupying below the notice board in the foyer. The man stepped out in front of him.

"Who are you?" Jack said, freeing one arm and struggling with the other.

"Gerald Alexander," the man said.

Jack glanced around at Andy Brewer, who gave an apologetic shrug, "Mr Apollo's solicitor, sir," he said. "He *has* been waiting a long time."

Jack finally freed his arm. "I don't care," he said. "I'm sorry, Mr Alexander, but I've been out investigating a homicide. I take it you're here about your client."

"Of course. That's exactly why I'm here," Alexander said, his voice becoming shrill. "Two hours I've sat here, and all I've had is prevarication from your sergeant there, and a string of his feeble excuses. I demand to see my client."

"Okay," Jack said.

"What does that mean?"

"It means okay. Yes, you can see him now," Jack said, folding his coat across his arm, and moving towards the stairs. "In fact, I'll go one better. You can take your client with you when you leave." He took another step.

"Now, just one moment," Alexander said, his ruddy, bellicose face returning to a more natural colour. "What do you mean, I can take him out of here?"

Jack sighed, and looked up at the clock of the foyer wall. The hands were nudging towards five o'clock. "Look, Mr Alexander, I'm sorry you've had to wait so long, but it's been a very busy day, and sometimes it's as much as we can do to keep on top of things, but we try. So, what I'm telling you now, is that your client has not been charged with anything, and is now free to go."

"And that's all you have to say?"

"Pretty much," Jack said. He turned to Brewer, "Sergeant, ring through to the cells and have Mr Apollo brought up to meet Mr Alexander."

"Do we have a problem here, Chief Inspector?" Chief Superintendent Watkins was standing at the top of the stairs, watching the scene being enacted below, an impassive expression of his face.

"It's all in hand, sir," Jack said.

"Is that the case, Mr Alexander?" Watkins said, walking slowly down the stairs.

"No, it damned well isn't!" Alexander said, colouring again. "First they refuse to let me see my client, then they keep me hanging around here for hours, making excuse after excuse, and then this fool strolls in and tells me that my client has no charges to face and I can take him home."

"Would you care to elaborate on that, Chief Inspector?"

Jack rolled his eyes and laid his folded coat down on a vacant chair. "Tommy Apollo, Mr Alexander's client, has been here since last night, helping us with our inquiries. I didn't charge him earlier because the investigation was on-going, and I didn't think it was apposite to do so.

"Before Mr Alexander arrived, I was called away to another murder scene, and what we found there puts Mr Apollo in the clear, so I apologised for keeping him waiting, and told Mr Alexander that he can take his client home."

"That's it?" Watkins said.

"Yes, sir."

"Anything to add, Mr Alexander?"

"That's about the long and the short of it," Alexander said grudgingly.

Watkins rocked on the balls of his feet. "Well, Chief Inspector Callum's explanation of events seems perfectly reasonable to me. I'm sorry for the inconvenience, sir."

"But...but..."

At that moment the door to the cells opened and Martin Follett led Apollo into the foyer still handcuffed, the lump on his head now a nasty shade of purple.

"Release him, Sergeant," Jack said to Follett. "That's it, Tommy. You're free to go."

Apollo's face split into a grin as the handcuffs were removed. "Seriously?"

"Yes," Jack said. "There are no charges to face, but I would warn you about striking young ladies in future. It's not something I take lightly, and if I wasn't involved in a much more serious matter, and if the young lady in question wasn't deceased, I'd arrest you on the spot, and charge you with assault. Do I make myself clear?"

Apollo blushed. "Yes...sir."

"Right. If you ask Mr Alexander nicely, I'm sure he'll drive you over to Hertford to pick up your car."

"No need, sir," Andy Brewer called. "The officers you sent to investigate Mr Apollo's motor took the liberty of bringing it back here. It's in the car park."

"Well, that will save you a trip," Jack said. "If you could just leave Dawn's raincoat here. I'd like to return it to her father."

"Right," Apollo said. "I'll be off then."

Alexander stepped forward. "Just a minute, Tommy." He turned to Jack. "How do you explain the state of my client's forehead? Such an injury could be dangerous. There could be brain damage."

"Leave it out, Gerry," Apollo said. "I get a lot worse than this in the ring every week."

"Mr Apollo tripped when leaving his cell earlier."

"That's it," Apollo agreed. "Tripped as I was coming out of the cell and smacked my head on the doorframe – clumsy sod that I am. Come on, Gerry. Let's get out of here."

"You haven't heard the last of this," Alexander said.

"Oh, I believe we have, Mr Alexander," Watkins said. "Chief Inspector, I take it you're not pursuing the earlier charge of assaulting a police officer?"

"In light of the inconvenience Mr Apollo has been subjected to, no, I'll let that one slide."

"Then your client can consider himself a very lucky man, Mr Alexander."

Apollo tugged the solicitor's sleeve. "Come *on*, Gerry."

Alexander opened his mouth to say something more, but thought better of it, clamped his lips tightly together, and marched out of the station. Tommy Apollo trotted along behind him, trying to keep up.

Jack retrieved his coat and tried again to walk up to his office.

"Just one moment," Watkins said.

Jack stopped and turned slowly to face him. "Yes, sir?"

"Just to let you know, Chief Inspector, I support my men, regardless of how dubious I find their methods. But my tolerance is discretionary. Am I making myself clear?"

"Yes, sir," Jack said.

"Just watch it in the future," Watkins said, and strode up the stairs without a backward glance.

Before he could take another step, the doors burst open and Tommy Apollo ran into the station, bundling Dawn's raincoat into Jack's arms. "There you go, and thanks again." He turned and ran from the station.

Jack yawned, shook his head and shrugged into his overcoat. "That's it, Andy. I'm off. I've had more than enough for one day."

"Goodnight, sir," Brewer said and threw him a salute.

*

The caravan on Plot six directly next to Marshall's couldn't have been more different. It looked as though it had just rolled out onto a showroom forecourt and, apart from its pristine condition, it was surrounded by neatly trimmed turf, and large ornamental flowerpots containing dwarf conifers and standard roses.

The door was open, and Fuller poked his head inside. "Hello?" There was a man standing at a small enamelled metal unit containing a plumbed in sink, complete with its own draining board. He was in his forties, and his face was covered with soap lather. He grabbed a clean towel from a hook at the side of the unit and dabbed at his face. "Excuse me. I've just come in from work. Just freshening up."

"I'm with the police," Fuller said.

"So you're the one responsible for turning the Park into a circus," the man said, looking beyond Fuller and out through the door to the small crowd, who were watching the police activity avidly.

"Sorry," Fuller said.

The man smiled. "Don't worry about it. Besides it's providing that lot with some entertainment, and heaven knows that's in short supply in a place like this." He hung up the towel, and opened a small refrigerator in the base of the unit and took out a bottle of pale ale. "Can I get you one?"

"I'm on duty, I'm afraid."

"My word," he laughed. "You actually say that. I thought that was just for those Edgar Lustgarten films."

Fuller nodded.

"Fair enough. Why are you here?" he said, as he removed the cap and poured the beer into a clean tumbler.

"We're investigating the death of your neighbour, Dougie Marshall."

"So Doug the slug – that's what my wife calls him – is dead eh? Well. I can't say I'll miss him." He sat down on a padded bench that ran the length of the neatly decorated and very tidy caravan, and sipped his light ale.

"How well did you know Mr Marshall?"

The man shook his head. "I barely knew him, rarely saw him, but heard him more often than was good for me."

"What exactly do you mean by that Mr…"

"Sorry," the man said, extending his hand. "Linden. George Linden."

Fuller shook his hand.

"What I mean is that our paths rarely crossed. I'm out at work all day, and he was rarely here in the evenings. But I would hear him, either coming home drunk late at night, or playing his records into the early hours. These places aren't soundproofed you know, so you have to be considerate to your neighbours, and Doug the slug wasn't the considerate type. If he wasn't playing music, he'd be entertaining his guests."

"His guests?"

"His pals who he'd been drinking with, and women, lots of women."

"Was there one woman in particular he used to see?" Fuller sat down on the bench opposite.

"Funny you should say that, and had you asked me that two months ago, I would have said no. But recently there *was* one who kept showing up here, even when the slug was out. Pretty girl. Dark hair and big eyes."

"Did you catch her name?"

Linden shook his head. "The wife might know." He stood up, walked to the door, peered out, and spotted his wife in the crowd of onlookers. Sticking two fingers in his mouth he gave a shrill whistle, and beckoned her across.

"Maggie?" he said, as the woman walked into the caravan. "Maggie, what was the name of that girl who used to hang around the slug's caravan?"

"Dawn," Maggie said.

"Just Dawn?"

"I didn't ask for her biography, George. We just used to chat if I saw her around. Now is there anything else. I'm missing all the fun."

"I'm having fun in here," Linden said. "This is Inspector Fuller. He's with the police."

Maggie turned to look at Fuller, as if noticing him for the first time, and her eyes widened. "Perhaps *you* can tell me what's going on?" she said. "The policeman out there won't tell us a thing."

"Come and sit down, Mrs Linden, and I'll tell you what you want to know."

"Really?" She glanced wistfully back at crowd, hesitated for a moment, and then made her decision. "All right then," she said, coming across and sitting down next to her husband.

Maggie Linden was an attractive woman in her late thirties, with curly blonde hair, and blue, lively, inquisitive eyes.

"I'm afraid your neighbour, Mr Marshall was killed, we think, early this morning," Fuller said.

Maggie looked at him incredulously. "Killed? Murdered you mean?"

"I'm afraid so."

"So that's what all the kerfuffle was about," she said. "I wondered."

"Perhaps you can both tell me what you witnessed?"

"I didn't notice anything." George Linden said.

"That's because you left for work an hour before it all kicked off," Maggie said.

"What time did you leave this morning, Mr Linden?"

"The same as I always do, about five. That's why I never appreciated being kept awake 'til one or two in the morning. I work the early shift at Pelham's, the non-ferrous company. I'm a charge hand, and pretty exacting work it is too."

"What did you witness, Mrs Linden?" Fuller steered the conversation back to Maggie.

"Well, I didn't *see* anything, but I heard part of it. I was still in bed, and had my head under the pillow to block it all out, so I only really heard the slug bellowing and that bloody dog barking."

"What exactly was he bellowing?" Fuller said.

"Umm."

"Take your time."

20 WEDNESDAY

"It was like listening to one end of a telephone conversation," she said. "I heard what he was saying, but I couldn't hear the responses," Maggie said. "Can I have one of those?" she said to her husband, pointing to his glass of beer.

Linden rose from the bench and went to the fridge.

"Did it occur to you that a telephone conversation might have been exactly what you were listening to?"

Maggie smiled indulgently. "Look around you, Mr Fuller. Do you see a telephone? No. Look outside. Can you see any telegraph poles? No. I'm afraid we had to give up so many creature comforts when we came here to live in this dustbin. The telephone was one of them. Thanks," she said to her husband as he passed her the cold beer.

"Have you been living here long?"

"Two years," Linden said gloomily. "Since I lost my job at Browning's —that's an architects' in Letchworth. County Council budget cuts. They had to let me go. We couldn't keep up the repayments on the mortgage. Luckily, I'd saved a small nest egg, so we bought this place."

"And regretted it ever since," Maggie said bitterly.

"It's not that bad, love," Linden said.

"I don't recall our old next-door neighbours getting murdered, do you?"

Linden shook his head. "You have a point," he said.

Fuller once again had to steer the conversation back on track. "What kind of thing was Marshall shouting?"

"Oh, he was in a right old temper. 'I'm not paying that!' 'What do you think I am? Made of money?'"

"Anything else?"

Maggie's face darkened. "Now, I'm not sure I heard this right. Like I said, my head was under the pillow, but I'm sure he said, 'She wasn't going to tell no one. You didn't have to kill her.'" Maggie looked at Fuller, trying to judge his reaction but his face was inscrutable.

"Bloody hell," Linden said. "Did he really say that?"

She nodded her blonde curls. "I'm pretty sure that's what he said."

"You're sure you didn't hear the other half of the conversation?"

She shook her head. "It was muffled. Like someone was speaking from the bottom of a well. That's the best way I can describe it. I couldn't hear the words, just a sort of rumble. I even took the pillow away from my ears, but it didn't improve any, or maybe the other person just stopped talking. Anyway, just then the dog started barking, and I hear the slug's door slam, followed by a motorbike starting up and roaring away."

"Are you sure it was a motorbike?"

"I know the difference between a bike and a car."

"How long between the conversation stopping and the dog barking?"

"Not long. Thirty seconds, a minute perhaps."

Fuller leaned his head back against the fibreglass wall. "I wonder if anyone else on the site heard anything?"

"They didn't," Maggie Linden said. "Geoff Baker, the man in the next caravan down, said he heard the bike roaring away, but he heard nothing of the argument."

"You asked everybody?"

"Of course. We were all gossiping about what could have happened after your lot arrived. Remember, this was all kicking off about six this morning. Oh, and I've just remembered, a woman heard the dog barking, but just dismissed it as nothing particularly unusual. The bloody thing was always yapping. Nobody took much notice of it."

Fuller heard his name being called outside. He glanced round at the open door, and saw one of the forensic team walking around, looking into the spaces between the caravans, searching for him. "I'll be right with you!" he called back. He turned to Maggie Linden. "One last question. Could you tell if Mr Marshall was speaking to a man or a woman?"

She looked blank.

"You must have formed some kind of impression."

"A man," she said at last. "But it could have been a woman with a deep voice...I'm sorry. I really can't be sure."

"No matter. You've been very helpful. Thank you."

Fuller stood up and left the caravan.

"We're done in there," the forensic officer said.

"Anything interesting?"

"The place is covered in prints. We'll process them and let you know if we get any matches, apart for the victim, of course."

"Of course," Fuller said. "Has anyone seen my constable? He was taking the dog for a walk."

The officer was grinning. "Not a natural dog person, is he?"

"No," Fuller said.

"The last I saw of him, he was heading for a group of trees, over there." He waved his arm in the direction of the road.

"Christ!" Fuller said. "He'll probably be half way to Royston by now."

"Are you up for it," Myra Banks said.

Constable Brian Peck looked uncertain. Peck looked a lot younger than his twenty-three years, almost as if he'd stepped straight out of the sixth form, and into the police service.

"Well? Are you?" Myra said, waiting patiently for his response.

"Who else is going to be on this special team?"

"You, me, Helen Carter when she gets back tomorrow…and Inspector Fuller."

"Well, if the inspector's involved, then count me in."

Myra avoided his eyes.

"What aren't you telling me?"

"Well, it's like this, Inspector Fuller doesn't know he's on the team yet."

Peck took a step away from her. "Oh, no. I'm not falling for that one. If the inspector is in on it then you can count me in, but I'm not going against him. I'm his bagman after all."

"I know that, you idiot. It was me who recommended you for the job. Who do you think was the inspector's bagman before you came along?"

"You?" Peck said disbelievingly, and looked across at Andy Brewer behind the desk for confirmation.

Brewer gave an almost imperceptible nod.

"But you're a …" Peck stopped himself.

"Careful, Brian. I'm a detective constable, just like you."

"Well, thanks for putting me up for it," Peck said.

"You're welcome, and you can thank me properly by joining my team."

Peck was shaking his head. "I'm sorry, Myra, but I stand by what I said. If Inspector Fuller is on the team, then so am I. But if he doesn't sign up for it…well, sorry."

Myra sighed. "Okay, Brian. I'll let you know the upshot once I've spoken to the inspector." She glanced at her watch. "It will have to be tomorrow now. Goodnight, Brian. 'night, Sarge," she said to Andy Brewer, and made her way to the front door. She stopped in the doorway. "Another thing, Brian. You *do* realise that it was Jack Callum who suggested you for my team?"

Peck looked surprised. "Really? Chief Inspector Cal…" He pulled himself up short. "Oh, nice try, Myra, but I hardly know the man. Why would the chief inspector suggest me? Try pulling the other one next time. It might not ring as loudly."

Myra shook her head and pushed through the doors. "Suit yourself," she muttered. "You bloody fool."

"Is DCI Callum in the building, Sarge?" Peck asked Andy Brewer.

"No, lad. He went home about half an hour ago. Why?"

"What Myra said about Mr Callum suggesting me for a role on the team she's putting together to look into Boswell House."

"Well, what about it?"

"Do you think she was making it up? I mean, I've hardly spoken to him since I arrived here."

"But that doesn't mean he hasn't noticed you."

"Yes, but…"

"Yes, but nothing. Listen, Jack Callum is the best detective working at this station. If he's suggested you for a job, it's because he thinks you're good enough to do it and do it well. He's not a man to waste his time. Or anybody else's for that matter. So if you're thinking of turning it down, I'd think again."

"No, Myra's just pulling my leg. Besides, I'm Inspector Fuller's bagman."

"Yes, so you keep telling us," Brewer said. Do you know where your precious inspector is now?"

"He's out, investigating a suspicious death."

"Yet you're here. If you're his bagman, why aren't you with him?"

"He took Harry Grant instead."

"Why was that?" Brewer said.

Peck looked uncomfortable. "He said he needed someone with more experience, and Grant fits the bill."

Brewer raised his eyebrows. "Have you got time for a cuppa, lad?"

Peck glanced at the station clock. "Yes, why not?"

Brewer lifted the flap in the desk. "Come through."

In the back-office Constable Robert Meadows was laboriously copy typing a report from a notebook lying on the desk beside him.

"You can finish that in the morning, Bob."

Meadows looked up from his task. "But I'm nearly done, Sarge, Another half an hour."

"In the morning, Bob."

"But…"

"Bugger off home," Brewer said.

Meadows looked from Brewer to Peck and back again, and then got to his feet. "Right," he said. "See you tomorrow."

"Goodnight, Bob."

As Meadows left the office Brewer switched on the electric kettle. "Take the weight off your feet, lad," he said to Peck, who duly obliged, settling into Meadow's still warm chair.

Brewer made the tea quickly. 'Milk, sugar?"

"Both. Two sugars."

"How long have you been here now, Brian…it is Brian isn't it?" Brewer said as he set the mug of tea down in front of him.

Peck nodded. "Six weeks."

"And you came here straight from Hendon?"

"That's right, Sarge."

"Then the inspector's right. You are lacking in experience."

"But how am I going to get that experience if I'm not allowed to go out on a case with him?"

"Learn to walk before you can run, lad." Brewer sat down and took a long swig of tea, wiping his mouth on the sleeve of his tunic. "The case the inspector's working on is, by all accounts, pretty involved."

"I know, and I believe…"

Brewer raised his hand to stop him. "And the way I understand it, looking into Boswell House is pretty pivotal to the investigation as a whole."

"I suppose so."

"Myra Banks, despite her age, has been involved in some of the ugliest cases I've seen in my twenty-five years in the force. As well as that, she's the only female CID officer in the Hertfordshire Constabulary. What does that tell you about her?"

"She's good at her job?"

"Oh, yes, she's good. Damned good, and, because DCI Callum suggested you, she wants you on her team." Brewer took another mouthful of tea, swallowed, belched and put his mug down. "And you're pissing her about, being too grand, and too full of your own self-importance to agree to join her. Now what does that say about you?"

Peck thought about it for a moment. "That I'm a bit of a prick?"

"By George, he's got it!" Brewer said.

Peck was blushing furiously.

"Don't feel too bad about it, son. We all make arses of ourselves sometimes."

"What do you suggest I do?"

"Make amends. Get in here early tomorrow morning, and I mean early because Myra's always here before eight, and tell her that you're happy to join her team, and you're sorry you couldn't give her a straight answer this evening."

"Do you think she'll accept my apology?"

"Yes, lad, I do…mind you, she'll probably rib you about it for weeks to come, but you've brought that on yourself."

"You're right, Sarge. Thank you."

"You're welcome. Now, drink up and piss off home. The night shift will be along any minute and, if they see you still here, they'll find jobs for you to do and you'll still be here at midnight."

Peck swallowed the last of his tea, "That's it. I'm off."

"See you tomorrow," Brewer said. "And remember, bright and early."

21 THURSDAY October 20TH 1960

"I can't, Jack," Eddie Fuller said. They were sitting in Jack's office.

"Why not?"

"I can't join Myra's team if Helen Carter's going to be on it."

"Again I ask, why not?"

"There's history between Helen and me. It could get ugly."

"Oh, Jesus wept, Eddie. How many times have I told you to keep your work life and your personal life separate?"

"I know, I know. It was just one of those things that happened. I realised my mistake almost at once and tried to put a stop to it, but she didn't take it well."

"I don't blame her. She probably thought you were taking advantage of your rank and just using her."

"It isn't like that, Jack. I really like her, and I thought she liked me."

"So, it has nothing to do with you not being able to keep your flies buttoned up?"

"No...well... maybe, just a bit."

Jack shook his head. "Sorry, Eddie, I'm not giving you a choice. This is vital to the investigation. We need to look into Boswell House, and especially into Farlowe and Gerard, and Myra seems to have very good contact in Leo Keating that we need to exploit."

"I'm not being on a team led by a Detective Constable," Fuller said adamantly. "I have my reputation to think of."

"Oh, stop being an arse, Eddie. You'll be leading the team in name, but I want Myra to co-ordinate it. She's bloody good at that sort of thing, and as for Helen Carter, you're just going to have work it out between yourselves. I like Helen. She's good at her job, and I won't have her sacrificed on the altar of your bloody libido. She has a place on the team, okay?"

"Bloody hell!" Fuller said. "All right."

"So, what are you waiting for? Go and see Myra and find out what she wants you to do."

"Have you seen Myra," Fuller asked Peck when he reached the squad room.

"She's gone to the library, sir, to see what she can dig up on Farlowe and Gerard."

"So, what are we supposed to do while she reads through some books?"

"Well, I've just called Boswell House, and told them we'll be calling in later to speak with the residents on the old whistler's list."

"Did you speak to Farlowe or Gerard?"

"Neither of them is there today. I spoke to the nurse who seems to be running the place in their absence."

"What did she say?"

"It was a *he*, sir. A Rodney Barton."

"Well, what did *he* say?"

"He'll have them ready for us when we get there. Myra told me to say twelve o'clock. She reckons she'll be finished at the library by eleven thirty."

"Okay," Fuller said. "In the meantime, I'll just go back to my office and twiddle my thumbs, shall I?"

"Yes, sir…I mean no, sir…I mean…"

Fuller gave a silent curse, and walked out of the squad room. Brian Peck sighed. He had a feeling that today was going to be very long indeed.

"These are the other titles you asked for," the librarian said, laying two books down on the table at Myra's elbow.

Myra peeled her gaze away from the large picture book she was currently perusing and glanced up. "Thanks, Carol," she said. "Is there anything more specific you can recommend? This book covers too wide an area. I'm not interested in trapeze artists and circus clowns. I need something that's going to give me potted biographies of the people who were big in Variety between the wars, even up to the 'mid-fifties."

Carol, the librarian, looked thoughtful, and then smiled as an idea occurred to her. "What you need is something like *Finch's Almanac of the Music Hall and Variety Theatre.*"

"Does that cover the period I'm interested in?"

"It's subtitled, *Sixty Years of Variety and Music Hall Turns, from 1890 to 1950.*"

"That sounds perfect. Do you have a copy?"

"No. At least we don't have a copy here at Hatfield, but I think they might have one at the Welwyn branch. I can call them and find out."

"Would you?"

"Two ticks," Carol said, and hurried back to her desk.

She returned a few minutes later. "No luck at Welwyn, but they do have a copy at Letchworth," she said.

"How long would it take to get it sent here?"

"Tomorrow morning."

"Damn!" Myra said under her breath. "I really need to look at it today."

"Sorry. Tomorrow morning is the earliest we can do," Carol said.

"I don't suppose I have much choice then."

"Did you come here by car?"

"Yes, I did, as it happens."

"Well, you could always drive over there. They can have it waiting for you when you arrive."

Myra nodded, then stopped. "But, Carol, you've just spent twenty minutes sorting these out for me." She lifted the books from the table.

"That's not a problem. You can take them with you."

"I don't have a library ticket."

"That's all right. You don't need one. It's not as if you're taking them home. You're simply moving them to another branch. All the Hertfordshire libraries are connected. Just like one big happy family really. We're swapping reference books between branches all the time. They'll find their way back here eventually."

"You're a lifesaver," Myra said. "May I use your phone? I need to call the station."

Helen Carter walked through the double doors of the smart Art Deco styled building and approached the desk. "Hello," she said brightly. "I'm looking for the reading room."

The librarian behind the desk was a stout, middle-aged woman, who wore a tweed suit, and had her grey-streaked brown hair in an old-fashioned style – long plaits rolled into perfect circles, and secured either side of her head like a pair of ear muffs. She glared at Helen and transferred the glare to the sign hanging above the desk. SILENCE.

"How am I meant to ask a question if I can't speak?" Helen said.

With an economy of movement, the librarian inclined her head towards another sign, this one showing an arrow and the words READING ROOM.

"Fine," Helen said. "Thank you." She turned and followed the sign.

She found Myra seated at a desk by the window, surrounded by piles of books, and scribbling furiously on a pad of foolscap paper.

"Are you ready for the off?" Helen said, and an old man who looked like a retired army officer, and was reading a copy of the *Times,* raised his fingers to his lips.

"Sshh!"

"Christ! Is it always like this?"

"Sssh!"

Myra gathered up her notes and closed the book she'd been copying from. "Come on," she hissed. "Let's get you out of here before the Major has you shot."

"Is it always that bad?" Helen said once they were out on the street.

Myra shrugged. "You get used to it. This library is worse that Hatfield. At least they let you talk at Hatfield…well, quietly anyway. Whose car are we going in?"

"Let's take the squad car," Helen said. "I'll bring you back here when we've finished, and you can pick up yours."

"Are the others meeting us there?"

"As per your instructions.

Myra checked her watch. "I'll drive. You can gen up on these." She handed Helen the sheaf of notes she had made at the library.

Helen exchanged them for the car keys. "What are they?"

"Everything I've managed to find out about Duncan Farlowe and Elise Gerard, plus there are thumbnail sketches of the Boswell residents we're going to interview."

Helen flicked through them as they walked to the car. "You're thorough, I'll say that for you."

"Not as thorough as I'd like. If I hadn't had to drag over to Letchworth, that would have given me an extra half hour. I'm sure I could have dug up more on Farlowe and Gerard, and as for the residents, there are two on the list that I couldn't find at all, and I scoured three different reference books."

"Well, you've done well considering you were against the clock."

"Boswell serves lunch between one and two, so I had that against me as well." Myra unlocked the car, and slid in behind the wheel. "How did the inspector take the news that he'd be working on the same team as us?"

"Like he'd been given socks for Christmas, instead of the Havana cigars he really wanted."

"That well, eh?" Myra started the engine.

"Eddie Fuller's an ass," Helen said, and flicked over the first page of notes.

"Oh, for Pete's sake, Helen. Haven't you buried the hatchet yet?"

"I'd like to bury it...in his head." Helen said venomously.

Myra looked at her. "He really hurt you, didn't he?"

"He made me feel cheap, Myra, and I've never felt that way before in my entire life, and yes, it hurt."

"Well, let's see if you can put it behind you while we work this case. I'll need everyone giving one hundred per cent on this."

"*I'll* certainly try, Myra. I can't speak for the ass."

Myra shook her head despairingly, changed gears to overtake a very slow-moving tractor, and put her foot down.

Eddie Fuller and Brian Peck were sitting in the Wolseley outside the gates to Boswell House.

Fuller rolled down the window as Myra drew alongside him. "You took your time. I'd almost given up on you."

Myra checked her watch. It was five minutes past twelve.

"National tractor convention," she said glibly. "Shall we go on up to the house?"

Once they had parked, Myra handed Fuller the notes, and explained what she'd been doing today so far.

Fuller scanned them quickly and passed them to Peck. "Very comprehensive, Myra. Good work." He smiled at her, and trotted up the steps to ring the bell.

"He's a happy boy, now he's got his precious bagman back," Helen whispered in Myra's ear.

Myra slapped her arm. "Stop it," she whispered back.

Helen shrugged.

The man who answered the door to them stood about six feet, had neatly combed fair hair and freckles He wore a crisp while medical jacket over his everyday clothes. "Rodney

Barton," he said. "Staff Nurse Rodney Barton. Won't you please come in? They're all ready for you."

He led them into the house, across the foyer, past the reception desk and down the corridor to the communal room, where Myra had seen residents gathered on Monday enjoying a sing along.

Today, though, the room contained only seven people, six sitting in easy chairs – four men and two women – being serenaded by Leo Keating, who was standing at the piano, giving them a whistled rendition of a classic Gracie Fields song.

The nurse ushered them inside. "I'll leave you to it." Then turned and walked back down the corridor.

As Myra and the others entered the room, Keating stopped whistling and stepped forward, his hand outstretched. "Myra! Wonderful to see you again so soon."

Myra took his hand. "Hello, Leo. Good to see you again too."

"Let me make the introductions," he said, and took them along the line of residents, announcing each of them in turn, and adding their bill matter to their names. "Leila Harris – *The Nottingham Nightingale*, Orson West – *A Lariat and a Laugh*, Henry Pickles – *He's Right Up Your Street*, Hetty Lester – *With Her Wizard Wheezes*, Vernon Evans – *Songs from the Valleys*, and last but not least, Paul Blaze – *He Eats the Flames*. Freddie Cotton sends his apologies, but his sciatica's acting up, and he's confined to bed." Leo took a step back, looking satisfied, and turned to his friends. "Ladies and gentlemen, the men and women from the police."

Myra smiled, waiting for Keating to provide a catchy slogan for them, but nothing else was forthcoming. She stepped forward. "Hello," she said. "It's good of you all to give up your time today."

"It's not as if we've got anything better to do," Leila Harris said.

Keating clicked his tongue. "Now, Leila. Show a bit of gratitude. Myra and her friends are here to help us out."

Leila said nothing more, but folded her arms across her chest, looking disgruntled.

"Sorry about Leila," Keating said quietly to Myra. "She wasn't in favour of this. Doesn't want to upset the applecart."

Myra smiled at the woman indulgently, and received a frosty stare in return. "Right then," she said. "Shall we make a start? Who would like to go first?"

22 THURSDAY

"I suppose that had better be me." Henry Pickles got slowly to his feet. "How do you want to proceed?" he said to Myra

Myra took in the room and saw a small table on the far side with a stack of ten chairs beside it. "We can go over there and sit down."

"That'll be fine," Pickles said, and limped towards the table. Myra hurried to join him, quickly removing two chairs from the stack before Pickles injured himself trying to liberate them.

"I'd give you a hand, but this damned leg…"

"Rheumatism?" Myra asked,

"Bloody arthritis. They don't tell you when you're younger and kicking a football around the park, playing tennis, and just running for the bus, that one day your body will pay you back for everything you put it through."

Myra regarded him sympathetically as he eased himself into one of the chairs, and then sat down herself, facing him.

"I take it Leo told you why were conducting these interviews?"

"Because that baggage, Elise Gerard, is drugging us to keep us sweet and easier to control," Pickles said.

"Do you believe she is?"

"Come off it, love. That's exactly what she's doing. Leo said he showed you the collection of tablets he's managed to hide away."

"Yes, he showed me."

"Did you get them tested?"

"They were *Mogadons*."

"There you are, Leila," he called across the room. "She was giving us *Mogadons*. Bloody *Mogadons*, but you wouldn't have it. Vitamins, my arse." He leaned forward and lowered his voice. "That's what Elise told everyone the tablets were. Vitamins, my arse! No wonder everyone in here walks around like bloody zombies."

"But not you?"

He shook his head. "No. I got wise to her after the first pill she gave me. Vitamins are meant to be good for you, to perk you up, not make you feel like you've suddenly got one foot in the grave. So I told the others who live here, and this lot agreed to stop taking them. Even Leila, who refuses to believe anything bad about Elise, started hiding them away, because she couldn't deny the tablets were making her feel bloody awful."

"So, you believe that Elise Gerard was deliberately trying to harm you."

"I think she's a conniving cow. Dope us up to keep us quiet, but don't give us enough to kill us off."

"Then you don't think she's out to kill you."

"What would be the point of that? You can't charge rent to a corpse, can you? Like I said, a conniving cow."

"Are you one of Dr Maitland patients?"

"No. I've got my own doctor, and I've had him for forty years."

"Did you tell him about Elise's medical regimen?"

Again, Pickles shook his head. "I should do really, but he lives in Hove, and he's even older than me. I wouldn't want to bother him with this nonsense."

"I think you should," Myra said. "You can't be too careful."

Pickles smiled. "I last saw him in '51, and then it was only because I had a hernia – wouldn't have bothered him otherwise. I was always too busy working, travelling all over the country."

"What act did you perform?" Myra said. "I heard Leo add, *He's Right Up Your Street* to your name. I can't imagine what the act was."

Pickles laughed. "It wasn't an act, love...then again, maybe it was."

Myra looked puzzled.

"I was on the wireless. *Right Up Your Street*."

Myra looked blank.

"Not a radio lover, eh?"

"I listen to Luxembourg, or if the reception's poor, the Light Program."

"That would explain it. RUYS did what you're doing now. Interviewing people. I'd go to a town, select a street, and talk to the residents about local issues. It could be tragic one week, a real hoot the next. You could never be sure what you would get."

"Was it popular?"

"It ran for thirty years, so what do you think?"

"Why did it finish?"

"I retired, love, and the show retired along with me. They were going to keep it going, but they couldn't replace me – and that's not ego talking. It's just that I wasn't like any other presenter out there. Listen to me. I don't talk with plums in my mouth. I was born in Brighton, went up to London, and got a job as a tea boy at the BBC. I made lots of friends in the business, and I was very lucky. I suggested the idea to a producer I knew, and suggested myself as the presenter as well. I've always been a bit of a talker – or a bleedin' natterer, as my late wife used to say – and I pitched it as 'a common lad talks to common folk', and *Auntie*, as they call it now, went for it. The happiest years of my life," Pickles said wistfully.

"Thank you for your time, Mr Pickles. It's been most informative."

"Is that it?"

"For now, yes."

"Shame. I was enjoying myself." He reached across the table and shook Myra's hand, pushed himself out of his chair, and went back to join Leo, who was sitting at the piano, watching the proceedings with interest. "You were right, Leo. A little cracker, that one," he said.

Myra smiled as she added a few more notes to her page on Henry Pickles.

By the time Myra looked up again, Keating and Pickles had been joined by the Welshman, Vernon Evans. Of the others, Orson West, Paul Blaze and Hetty Lester were being interviewed by Fuller, Peck and Helen Carter. Which left Leila Harris, sitting by herself at the front of the room, still looking disgruntled.

Myra went across and sat down next to her. "I'm sorry," she said. "I know you're not enjoying this."

Leila sniffed her disapproval. "I think it's disloyal," she said. "Elise gave these people a home. Their families didn't want them and, if it wasn't for her, where would they be?"

"I think Miss Gerard has a case to answer," Myra said. "You yourself stopped taking the pills she was giving you."

"Only after pressure from the others, Leo especially. He wouldn't let it lie until I agreed to stop taking them."

"Did you know Elise Gerard before coming here?" Myra said.

Leila nodded her grey curls. "We were friends before the war," she said. "I remember her when she and Duncan first entered the business. Being a singer myself I took a particular interest. We didn't often appear on the same bill. With both of us being sopranos, it rather flies in the face of calling it Variety, but occasionally we'd run into each other.

"Of course, it was very different then...*we* were very different. I'm fifteen years older than Elise and I suppose you could say, I took her under my wing somewhat."

"In what way?" Myra said, relieved that the woman was actually talking to her. She thought this was going to be a difficult interview, but Leila Harris seemed quite happy to reminisce.

"She was so young – stunningly beautiful, but a little naïve. I helped her deal with some of the theatre managers who acted like little tin gods, and expected certain favours from the prettier artistes in return for a good placing in the shows they put on."

"But surely she was with Duncan. I would have thought that would have put off any amorous advances."

"Not once you got to know Duncan. They were partners in music – their voices blended so beautifully – but they were never a couple, if you know what I mean."

"I'm not sure I do," Myra said.

Leila gave her an old-fashioned look. "Duncan Farlowe's tastes veered more to the *outré* when it came to S. E. X." She spelt out the word, blushing furiously.

"You mean he was a homosexual?"

"Sometimes he was, sometimes he wasn't."

Myra looked at her, puzzled.

Leila rolled her eyes. "It didn't matter to him if they were boys or girls, but they had to be young. That was the key. He was attracted by their youth. Elise, at just five years younger than him, was simply too old for him. He just wasn't attracted to her, despite her beauty."

"So, he was lying when he told us he spent Sunday night with her in her bed," Myra said.

Leila looked surprised. "If they've suddenly developed feelings for each other, then it's news to me…especially now."

"I'm sorry, Miss Harris, what do you mean, especially now?"

"Well, I can imagine today's Duncan Farlowe falling for the Elise I first knew, all those years ago, but the Elise of today is a completely different proposition. It was a total shock for me when she came back from abroad. She looked like a completely different person."

"When was she abroad? And what do you mean, she came back a different person?"

Leila's reservations about being disloyal to Elise Gerard seemed to have melted away. Myra guessed she was either enjoying the attention she was receiving, or she was just savouring a good gossip.

"She and Duncan left the country in late '38, a few months before war broke out. They came back in 1945, and tried to resume their career, but nobody seemed interested. It had a lot to do with how Elise had changed, I suppose."

"How was that?"

"Well, Duncan came back after nearly six years, and in appearance he looked no different, but Elise…I really don't know what happened to her. She had gained at least three stone, and her golden hair had gone, cut short and a kind of mousy brown, and she looked…how shall I best describe it…well, not a lot different from how she looks now really. Plain. Not the type of woman to make other women envious, and to make men swoon. That had been lost forever."

"You say *abroad*. Do you know where they went?"

Leila shook her head. "They never said, and I never asked. I just assumed they went somewhere to sit out the war, maybe Switzerland or somewhere like that. That was another reason they found it so hard to re-establish themselves. While so many of us in the business joined in and did what we could to help the war effort at home, joining ENSA and travelling all over the place to entertain the troops and boost their morale, it was widely thought that Duncan and Elise had put their own interests first, making sure they were safe and sound while the rest of us suffered the worst the Nazis could inflict upon us. There was a lot of bad feeling within the business, and doors that had been open to them were suddenly slammed in their faces. It wasn't long before they dropped out of sight again, only to open Boswell House a few years later."

"Surely people's memories aren't that short. I would have thought that resentment like that would be slow to fade away."

Leila smiled. "The reason they have any guests at all is because Boswell is so much cheaper than Brinsworth and Denville."

"What about the stories of drink problems and breakdowns?"

"All true, I suspect. It must have been hard for Elise to take, being shunned by a world that had once valued her so highly, and it was obvious that she wasn't a stranger to the bottle. How else could you explain the physical change in her after those few short years away? You can't blame food. She still eats like a sparrow, but drink can have a devastating effect of beauty. I've seen it happen to others in the past, I'm afraid. A rumour was going around here when I first arrived, that Elise was a regular visitor to a rather notorious sanatorium in Cambridge, but I never asked her whether it was true or not?"

"What is the meaning of this?"

Every head in the room turned to stare at Elise Gerard, who stood in the doorway, her face bleached white with fury and outrage.

23 THURSDAY

Panic flared in Leila Harris's eyes.

Myra laid a comforting hand on her arm and stood up, going over to the doorway to confront Elise Gerard. "Excuse me, Miss Gerard, but we're still engaged in police business, and we're following up an issue raised the last time I was here."

"Without my permission," Elise snapped.

"I tried to contact you but was told you were unavailable today, and actually your permission wasn't needed."

"Well, really! That is totally unacceptable."

"But true nonetheless." Eddie Fuller appeared at Myra's side. "This is an investigation into a homicide. Any objection you might have is irrelevant."

Elise bridled. "We'll see about that. I will take this up with your chief inspector."

"We're here with Chief Inspector Callum's full knowledge and approval," Myra said, emboldened by Fuller's support.

"Then I shall take it higher."

"You do what you have to do, Miss Gerard," Fuller said. "But it won't alter the outcome. We're conducting our interviews, with or without your consent."

Elise glared at him. "We'll see about that." She turned to the guests. "Listen everybody, lunch is being served in the dining room at this moment. Any of you who don't attend this instant will, I'm afraid, forfeit your meal. You will not, I repeat, *you will not*, be given a replacement. Am I making myself clear on this?"

Leo Keating shuffled towards her. "We'd finished anyway." He looked back to the room. "Come on, everybody. Let's go and have lunch." He caught Myra's eye, and winked at her.

Elise Gerard glared at each of the guests in turn as they trooped by her, saving a special, withering look for Leila Harris, who ducked her head, and hurried by her.

Elise spun on her heel to follow them.

"Just a moment, Miss Gerard," Myra said. "I need to ask *you* something as well."

"And when Detective Constable Banks is finished, I'll require you to show me the Boswell House dispensary," Fuller added, ignoring the look of fury and outrage on the woman's face.

"Please come and sit down," Myra said.

The woman hesitated.

"The sooner you answer my questions, the sooner we'll be on our way. An outcome, I'm sure, you'll be happy with."

Elise took a breath. "Oh, very well," she said, and went to sit at the table.

Myra looked at Fuller who indicated she should continue. She pulled out her notebook. "When we spoke to Mr Farlowe on Tuesday, he told us that he spent Sunday evening with you at your house. Is that correct?"

"Yes," Elise said warily.

"And that he stayed the night?"

"Yes. It wouldn't have been safe to drive back to Benington. We'd been drinking."

"So I understand," Myra said. "Mr Farlowe also led us to understand that you shared a bed that night."

The outrage flared again in Elise Gerard's eyes. "How dare you?" she spluttered. "What I do in my private life has nothing whatsoever to do with you."

Myra remained unmoved by the woman's outburst. "Just answer the question, Miss Gerard."

"I haven't heard one yet, just a scurrilous and impertinent suggestion."

Myra sighed. "Did he, or didn't he, spend the night in your bed?"

Elise Gerard started to rise from the chair. "I refuse to answer that question."

"Sit down, Miss Gerard," Fuller said, coming to join Myra at the table. "It will look extremely bad for you if you don't co-operate with Constable Banks. It makes it look like either Mr Farlowe's lying about Sunday, or that you've got something to hide. Either way, it doesn't look good for you when we're here investigating the death of a member of your staff."

"Oh, very well then. Yes, Duncan stayed the night in my bed and we had wild, abandoned sex...with the lights on. There, satisfied?"

"Not really," Myra said. "But if that's what you're telling me then I have no choice but to believe you. What time did he arrive on Sunday?"

Elise seemed thrown by Myra's sudden change of tack. "What do you mean?"

"It's a simple enough question, Miss Gerard, like the last one. What time did he arrive at your house?"

"I really can't say. I don't spend my life staring at the clock."

"I wasn't suggesting you do, but you were cooking a meal for him that evening, and, although I'm not much of a cook myself, I know enough to understand that timings are pretty important when you're cooking."

"It wasn't that kind of meal."

"What did you cook?"

"I don't remember."

"Cold cuts and salad perhaps," Fuller said.

Elise seized upon his suggestion. "Yes, that was it. Ham, tongue and cold roast beef with salad and new potatoes."

"In October?" Myra said. "Where did you manage to get new potatoes in October?"

"I meant boiled, boiled potatoes."

"How long did you boil them for," Myra said. "Twenty minutes?"

"Yes, probably."

"How did you time them?"

"With my watch of course."

"You looked at your watch to see that the potatoes were cooked, but you didn't notice what time it was?"

"Yes…er…no… What have potatoes got to do with Dawn's murder?"

"Nothing at all," Myra said. "But then they could have everything to do with it. What time was it when you checked the potatoes?"

"Eight o'clock."

"So, are you saying that Mr Farlowe walked through the door on Sunday evening, and he had no sooner sat down at the table and you served him dinner, along with the potatoes, at eight o'clock?"

"Yes," Elisc said.

"What no aperitifs, no pre-dinner conversation?" Fuller said.

"I don't know what you're trying to make me say," Elise said.

"We're not trying to make you say anything," Myra said. "I just wanted an answer to a very simple question. What time did Duncan Farlowe arrive at your house on Sunday evening?"

"Eight o'clock," Elise said, folding her arms across her chest in a gesture of finality.

"Do you have any further questions, Constable?" Fuller asked.

Myra shook her head. "No. That will be all for now."

"Right," he said. Then perhaps, Miss Gerard, you can show us your dispensary."

"You two go back to the car," Fuller said to Helen and Peck. "We'll be along shortly."

"Yes, sir," Brian Peck said. Helen Carter said nothing, but turned, stony faced and stalked from the room.

"You're still not flavour of the month," Myra said quietly to him.

"Don't I know it."

Elise Gerard led them to a door off the main corridor, then pulled a bunch of keys from her cardigan pocket and inserted one in the lock, turning it sharply and pushing the door open. "There you are," she said. "But I don't know what you're expecting to find."

"Thank you," Fuller said, stepping past her and entering the room, with Myra at his heels.

The room was nothing more than a very large cupboard, about ten-foot square, and three of the walls had been racked with wooden shelves. Taking a wall each, Myra and Fuller examined the contents of the shelves with a growing sense of disappointment.

There were boxes of bandages, cardboard boxes containing sticking plasters, bottles of liniment and embrocation, a whole shelf devoted to Epsom salts, another holding boxes of ointment for minor burns and scrapes, bottles of camphorated spirit, cough mixture and calamine lotion. The only pills in evidence were large brown bottles of aspirin, paracetemol and laxatives.

"There's nothing much to see here," Fuller said, as they moved onto the third shelf, this one containing three walking sticks and a pair of crutches and very little else.

Elise stood in the doorway, a vaguely smug expression on her face. "Have you found what you were looking for?" she said as they moved away from the shelves without further comment. "No, I didn't think you'd find anything. I keep the cyanide and strychnine in a different room."

"May we see?" Fuller said brightly.

"Really!" Elise huffed, as they walked out of the room ahead of her.

"Andy," Jack said, as he walked up to the desk. "The raincoat that Tommy Apollo dropped in yesterday. Did you hang it somewhere safe as I asked?"

"I did indeed," Brewer said. "Give me a moment and I'll fetch it for you," He disappeared into the room behind the desk, re-emerging moments later with the raincoat, neatly draped on a clothes hanger. "Here you are, sir," he said, and passed it across the desk.

"Thanks for keeping it safe, Andy." Jack unhooked the coat, passing the hanger back to Brewer. "You can keep the hanger. I'll fold it and put in the back of my car, then I can take it back to the Peterson's after work. Hold on a moment." As he was smoothing the coat over his arm, his fingers encountered a small lump in one of the raincoat's voluminous pockets.

Spreading the raincoat out on the desk, he delved in, but all his fingers connected with was the smooth material of the inside of the pocket. "Strange," he muttered, and turned the coat over.

"There, sir," Brewer said, and pointed to a small slit in the lining. "It looks like a secret pocket.

Jack slid two fingers into the slit and encountered smooth plastic. He scissored his fingers, and withdrew a small white plastic bag, secured at the top with a strip of adhesive tape. He peeled back the tape and emptied the contents of the bag onto the desk – three triangular blue pills.

"*Purple Hearts*," he said.

Brewer stared down at them. "Forgive me saying, sir, but they don't look very purple. They look more blue to me."

"Yes, Andy, they do, but for some reason *Drinamyl* acquired the name, *Purple Hearts* and it stuck."

"I suppose it's catchier than *Blue Triangles*…or *Drinamyl* for that matter. There's not many of them, if the young lady was planning to deal in them."

"I think these were for her own personal use. She must have been very upset when Apollo drove off with her coat still in his car."

"Furious probably," Brewer agreed. "What do you think she did?"

"What would you do, Andy, if you were hooked on these, you only had three left, and some clown drives off with them?"

"Try to get some more, I suppose."

"Hmm," Jack said, trying to picture Dawn outside the abandoned factory, distraught and angry, wanting so much to pop a pill, to make the distress go away. What would *he* do? "I'd try to contact my supplier, and get him to bring me some more. That's it, Andy, the phone box."

"Sir?"

"There's a bloody telephone box outside the old factory where we found her. It's the one the tramp used to call us. She must have used it to call her supplier. She couldn't go to him because she was stranded there without a car, so all she can do is wait, probably inside the factory, for him to deliver some more pills to her."

"Are you making this up, sir?"

"Yes, Andy, I am, but I'm also sketching out a possible scenario for what could have happened on Sunday evening. What if her supplier arrives, they argue over something? Possibly she doesn't have any money to pay him, possibly they fight over something else, and he attacks her, garrottes her, and leaves her dead on the mattress in a derelict factory. It's not as if she's going to be easily found, if you're unaware of the comings and goings of the area's vagrant population." He rubbed his chin thoughtfully. "It's a possibility."

"But who was her supplier, sir?"

"That, Andy, is the question. Who indeed? Thanks. You've been a great help."

Andy Brewer looked bemused. "I have?"

"Indeed you have. I would never have thought of it without you."

"Only too happy to help, sir."

Brewer watched Jack take the stairs up to his office two at a time, and then he stood up straighter, adjusted his uniform and muttered, "Well done, Sergeant. Well done." He retreated to the back room, and made himself a celebratory cup of tea.

24 THURSDAY

They sat in Jack's office, Fuller, Peck, Helen and Myra, and reported on things that were said at Boswell House.

"It left me in no doubt that Elise Gerard couldn't tell the truth if her life depended on it," Fuller said.

"I agree with the inspector," Myra said. "The alibi she and Farlowe have for Sunday night is so shot full of holes it could be a garden sieve."

"Especially in the light of the new time of death we have," Fuller added. "She says Farlowe got to her house at eight o'clock, which puts him squarely in the middle of the time-line."

"And as for their drugging the residents," Peck said, "the guest I spoke to corroborated Mr Keating's story. He was given *Mogadon* to sedate him on the pretext that he was being given vitamins."

"Did they hold onto the tablets?" Jack said.

Peck shook his head. "I had Vernon Evans, and he flushed them down the toilet when no one was looking."

"It was the same with Hetty Lester," Helen said. "She flushed hers away as well."

"Paul Blaze is a cannier customer," Fuller said. "He's kept his. He keeps them in a sock in his dressing table. He didn't believe the vitamin story at all and, as well as being a fire-eater, he's also a gifted conjurer. He told me it was easy for him to appear to take the tablets when he was given them by the nurse, but palmed them, and popped them into his pocket when the nurse wasn't looking.

"As for Orson West, I don't think the tablets would have had much of an effect on him. He's not quite the ticket."

"You mean he's senile?" Jack said.

"I think so. He kept calling me Dai, and tried to get me to sing *We'll Keep a Welcome in the Hillside*."

"You should have humoured him, Inspector," Peck said. "I hear you singing in the car sometimes. You have a fine tenor."

"Leave it out, Brian," Fuller said. "That's a song my nan used to sing to me to get me to sleep."

"A strange choice of song for a lullaby," Myra said.

"What can I say?" Fuller said. "She thought Welsh blood ran in her veins."

"Can we crack on," Jack said.

"Sorry, sir. Anyway, from what I've learned today, I'd say Elise Gerard has a case to answer," Fuller said.

"Did any of you get a clue to where she could be getting her supply of *Mogadon*?" Jack said.

"A few years ago," Myra said, "she was in and out of a sanatorium in Cambridge to deal with her drink problems. It's possible she made friends with a member of the staff there. She could be getting the pills from them."

"Does this sanatorium have a name, Myra?"

"I've done some digging, sir. There are a couple of clinics in Cambridge, but only one that specializes in alcohol and drug addiction. The Fallowell Institute. On the surface it appears to be very respectable, but there were stories in the papers a few years ago about inappropriate treatments offered to their patients. I've been researching, but so far I haven't found out what the treatments were."

"Still," Jack said. "It seems a good place to start, and it's fairly local as well, which could be significant."

"In what way, sir?" Myra said.

"It's what, a forty-minute drive to Cambridge, even shorter if you meet your source halfway. Convenient, wouldn't you say?"

"Could the Institute also be a source for the *Purple Hearts*?" Myra said.

"It's possible. Keep digging, Myra. Find out as much as you can about the Fallowell Institute."

When they had finished reporting on their day, Jack told them about Dawn's raincoat, the pills, and his theory of how she could have summoned her killer. As he was relating it, his scenario was answering a slew of questions that had been bothering him since interviewing Tommy Apollo. He believed Tommy's story about having a row with Dawn in his car, and her storming off to take refuge in the factory. But it didn't explain her killing. How did her killer know she was there? Why was the killer there himself? The fact that Dougie Marshall, one of Dawn's clients for *Purple Hearts*, had been killed in an identical fashion, made it pretty certain that they were looking for one person who was responsible for both murders. Could it be that she actually brought death towards her?

He turned to Helen Carter. "Helen, when we've finished here, get onto the Exchange and find out if the telephone box was used on Sunday night, and if so, what numbers were called from it."

"Yes, sir."

Jack was starting to wonder if the drug abuse at Boswell House was muddying the waters in the murder investigation. There was obviously a connection there but, so far, the only common links were Dawn herself, and the fact that both cases involved the misuse of drugs, but in a completely different way.

Wrestling and Variety theatre – two very different worlds. *Mogadon* and *Drinamyl* – two very different drugs. He scrubbed his eyes with the balls of his hands.

"Is Frank Lesser in the building?" he asked.

"I think I saw him earlier in the squad room, sir," Peck said.

"Pop down there and see if you can find him, Brian."

"Why do you need Sergeant Lesser, sir?" Fuller said.

"Because I don't think we're seeing the complete picture here," Jack said. "The murders of both Dawn Peterson and Dougie Marshall were cold, clinical and brutal, and the way this investigation is going, the prime suspects seem to be Duncan Farlowe, an aging lothario who has a penchant for young girls and boys, and the other is Elise Gerard, a fading chanteuse who likes a drink and has control issues. It just doesn't seem likely, somehow, that these two could be ruthless, cold-blooded killers. What do the rest of you think?"

"I think this investigation is proving to be a problem," Fuller said.

"Ah, Frank," Jack said as Lesser came into the room followed by Peck. "Tommy Apollo. Do you know how to get hold of him?"

"I've got several addresses he uses when he's wrestling in the area. I'm sure I can pin him down. Why?"

"I want to talk to him again."

"Do you know this part of Stevenage?" Lesser said, as he steered the car carefully down a narrow side street, that branched off from the main road.

"Not well," Jack said. "Tommy Apollo's living in digs down here? Number thirty-two, a place belonging to Florence Gafney." He looked out at the houses they were passing. For the most part they were a collection of terraced cottages, but there was nothing rural and romantic about these. These had the distinct feel of a run-down urban area that had been sadly neglected by the march of time. There seemed to be a uniform greyness about the street, and he half-expected doors to open to reveal children in ragged clothes, and careworn women on their hands and knees, cleaning filthy doorsteps with a worn-out scrubbing bush and a pail of dirty, soapy water.

"Rather bleak isn't it?" he said.

Lesser nodded. "Workers from the local paper mill used to live in these cottages. The mill owned the buildings and rented them out for peppercorn rents to keep their staff living in the area. Of course, it closed down during the war, and never re-opened, so the county council bought them up, and still rent them out for a pittance. They're slowly falling into disrepair these days, not that they were ever salubrious back in the first half of the century."

"You're a walking social history lesson, Frank, did you know that?" Jack said.

"I just take an interest in my local area," Lesser said, stung by Jack's comment. "It's not a crime, is it?"

"Not at all. If fact it's commendable. It helps to know the seedier parts of town."

Lesser allowed himself a wry smile. "Tommy's staying in digs, just up here," he said, and pulled into the kerb.

The cottage they parked outside was distinguishable from its neighbours only by the sad-looking window boxes on the sills, containing unrecognisable, browning and desiccated plants.

Lesser lifted the black cast iron knocker and let it fall. It thudded hollowly on the door.

Florence Gaffney opened the door, and she was exactly the type of woman Jack had pictured living in places like this. She wore a grubby, flower-patterned overall, and her grey hair was held in a bun at the back of her head. The carpet slippers on her feet were threadbare, with the line of fur across her instep grey, and slightly greasy.

"Yes?" she said.

Lesser stepped forward. "I understand that Tommy Apollo rents a room here," he said.

"He does," the woman said incuriously.

"Would it be possible to speak with him?"

"He's probably asleep in bed, but come in. I'll knock him up."

She went back into the house, and glanced back over her shoulder to check that they were following her.

They found themselves in a small living room dominated by a rectangular dining table surrounded by four plain wooden chairs. There was a tiled fireplace with a dusty over-mantle populated by cheap plaster ornaments, mostly cats and dogs, and the occasional framed photographs of random men, most dressed in military uniform, apart from one Edwardian-looking gentleman, who was dressed as an undertaker, and had the demeanour to match his profession.

Stairs led off from the middle of the room, and a small kitchenette was visible through a door to their right. There was another door directly opposite the kitchenette. Mrs Gaffney rapped on it sharply with her knuckles. "Thomas? You have visitors."

"Coming," Apollo's voice floated back through the door.

When he emerged a few minutes later he was wearing only pyjama bottoms and a grubby string vest, His feet were bare, and his thick, wavy hair was awry. Even his tanned and toned physique looked a little grey and loose in the dim light provided by the naked, low-wattage, bulb hanging from the overhead light.

The welcoming smile dropped from his lips when he saw who was waiting for him in the living room. "Oh," he said. "I thought I'd seen the last of you."

"I'm afraid not, Tommy. Don't worry. You're not in any trouble," Lesser said. "We just want to ask you a few more questions."

"All right," he said uncertainly. He turned to the landlady, who was watching the exchange with frank curiosity. "Florrie, is there any more tea in the pot? My mouth feels like a rat's been sleeping in it."

She grimaced. "Don't worry, pet. I'll make you a fresh one." She went across to the Butler sink, and filled the kettle.

Apollo indicated the chairs around the dining table. "Take a seat. Make yourself comfortable."

Jack looked at the chairs sceptically. They didn't look as if they had been designed for comfort. He sat down anyway, at the head of the table, and waited for the others to join him, and for Florence Gaffney to make the tea, before he began.

25 THURSDAY

When the tea was served, and the landlady grudgingly took her leave Jack said, "*Purple Hearts*, Tommy, did you buy a lot from Dawn?"

Apollo swore. "You tricked me. You said I wasn't in any trouble."

Jack sipped his tea. "You're not...but you will be if you don't answer my questions honestly, and completely."

Apollo took a mouthful of tea and swilled it around before swallowing. "That's better. Yes," he said. "I used to buy them every week, but I wasn't the only one. Most of the lads bought from her at one time or another."

"She had enough of the pills to satisfy everybody's needs?"

Apollo nodded. "Supply was never a problem. If she couldn't fulfil an order one night, she'd meet at the next show, and make up the balance."

"Is this common at wrestling shows?" Jack asked, "Drugs being handed out like sweets."

"Oh yes," Lesser said. "If it's not pep-pills, uppers, it's downers. Sometimes a wrestler can get so strung out on adrenaline he'll takes pills just to calm himself down, and get some sleep. Drugs go with the territory, I'm afraid."

"That's so true?" Apollo said. "When I first entered the game, I swore I'd never touch them, but this way of life can erode your willpower, and cripple your best intentions. Sometimes you have to rely on chemicals just to survive, and drink. You'd be amazed at some of the lads who can wrestle with half a bottle of scotch inside them, and then have the rest after the match to wind down. I haven't even mentioned painkillers yet."

"Painkillers?" Jack said.

"Do you think we throw each other around the ring night after night, take horrendous bumps, landing on wooden boards with just a quarter of an inch of padding, and don't get hurt? Why do you think I was still in bed today at four o'clock in the afternoon? Sometimes it takes me all my strength just to roll out of my kip."

"Did Dawn supply painkillers as well?"

"Dawn could supply anything you wanted," Apollo said. "She was a walking chemist's shop – a damned sight more useful than some of the other ring rats – and the boys took care of her because of it."

"Evidently not well enough," Jack said.

"Any idea where she was getting them from?" Lesser said.

"I asked her once but she was keeping *schtum*. I don't really blame her. I expect she figured out that if she told us who her supplier was, we could go to him direct, and cut her out of the deal."

"Okay, Tommy, you've been very helpful," Lesser said, and stood up to go.

Jack stayed seated. "Just one more thing. Do you know if Dawn upset one of the other wrestlers? Did anyone you know in the business have an issue with her? If not the wrestlers, then perhaps one of the other ring rats."

Apollo shook his head. "No. I would have heard. The rumour and gossip mills run smoothly in our business. Everyone knows everything about everybody else. It's why we all get on so well and don't kill each other in the ring. Can you imagine how dangerous it could be otherwise?"

They got back into the car, and the radio crackled into life. Lesser picked it up. "Helen Carter would like a word, guv," he said, handing the radio to Jack.

"You were right, sir. A call was made from that phone box at six forty Sunday evening."

"Yes." Jack slapped a hand on his thigh. "Helen, does the Exchange have a record of who the call was to?"

"They do, sir and – you're going to like this – the call was made to Boswell House."

"Were there any other calls from the box that evening?"

"No. That was the only call until Monday morning."

"Excellent, Helen."

"Tomorrow first thing, Frank, Myra and I are going to see Duncan Farlowe and Elise Gerard, and find out which of them are lying through their teeth."

"We could get to Boswell House this evening," Lesser said.

"No, we'll leave it until tomorrow, Frank. I want to give Myra some more time to dig up all she can on them, and I need to take Dawn's coat back to her father. While I'm there, I'm going to pop along to speak to Danny Hutchence again, to see if he can shore up his alibi in light of Professor Strong's new time of death estimate. I'm also interested to see if he can account for his movements early yesterday morning, when Dougie Marshall was killed."

"We seem to be collecting suspects like Green Shield Stamps," Lesser said.

Jack chuckled. "It does seem that way, but only one of them is responsible for the murders. The trick is going to be finding out which of them it was."

"My wife's out at the moment," Wilfred Peterson said. "She's visiting her mother."

"Actually, it was you I came to see," Jack said, and handed him the raincoat. "Dawn was wearing this on Sunday evening. I thought you might like it back."

Peterson took it without comment.

"And here's your photograph back." Jack produced an envelope from the pocket of his coat, and handed it to him.

Peterson tucked the coat under his arm, slid the photo from the envelope and stared at it, tears welling in his eyes. "Thank you," he said softly. "She looks so happy."

Jack smiled indulgently, remembering what Myra had said about the girl's beautiful eyes, that there was nothing behind them. No spark.

Had living in this house with an indulgent father, and an indifferent stepmother, been the factor that extinguished it? *Impossible to say*, he thought. All he knew was that Dawn Peterson had drawn a handful of life's many short straws, and not survived them.

He thought of his own daughters. Both had been through their trials and tribulations, but Joanie and Rosie were survivors, and had fought back. He was under no illusions that they had got their resilience from him. Their strength was drawn from their mother. Annie was a remarkable woman. Had Dawn Peterson's real mother lived, he doubted that recent events would have happened, and Dawn might still be alive.

Whilst he had sympathy for Wilfred Peterson, he could find no empathy for the man. He had chosen his own personal happiness over a father's duty to love one's child unconditionally, and he had let his daughter down, terribly.

"Right," he said. Good day to you, and my condolences once again."

"Yes, yes, thank you," Peterson said distractedly, stepped back inside and closed the door.

As he stepped away from the door, Jack heard that almost ethereal wail of a wounded animal, as Wilfred Peterson was left alone with his grief, his guilt and his shame.

Jack walked down the street, and rang the doorbell of the Hutchence residence.

There was no reply.

Danny could probably still be at college, and the garage door was open, the garage empty, so it looked like Irma Hutchence was out as well.

He looked at his watch.

It could wait. He would send a car out to meet Danny Hutchence from college tomorrow, and bring him into the station for an interview. He had a feeling that Friday could be quite a busy day.

"Are you sure about that?" Myra said into the phone.

"Definitely," said the voice on the other end of the line. "Everything I've told you about her is true, and I have documentary evidence to support it. I spent an awfully long time researching her for the book. It's just a shame there was so much I couldn't use, even down to the fact that Elise Gerard is not her real name."

"What *is* her real name, Mr Finch?"

"Elise *Giroud*. It's French – as is she – and she was born 1901 in Montmartre."

"What about Duncan Farlowe?"

Archie Finch laughed. "Much simpler. The name Duncan Farlowe is a much more romantic sounding name than Cyril Sharples, wouldn't you agree?"

"It certainly is," Myra said.

"Was there anything else?"

"I don't think so, but I would like to thank you for giving up your time to talk to me."

"Not at all. I assure you the pleasure was all mine. I'm delighted my book found its way into your hands. I imagined it sitting on a dusty shelf in some library somewhere, never looked at from one year to the next."

"No," Myra said. "It was an absolutely fascinating read. So much information to uncover."

"As I myself discovered when I was compiling it."

"Well, thank you, good bye," Myra said quickly, sensing the man was about to launch into a whole new chapter.

"Who were you talking to?" Helen Carter said.

"Archibald Finch. He wrote that book I was telling you about: *Finch's Almanac of the Music Hall.*"

"You seemed excited."

"I wouldn't say excited exactly, but what he said was interesting. Elise Gerard and Duncan Farlowe are not their real names."

"No?"

"No. He's Cyril Sharples and she's Elise Giroud. He obviously changed his to sound more like a romantic operatic tenor, she to make herself seem more the English Rose."

"Is that significant to the case?"

"It could be. Not him so much, but her definitely. How old would you say she was?"

"Late sixties, early seventies."

"Yes," Myra said. "I would have pegged her about the same. She's fifty-nine."

"Never."

"Born in 1901."

"She must have had a hard life."

"I saw a picture of her, taken in the late thirties. Helen, she was stunning. Slim, beautiful, blonde."

"What happened?"

Myra shook her head. "I can't tell you until she's confirmed it, it occurred while she was out of the country, because she came back fat and mousy, and, by all accounts, an alcoholic."

"Could drink really affect someone's looks that much?"

"It's feasible, but I'll keep digging."

"Good luck," Helen said. "I'm glad you're the detective and not me. I wouldn't have that kind of patience."

"Horses for courses, Helen. I did your job when I first started, and hated every predictable minute of it. I always wanted to be a detective. I think I read too many Dorothy Sayers and Ngaio Marsh novels when I was growing up. I love solving puzzles. And this case is a puzzle and a half."

26 FRIDAY October 21ST 1960

"Oh, it's you again," Veronica said, as she opened the door to Duncan Farlowe's Benington house.

"I'm afraid so," Jack said. "We'd like to see Mr Farlowe."

"All right then."

She pulled the door open wide for them to enter.

Myra noticed the young woman was much more conservatively dressed this time. Her hair was in a tight, business-like bun; the tinted, steel-framed glasses had been replaced by dour, heavy horn rims, and her face was free of any trace of makeup. She was still very attractive, but much more severe, almost matronly.

"He's in the study. You know the way." She turned and left them, her short heels clacking on the tiles as she made her way to another room, opposite from the study.

"Not so glamorous today, I notice," Myra said. "She must be learning."

Jack knocked on the study door.

"Come."

Jack pushed it open, and they walked into the room.

Farlowe was sitting at the desk. He was dressed more casually, with a pink cashmere sweater over a light grey shirt that almost matched the slacks he'd worn on Tuesday.

"Is this really necessary?" he asked as he lit a *Sobranie*.

"I'm afraid the answers you gave us the other day weren't exactly truthful," Jack said, "and we were wondering why."

"Well, if you'd like to outline the part where you thought I wasn't being entirely candid with you, then maybe we can progress from there."

"You said you stayed the night with Miss Gerard, in her bed."

"A fact that Elise Gerard flatly denies." Myra said.

Farlowe grimaced. "Yes, I thought she might."

"Then why tell us if it wasn't true?"

Farlowe spread his arms helplessly. "Elise and I have had a partnership for thirty years, and in that time we've had to deal with rumour and innuendo about our relationship, and in all those years we've managed to keep the newshounds at bay with a combination of misdirection and subterfuge."

"So which of you are telling us the truth?"

Farlowe smiled. "In a way we both are."

"Would you like to elaborate?" Jack said.

"I think I summed up the evening thus. We had a meal, we listened to music and, I think I said, that we went to bed together."

"That's right."

"What I forgot to say was that, although we went upstairs to bed together, we slept in different rooms. She at the front of the house, me in the room she kindly lets me use, at the back." He smiled broadly. "There. Mystery solved. You just assumed that we slept together, in the biblical sense, when in fact we were yards away from each other in different parts of the house, and therefore I can't be held accountable for your misguided assumptions, can I?"

"No." Jack said. "You certainly can't."

"So, when Elise said you had wild, abandoned sex, she was making that up too?"

Farlowe laughed. "She told you that?" he said. "As I say, misdirection and subterfuge. It works. Never give them something solid to work with."

"Were the potatoes nice?" Myra said.

Farlowe's smile faltered. "Pardon?"

"Miss Gerard told me that for your meal you had a collation of cooked meats, salad and new potatoes – *Jersey Royals*, I think she said."

"Ah, yes," Farlowe said with a renewed smile. "Beautiful. Such an exquisite flavour."

Myra turned to Jack. "He's lying again, sir. Miss Gerard told me she served boiled old potatoes. *Jersey Royals* are seasonal and they're only available between late March and July."

"Care to explain, Mr Farlowe?"

"An honest mistake, Chief Inspector. I wouldn't class myself as an epicurean by any stretch of the imagination. I must have misunderstood what Elise meant. I know they were delicious. Further than that, I can't really say."

"Okay. What time did you arrive at Miss Gerard's?"

"Early evening."

"Six? Seven?"

"More like eight actually. Early evening by my standards."

"Moving on," Jack said. "Did you see Miss Peterson earlier that evening?"

"Gracious, no. I would have said." Farlowe stubbed out the cigarette in the ashtray.

"Do you have any more questions? Because I really should get on."

"Are we keeping you from something, sir?" Myra said.

"I'm expecting a very important telephone call."

"Don't worry," she said. "As soon as the phone starts ringing, we'll go and leave you in peace but, until it does, can you tell us where you and Miss Gerard disappeared to in 1938? We know you went abroad, and spent the war years there, returning in late '45."

"I don't see what bearing that has on a murder in 1960."

"Just answer the question please," Jack said.

Farlowe lit another cigarette. "Well, if you must know, I went to Switzerland and spent the war with relatives."

"And Miss Gerard?"

"Elise is of French descent, you know? She went back to her family home in Montmartre."

"So you didn't see each other at all for the entire duration of the war?" Myra said.

"No," Farlowe said. "And the years went by so painfully slowly. They took their toll, especially on poor Elise."

"What happened to Miss Gerard?" Myra said. "During that time."

"I can't say. To do so would be to betray a confidence that I vowed never to do."

"I could compel you to tell us," Jack said. "I could haul you up in front of a judge and make you tell the truth."

Farlowe gave one of his expressive shrugs. "Then I'm afraid, Chief Inspector, that is what you are going to have to do because, as of this moment, my lips are sealed."

Jack and Myra glanced at each other. It was Myra who spoke. "Okay, Mr Farlowe. Could you tell us, in your own words, what you were doing earlier on Sunday evening?"

"Must I?"

"You must."

Farlowe took a deep breath. "I went to church."

"Church?"

"Yes. St Peter's, in Benington."

"Are you a religious man, Mr Farlowe?" Jack asked.

"Not in the slightest. In fact, I would have said I had leanings towards atheism, but I do like a good hymn, and singing with a congregation I find uplifting, and good for my soul…if I had one, of course."

"Can anyone confirm that you were there on Sunday?"

"I doubt it. I tend to slip in when everybody else is inside and then I sit at the back. That way my voice, which is still extremely strong, blends in with the rest. I do hate to draw attention to myself."

"But you were on the stage," Myra said incredulously.

"Yes, I know, but that's different. That was a performance and I was getting paid for it. Singing with the other churchgoers on a Sunday is for my pleasure only. I have no need to stand out from the crowd."

"We only have your word for it that you were actually there," Myra said.

"Why on earth would I lie about such an innocent pastime?"

"To give yourself an alibi for early Sunday evening."

"But why would I need one? My conscience is clear."

The telephone on the desk started to ring, stopped for a few seconds, and then began ringing again. Farlowe picked it up and listened. "Yes, Ronnie. I was expecting it. My guests are just leaving."

He held the receiver to his chest and looked at them expectantly.

"Come on, Constable," Jack said. "Let's leave Mr Farlowe to his important telephone call." He turned and walked to the door. Myra followed two paces behind.

When they got back to the car the radio was squawking. It was Eddie Fuller. "Professor Strong would like you to call in and see him if you're anywhere near the hospital, sir."

"This morning, Inspector?"

"He said it could be fairly urgent."

"I don't see how," Jack said. "Dougie Marshall isn't going anywhere, is he?"

"I'm just reporting what he said, sir."

"Very well. I'll call in and see him on our way to Boswell House."

He disconnected.

"Myra, turn the car round. I'm needed at North Herts Hospital."

Myra indicated, pulled the Wolseley into the side of the road, waited for a gap in the traffic, made a smooth U turn, and soon they were travelling back in the opposite direction.

"Church, sir? Really?" Myra said.

"On that, I believe him. Anyway, it would be easy to check. We'll just ask the vicar. He, if no one else would have seen him."

"But he said he doesn't like to stand out from the crowd, likes to blend in."

"Really, Myra, sometimes I wonder about your gullibility. Duncan Farlowe is a rampant egotist. I doubt he's ever blended in his life, but, if you're not convinced, phone the vicar at St Peters and ask him if Farlowe was there on Sunday, but you'll be wasting your time. I'm sure the vicar will confirm his presence, and I'm equally sure that half the congregation will as well. I don't think Duncan Farlowe can live without an audience. Every breath he takes is a performance, and he expects applause for it."

"I will check though, sir."

"As you wish, Myra."

"Professor Strong, you wanted to see me?"

"Ah, yes, Chief Inspector. Something interesting in the toxicology report that I thought I should bring to your attention. Come through."

Strong picked up a clipboard, and carried it like a shield before him, as he pushed through the rubber doors into the mortuary. Jack and Myra followed him into the chilly room, their noses assailed by the harsh disinfectant smell designed to mask the unpleasant odours of death.

Dougie Marshall's corpse lay on a metal dissecting table, covered to the throat by a white sheet. The sheet preserved his modesty, but far more obscene was the wound to his throat, that looked like nothing more than a grinning red mouth.

Myra shuddered.

"Are you okay?" Jack said.

"I've seen worse," she said. "It's just this place. I'll never get used to it, no matter how many times I come here."

He fished in his pocket and produced a roll of *Polo* mints. He opened the roll and offered her a *mint with a hole.* "Try one of these," he said. "I find it helps."

She nodded her thanks, took one and popped it into her mouth, letting the cool peppermint vapours quell the incipient nausea that was making her head spin.

"Now," Strong said. "Dougie Marshall. The same wounds as that poor girl the other day, or so it would seem."

"Yes," said Jack. "You're having doubts?"

"Not that the poor boy is dead. It's just the manner of his passing I take issue with."

"I would have thought it was self-evident. The wound to the neck speaks volumes."

"Sometimes the loudest voices say the least," Strong said, looking down at the notes on his clipboard. "I saw the photos of the crime scene and I noticed something odd, which in turn made me give the body a thorough external examination. It took a lot of searching, but I found it in the end."

"Found what?"

"Let me show you." He walked across to the table and lifted the sheet, pulling it back to Marshall's waist. To the side of the table was a large magnifying glass on an articulated metal stand. He pulled the lens forward, and positioned it over the body, at the same time depressing a button at the base of the stand with the toe of his shoe. A hidden light set in the rim, framing the lens, burst into life, illuminating Dougie Marshall's arm and shoulder.

Strong adjusted the lens and beckoned Jack across. "There," he said, pointing to a slightly obscene tattoo of a Hawaiian hula dancer on Marshall's forearm. "Just below her belly button. Do you see it?"

Jack peered through the lens, wondering what it was he was supposed to be seeing. He was aware of Myra at his elbow. She too was looking through the lens, her face creased in concentration.

"I see it," she said excitedly in his ear, and pointed at the tattoo. "A little red dot," she said to Strong. "Right?"

Strong beamed delightedly. "Yes indeed. You have good eyesight, Constable."

"Where?" Jack said.

"There, sir," Myra said, lowering her finger so it was almost touching the body. "There, just above my fingernail."

Jack looked closer. "Yes, I see it. What is it?"

"A hypodermic needle puncture mark," Strong said. "Once I saw that I hurried the toxicology test through."

Jack looked at him quizzically.

"Sorry, I'm getting slightly ahead of myself. Let's go back to the photos. What did you notice about them?"

Jack shook his head, not knowing where Strong was going with this. "They were pretty similar to the photos of Dawn Peterson," he said.

"Similar, yes, but with a striking difference."

"Which was?"

"Both bodies were found in similar circumstances, one lying on a mattress, one on a bed. Both victims had been garrotted, their throats cut through by thin wire, their carotid arteries severed."

"Agreed."

"Then why was there such a discrepancy in the amounts of blood found at the scene?"

"I wasn't aware there was," Jack said. "Both crime scenes were pretty bloody."

"Yes, they were, but think about it for a moment, Chief Inspector. The girl was killed on an old mattress. A lot of her blood would have soaked into it. This chap, on the other hand, was killed on a bed – a bed covered with something that looked a lot like an eiderdown, and unless they've changed significantly since I bought the one for my bed, they have a rather shiny, silky finish. The fabric is of a much finer weave than that covering the mattress which, if my memory serves me correctly, was striped cotton ticking."

"That's right," Jack said, wishing Strong would get to the point, but also knowing the man well enough to appreciate that he loved the drama of detection, imagining himself as something of a Sherlock Holmes.

"Both materials have some water repelling qualities, but the eiderdown does the job much more efficiently. So, I asked myself, where were the pools of blood? In both instances the carotid arteries and jugular veins were severed, and both bodies had been lying dead for a similar amount of time, yet the quantity of blood in the young man's case was significantly less than that of the girl." Strong paused, watching their puzzled expressions, enjoying the moment. "This brings us back to the needle mark on the arm."

"Dougie Marshall took drugs. God knows what junk he injected into himself," Jack said.

"Oh, I totally agree with you," Strong said. "But junkies inject into their veins, to get the drugs into the bloodstream that much quicker. Look where the hula girl's belly button is. It's right above the brachioradialis muscle. If you flex that muscle you can make the girl do a hula dance."

Jack's patience finally evaporated. "Look, Professor, this is all very fascinating, but we're investigating a murder, not how Dougie Marshall made his tattoo dance."

A pained expression appeared on Strong's face. "I was coming to that. I was about to say that I think this chap was dead before he was garrotted. He had been injected with a massive quantity of magnesium sulphate, certainly enough to incapacitate him, and make him much easier to garrotte, but I think the magnesium sulphate killed him before the wire had a chance to do its grisly work."

"And where would our killer get such a massive quantity of magnesium sulphate?" Jack said sceptically.

"Probably from his local chemist. You can buy it over the counter," Strong said.

"Epsom salts!" Myra said.

"That's right, common or garden Epsom salts – absolutely lethal in sufficient quantities.

"Boswell House has boxes of the stuff in their dispensary," Myra said.

"Thank you, Professor. You've been a great help," Jack said, moving towards the doors.

"Happy to oblige. You'll have my report in the morning."

27 FRIDAY

A rather plain, dumpy-looking girl in a starched nurse's uniform greeted them at the reception desk. Jack flashed his warrant card. "We're here to see Miss Gerard," he said.

"I'll deal with this, Sara." Elise Gerard emerged from the office behind the desk. "I thought after yesterday's fiasco you wouldn't be bothering us for a while."

"Which shows just how wrong you can be," Myra said.

Elise clucked her tongue. "Come along to the office," she said, and strode off without waiting for a response.

She walked into her office, leaving the door open for them to follow, and sat down at the desk, drumming her fingers impatiently on the blotter. "Well, take a seat. Let's get this over with."

"Nobody seems very pleased to see us this morning," Myra said.

"Who can blame them?" Elise said. "Barging into people's lives and turning them upside down."

"Mr Farlowe didn't seem very happy to see us either," Myra continued, as if the woman hadn't spoken.

"I hope you set him straight about Sunday night. I don't know what he was thinking, telling you that we slept together."

"That was an unfortunate misunderstanding," Jack said.

"Then I'm expecting an apology."

"I apologise," Jack said.

Elise speared Myra with look.

"Oh, me too," she said.

"Very well. I accept." Elise sat back in her chair, a slightly smug smile playing on her lips.

Myra wiped it off with her next question. "What happened to you when you went back to Montmartre in 1938?"

Elise Gerard's face blanched. "Who told you about that?" she said. "Has Duncan been talking?"

"Mr Farlowe kept your secrets, Miss Gerard," Myra said. "That's why I'm asking you now."

Elise pulled a lace handkerchief from her sleeve, and dabbed the perspiration from her top lip "I swore I'd never talk about it," she said in a voice that was little more than a whisper.

"Unfortunately, circumstances change," Myra said. "It's time you did."

Jack was watching Myra closely, not really sure where she was going with this line of questioning, but he trusted her enough to let her continue.

"1938. So many years ago," Elise said, almost dreamily. She pulled open a drawer in her desk, and pulled out a glass, and a bottle of whisky, unscrewing the cap and pouring half an inch.

Jack opened his mouth to speak, but caught the slight shake of Myra's head. He sat back in his seat and watched Elise Gerard down the scotch in one gulp, and pour herself another one.

"I received a letter from home in the August of that year. It was from my younger brother, Pierre, writing to tell me that my mother was very sick, and I realised I'd have to go back to Montmartre to be with her."

She stared down into the whisky, as she swirled it around in the bottom of the glass.

"Pierre was only fifteen, a child, and I knew he couldn't be expected to deal with it. I spoke with Duncan, and he agreed I should go, and that we should let our career rest for a while, and I'm grateful to him to this day that he persuaded me to return to my family.

"When I arrived home, I was shocked at how sick my mother was. Consumption, and she'd had it for some time. My father was a baker, and my mother ran a small *pâtisserie*, just across the street from the *Moulin Rouge,* and mother's shop was very popular with some of the dancers.

"As a child, perhaps four or five, I'd watch the dancers come in, sometimes in their street clothes, sometimes in costume, and I was captivated. They seemed to inhabit a magical world, so gay and carefree, and I think it was during those early years that I started to dream about a life on the stage."

Elise seemed to be drifting into reverie. She sipped her drink and looked across the desk at Myra,

"Please go on," Myra said encouragingly. "You were saying that your mother was very sick."

"Consumption, yes. I could tell she was nearing the end. Pierre was doing his best to keep the *pâtisserie* going, for my father's sake, but he was finding it impossible to do that, and to give my mother the care that she needed. So, I decided to sacrifice my career, and devote all my time to my family. I called Duncan, who was staying with family of his own in Geneva, to tell him of my decision, and he agreed that it would be for the best, and that we would stay in touch so, that if circumstances ever changed, we would get back together. Circumstances did change, but in a way we could never have foreseen."

She downed her drink, and reached for the bottle again, but hesitated, and dropped her hand to her lap.

"It's the smell of the tank fuel that I remember so well. Gasoline – choking, sickly. The smell of oppression and tyranny. Eventually they'd come into the shop. Nazi uniforms and jack boots, instead of ostrich feathers and sequins. The dancers and showgirls stayed away, and we had to be polite to our goose-stepping overlords." Bitterness dripped from her words.

"For my father it was the end. He'd survived the death of my mother, but he couldn't stand the sense of helplessness he felt, having to stand and do nothing while his country was raped. Drink, pastis, was his escape, and he escaped often. Fortunately he had trained Pierre to take over the bakery, should anything happen to him, and my brother was finding it a full time job just to keep the *pâtisserie* open. I did what I could, but I was little more than a shop girl by that time, so had to ensure our customers were happy.

"In 1944 we were just getting by. I had joined my father on his daily secret escapes, and I was drinking more and more. Living in a drunken haze made the unwelcome attentions of gutter-rough soldiers more tolerable somehow. I was doing what I had to do, just to survive.

"They came for me one night in July of that year. A dozen of them, some I had called customers, some I had called friends, now they were nothing more than a baying mob, out to punish me for that they called, *collaboration horizontale*.

"They cut off my beautiful hair – shaved me down to the scalp and left me in the street like a whipped dog. Pierre found me the next morning, huddled in the doorway of the *patisserie,* and took me inside.

"I made a sort of recovery, but something inside me died that night. We closed down the shop, and I stayed in the house, out of sight, until my hair had grown back to a short, mousy shag. Then I would go out, but only at night, and with my head covered by a shawl. I'd stand outside the *Moulin Rouge* and try to relive those childhood dreams, and to recall those beautiful days in England, touring the halls with Duncan.

"It was thoughts of those days that sustained me until the Nazis were defeated, and France was free. And it was Duncan who once again stepped into my life and rescued me. He took me back to England with him, and for a while we tried to breathe some life into our career, but times had changed, and things had moved on.

"The world of musical theatre and Variety was quietly dying, and we no longer fitted in with the nudie revues, and off-colour comics. It was time to retire.

"Duncan had made money in the years we'd been apart, so when he suggested opening Boswell House as a home for retired theatrical artistes, I supported him, offering to run the home for him while he concentrated on his other businesses."

She swallowed the rest of her whisky, lifted the bottle, and screwed the cap on tightly, before putting it back on the desk.

"So there you are. You see before you the ghost of the child who stood at the window of her parent's *patisserie,* and dreamed of gracing the stage of the *Moulin Rouge.* Do you like what you see?"

Myra sat back in her chair and clapped her hands slowly. "Oh, very good, Miss Gerard. Oscar-worthy acting. Bette Davis couldn't have done it better. How many performances of that one have you given over the years?"

Jack looked at her sharply.

Myra ignored him and settled in her seat. "Now, I'll tell the chief inspector here what really happened."

Elise glared at her.

"I must say, sir, she paints a very convincing story of a poor girl who sacrificed fame and fortune to care for her family. Unfortunately, ninety per cent of her saga was total fiction, but with just enough truth dropped in to make it appear credible." She stared frankly at Elise. "The part about the hair was a nice touch, guaranteed to gain our sympathy, but that's probably because it was one of the more truthful parts. You *were* hauled from your house, and branded a collaborator, because that was exactly what you were."

Elise Gerard's gaze had hardened into something resembling pure hatred.

"It was true that you were born in Montmartre, but your father was never a baker." She turned to Jack. "He was a banker, sir, with an office in Paris, a very rich man by all accounts, and her mother was the doyen of Montmatre society, who hosted parties where the great and the good would come to fawn, and curry favour with the powerful Girouds – Elise's real name, sir – and little Elise would be paraded before them and encouraged to sing. Quite the little Shirley Temple." Myra pulled her notebook from her handbag and flipped it open.

"As we know, the Germans invaded France, but, far from Nazi occupation driving your father to drink, he'd already made preparations for it back in the mid-thirties, and embraced them with open arms, seeing the coming conflict as a way to make even more money than he had already. Your mother, with your father's blessing, became a whore for German high command as early as 1936.

"The reason you were summoned home in '38 was not because of her ill health, but because your father realized your mother's charms were beginning to fade, and he needed to install a newer model to replace her, in order to keep his Nazi paymasters sweet, and who better to take her place her than her beautiful, talented daughter."

"This is slander," Elise Gerard said, rising from her seat in outrage.

"Since when was the truth slanderous?" Myra said. She turned to Jack again. "All these facts are verifiable, sir."

"Sit down, Miss Gerard. Carry on, Myra," Jack said gruffly.

Elise resumed her seat, and reached for the bottle again, removing the cap this time, and pouring more scotch into her glass.

"There was a particular German officer that meant more to you than the others: Major Otto Müller," Myra continued. "*Sturmbannführer* Müller was a wealthy man in his own right, and he set you up in a *pied-à-terre* in Paris, so he could guarantee your exclusivity – his songbird in her gilded cage.

"What was it Elise? Boredom? Or did you just miss the limelight – being the centre of attention? Because the arrangement didn't last, and in 1944 you left your Major, and returned to Montmartre to live with your parents. But you miscalculated badly, didn't you? By the time you returned the Resistance already had a strong presence in your hometown, and they weren't going to allow a family of Nazi sympathisers to live in their midst with total impunity.

"Later that year, your father was assassinated on his way to a meeting with his paymasters, and both you and your mother were dragged screaming from the house, and punished for your *collaboration horizontale.*

"I don't know how he did it, but Duncan Farlowe came to your rescue, and smuggled you out of France, but any hopes of restarting your career were dashed when rumours about how you spent your time in France started circulating within your business. You effectively became a pariah amongst the theatre owners in this country – many of them Jewish – and your name was mud. You had no alternative but to disappear from view, which is exactly what you did, resurfacing some years later, peddling the tale you just gave us here today, and setting up Boswell House to demonstrate what a thoroughly good egg you were.

"But we all know now what a crock that was. When did the residents start to irritate you so much that you began drugging them to keep them quiet, and out of your hair?"

Elise downed the rest of her whisky. "I'd like you to leave now," she said. "If you think you can prove any of your accusations then I challenge you to try."

"Oh, we will," Jack said. "I can assure you of that."

"Excellent work in there, Myra," Jack said, as he got into the car beside her.

"You can thank Archie Finch. He was the one who uncovered the truth about her. It was only the fear of being sued that meant he didn't go public with it."

"Why did she come up with all that guff about the *pâtisserie?*"

"Probably to excuse her weight gain. She certainly did pile on the pounds when she was in France."

"I must say, she *was* fairly convincing."

"What were you saying about *my* gullibility, sir?"

"*Touché,*" Jack said with a smile.

"Not that I blame you. She was very credible, but then she's had nearly fifteen years to perfect her story, and she's probably told it so often that she almost believes it herself. So much more palatable than the truth. I think it was Henry Pickles who called her conniving."

"He was right, but I don't have her in the frame for the murders. For those we're going to have to look further afield."

28 FRIDAY

"Mr Callum, it's Millicent Peterson. Thank you for returning Dawn's raincoat yesterday. My husband was touched by your kindness."

"That's quite all right," Jack said.

"Do you think you could you come back to the house today, only Wilfred's not here at the moment, and I was taking the opportunity to start clearing things out of Dawn's room, and I came upon some things I think you'll want to see."

"What would they be, Mrs Peterson?"

"Tablets. Lots of tablets, and a sheet of paper with names and numbers on it. Whether or not it's a list of people she was supplying the pills to I can't really say, but I thought you should see it."

"I'll be with you within the hour," Jack said.

He went down to the squad room. "Has anyone seen Myra?"

"In the canteen, having lunch," Helen Carter said, looking up from her typewriter.

"Damn," Jack muttered. He didn't want to interrupt her break. "Helen, can you spare an hour or two?"

"I'm just typing up a report. I'm sure it can wait a couple of hours."

"Good. Get your coat. We're off to Graveley."

*

Twenty-five minutes later they were pulling up outside the Peterson house.

Millicent Peterson answered at the first ring. "Come straight up," she said, turning and leading the way up the stairs.

Dawn's bedroom was fairly typical of a single, young woman's room. Pictures of film and pop stars adorned the walls, and a group of soft toys were clustered on the top of the bed by her pillow. There was a dressing table cluttered with pots of face cream, tubes of lipstick, eyebrow pencils, palates of eye shadow, plastic combs, a brush and two canisters of hair spray.

The scene was reminiscent of his daughters' rooms when they lived at home.

"They're in here." Millicent opened the door of a painted plywood wardrobe, the inside of the door plastered with black and white photographs cut from the pages of wrestling magazines. The images were of young men in swimming trunks, either posing to show off toned physiques, or trying to demonstrate how fierce and aggressive they were, their faces contorted into snarls.

Millicent dropped to her knees, and lifted out a cardboard shoebox. "Here," she said, handing the box to Jack.

He took it across to the bed, set it down on the pink candlewick bedspread, and lifted the lid, blowing through his teeth when he saw what the box contained.

There were a dozen polythene bags containing pills of various shapes and sizes. He lifted one with a hundred or more of the triangular blue tablets. "*Purple Hearts*," he said to Helen. "God knows what the others are for."

Tucked in the side of the box was a sheet of paper with *October 1960* written at the top. Beneath it was a list of over twenty names, each with a number by the side of it and, across the other side of the page, more numbers showing a price in pounds, shillings and pence.

"Quite the little entrepreneur wasn't she?" he said, and ran his finger down the line, making a quick calculation as he went. "And quite a successful one at that, if this was how much she was selling. For this month so far, she'd made in the region of forty-five pounds."

He flipped the paper over. Here there were more calculations, seeming to share the money out three ways. Sp = 25, Sa = 10, Da = 10. Total = 45.00.

Jack folded the paper and slipped it back in the box. "I'm afraid I'll v have to take this away with me," he said.

"That's all right. Wilf doesn't know about it," Millicent said.

"With your permission, I'd like to search the rest of the room."

"Be my guest. I doubt he'll be home for hours yet. He's taken to going out for long walks. I probably won't see him until it gets dark." She walked to the door. "I'll leave you to it," she said, and went out onto the landing, closing the door behind her.

"Where shall I start, sir?" Helen said.

"Check the dressing table, all the drawers. I'll see what else I can find in the wardrobe."

After ten minutes Helen said, "Sir, take a look at this."

Jack glanced round at her.

She was kneeling in front of a small chest of drawers. She had opened all the drawers, and had their contents stacked in piles on the floor beside her. She'd reached the last drawer, and was emptying it out onto the carpet.

Jack noticed that the newest pile consisted of many items still in their original packaging. Sheets, pillowcases, tablecloths, a small plastic box of cutlery, and random items of crockery, including a tea pot with matching milk jug and sugar bowl in an art deco design.

"Looks like Dawn was a romantic," he said. "That's her bottom drawer. She obviously saw herself getting married one day."

"Which was probably why she was saving so hard," Helen said, holding up a thick roll of bank notes.

Jack went across and she handed him the roll. "There must be a few hundred pounds here," he said. "Just how long had she been dealing in drugs?"

"Quite some time," Helen said, "if the money there's anything to go by."

Jack looked about the room. It looked like a bomb had hit it. "Okay. Helen. Let's put it all back tidily, and call it a day. I don't think we're likely to find anything else."

"I really don't think there's anywhere else to look, sir."

"No," he mused. "Good work."

"Ten minutes time, and you'll be back at your typewriter, finishing your report," Jack said as they drove back to the station.

"Back to the exciting world of St Patrick's High School, and the phantom tuck shop raider," Helen said. "Be still my beating heart."

Jack smiled. "Would you prefer to be doing Myra's job?"

"Good lord, no," Helen said. "I was only telling her the other day that I haven't got the patience to be a detective, or the dedication for that matter. I can see the attraction, but no, it's not for me."

"How do you see your career progressing then?"

"To be honest, I haven't given it much thought. I suppose I always saw my life following a fairly traditional pattern – marriage, kids, nice house, that kind of thing. I wouldn't want Myra's life."

"No, I can see that," Jack said. "Have you made your peace with Inspector Fuller yet?"

Helen stiffened. "Who told you about that...sir?"

Jack smiled. "Don't worry, Helen. I'm not going to lecture you about the perils of mixing personal relationships with work, but try to sort it out between you. I don't like disharmony in my team."

"Is that how you see me, sir, as part of your team?"

"Most definitely. You're not Myra, but then Myra's an anomaly, a one off, but you still have an important part to play – as important as Brian Peck and Harry Grant for instance. A team like ours relies on its foot soldiers. It can't function efficiently without them, and you're as important as any of them. Okay?"

"Yes, sir."

"Look, I know Eddie Fuller well, and I know he can be a bit of an arse sometimes, but I also know he has a great fondness for you, so try to get it sorted, for the sake of the team if nothing else."

"Yes, sir. Anything else, sir?"

"No. That's all for now."

Helen turned and stared out of the window, more to hide her blushes than anything else. *Sod you, Eddie,* she thought. *Sod you!*

The squad room was packed to capacity. Even Chief Superintendent Watkins had come down from his office, and was standing at the back of the room.

Jack walked to the front. "Constable Carter and I have just come back from Dawn Peterson's house, where we conducted a thorough search of the young woman's bedroom. In the course of the search we discovered a cache of drugs, several hundred individual tablets in number. I took them into the Stevenage lab on the way back here, and they visually identified uppers, downers, painkillers and various pills they could only guess at. They're running comprehensive tests on them all, and we should have the results within twenty-four hours. As well as the drugs, we also found bank notes to the value of four hundred and fifty pounds."

A series of low whistles echoed around the room.

Jack waited for the sounds of surprise to quieten down, and then continued. "Since Monday we've been treating the death of Dawn Peterson as the murder of an innocent girl who had fallen foul of circumstances beyond her control. As of now we shift emphasis. Dawn Peterson was no innocent. She was in fact someone who, while not being at its head, but was an important player in an ambitious and thoroughly ruthless gang, who distribute dangerous and illegal drugs to various levels of society."

He paused and took a sip of water.

"We also found a list, written in Dawn's hand, of over twenty names, who we think were her regular customers and, since we've been back, Helen has typed these names up, and is making copies for each of you. Some of the names you will recognise; some are names that have surfaced during this investigation; some, I can only say, surprised even me. I want you all to look through the list, and come to me with any ideas, or any knowledge you have of the names you think we might not know about. On the back of the Dawn's list were a group of initials and what looks like a breakdown of payments made to each. Helen has added those initials to the bottom of the list. Again, have a look at them. I'm open to any ideas that can put names to the initials."

Helen Carter came into the room, a sheaf of paper under her arm. "Make sure everyone has a copy, Helen. If anyone has any comments, I'll be in my office." Jack turned, and walked through the squad room.

"Oh, no," Myra said as he passed her. She was running her fingernail down the list. "Not Leo Keating."

"Keep going," Jack said. "And be prepared to be even more surprised."

"At least ten of the names are wrestlers, sir," Frank Lesser said, as he walked into Jack's office.

"Yes, I thought there'd be a high percentage of your lot. Any you know personally?"

"A couple, but I wouldn't go so far as to call them friends. They're both what we call blue-eyes."

"I've heard you use that term before," Jack said.

"Good guys, sir. White hats. Not the type who bend the rules."

"Unlike yourself."

Lesser grinned. "All part of the show, sir. The point is, because we operate at opposite ends of the spectrum, we rarely socialise, in case we get clocked by one of the fans. We don't want to shatter their illusions. That would never do."

"No, I suppose not."

"I can try and contact all the names on the list, if you think it will help."

Jack shook his head. "I think we'll just be muddying the waters of a case that seems to be getting murkier and more convoluted by the day. After finding the list and realising just what Dawn Peterson was up to, I'm having to rethink a lot of what this case is all about."

"Such as?"

"Such as Elise Gerard and Duncan Farlowe being on Dawn's list of customers. I can honestly say that I didn't see that coming. I started off believing them to be suspects in her killing. Now it seems pretty obvious that Elise was getting the extra *Mogadons* she was using to drug the residents of Boswell House from Dawn Peterson herself, and I'm guessing that Duncan Farlowe was using some kind of drug to pep up his sex drive. We know he likes them young. It's reasonable to assume that a man of his age was using some kind of chemical enhancement to either aid his libido, or his staying power, and Dawn was only too happy to supply him with the drugs he needed."

"The question is," Eddie Fuller said, as he came into the office, "where was Dawn getting all the drugs from?"

"A question that could be answered if we can find out who it was she spoke to when she phoned Boswell House on Sunday night."

"Well, if we discount Gerard and Farlowe, the only other two people on duty Sunday evening were Sara Clay and Rodney Barton, the two nurses," Fuller said.

"Could Sara Clay be the Sa on Dawn's list, where she seems to be dividing the loot?" Lesser said.

"She could be," Jack said. "If it *was* Sara Clay, then she was receiving the same cut as Dawn, and I think I met the girl this morning when I went to Boswell House. If we're assuming that whoever Dawn spoke to at Boswell House on Sunday, then drove to the print works and killed her, and then went on to kill Dougie Marshall the next day, then I can't think of a more unlikely suspect than Sara Clay. She's a small, overweight girl, who just wouldn't have the strength to take on Dawn, let alone a thug like Marshall, but I'm not ruling her out as Dawn's possible partner in crime."

"What about Rodney Barton?" Lesser said.

"Three sets of initials," Jack said. "Sp, Sa, and Da. No R's or B's. There might have been someone else there on Sunday apart from the nurses and the residents."

"So, you're discounting the residents as well as the nurses?" Lesser said.

"Yes," Jack said tiredly. "I'm dismissing the idea of a geriatric strangler, Frank. Somehow, I just can't see it, can you?"

Lesser shook his head. "I suppose not," he said.

"Let's pick this up in the morning," Jack said. "I really have had enough for one day."

29 FRIDAY

"Danny Hutchence is in Interview Room One, sir," Andy Brewer said, as Jack's foot hit the bottom stair.

"Hells bells," Jack said. "I forgot I'd asked for him to be picked up. Okay, Andy. Who's keeping him company?"

"Bob Meadows, sir."

"Okay. I'm just going to the canteen to get a coffee, and then I'll be along. So much for an early night."

He bumped into Eddie Fuller in the canteen, who was polishing off the remnants of one of Yvonne Morrison's legendary fry-ups.

"Not eating at home tonight, Eddie?" he said.

"Just a snack before I go," Fuller said. "Me and the boys are off to the pub when the shift ends. I'm just lining my stomach in preparation."

Jack ordered a coffee at the counter. It was pretty disgusting as beverages go, but preferable to Yvonne's tea, which was undrinkable. "I've got Danny Hutchence in the interview room. Do you want to sit in? He seemed quite intimidated by you last time. Your presence there might loosen his tongue."

Fuller mopped up egg yolk from his plate with a crust of bread and popped it into his mouth. "Sure," he said. "Don't you think he was telling us the truth last time?"

"I got the feeling that he was holding something back." Jack sat down at Fuller's table. "I'd like to try to shake something free. There was more to his relationship with Dawn than meets the eye."

"In what way?"

"When I saw her on Saturday, she was upset, and telling me that someone was going to kill her, and that someone was her *boyfriend*, Danny Hutchence. When I was driving her home she was in floods of tears, and I couldn't question her further. In the light of everything we've since learned about Dawn, I'm starting to think that, on Saturday, I became a pawn in a deceitful little game she was playing."

"What kind of game?"

"I'm not sure, Eddie, but think about it. Dawn spotted me at the Astoria and followed me as I was on my way back to the car. When I stopped walking, and confronted her, she was very quick to tell me that she went to school with Joanie, something I'm sure she thought would make me trust her, and to be honest it did have an effect. It might not have gained my trust as such, but it certainly made me feel more sympathetic towards her." Jack sipped his coffee and shuddered. "The thing is, when I mentioned her to Joanie, I got a whole other picture of Dawn Peterson than the one Dawn presented to me. *Dodgy Dawn*, Joanie and her friends called her, and by all accounts she was nothing but a tuppenny tart dispensing her sexual favours for a couple of cigarettes behind the bike sheds. As she's got older I think she's just raised the stakes from fags to drugs."

"But where does Danny fit into her game?" Fuller said.

"Danny was there, since the beginning. Joanie called him Dawn's pet. I'm willing to bet that he was totally aware of what she was like, but the fool was in love with her, and blinded himself to her shortcomings. It wouldn't surprise me if Danny threatened to expose her criminal activities."

"But he'd only make a threat like that if he thought he could get something back from Dawn, so what did he hope to get out of it?"

"Joanie put it rather well – *a chance to bask in her glory*," Jack said. "Instead of which Dawn brought me into the picture, and made up this story of Danny planning to kill her because of something she knew, hoping that I would lean heavily on the boy and, at the same time, distrust anything he was likely to say about her. The irony is that I think she was murdered because her killer thought she knew too much about the drugs racket, and couldn't trust her to keep her mouth shut."

"Phew!" Fuller said. "That's quite a theory."

"But it's the only one that's making any kind of sense to me."

"But why was Dougie Marshall killed?"

"Similar reasons. What did that Linden woman at the caravan park say Dougie shouted?"

"'She wasn't going to tell no one. You didn't have to kill her.'"

"That's right, so our killer made the mistake of pissing Dougie Marshall off as well. Let's face it, he's killed Dawn for fear of being exposed. What's another body along the way?"

"Are the stakes really that high, to warrant two murders?"

"Oh, I think this is far larger than Dawn and Dougie. You saw the amount of drugs Dawn had at her house, and that was just her working stock. I've a feeling that Dawn was just one of many, and whoever is behind this operation is making a fortune out of other people's misery."

"Then it's important that we find out who it is, and shut him down," Fuller said.

"I couldn't agree more. Finished?" Jack said, nodding at the empty plate. "Let's go and talk to Danny."

Danny Hutchence looked different again from when Jack last saw him. Dressed in smart, but casual clothes, wearing a navy-blue blazer, and with a yellow and purple striped scarf draped around his neck, he looked every inch a student, even down to his fair hair, that was styled neatly in what many young people were calling a 'college boy'.

He's a chameleon, Jack decided, *dressing and styling himself to fit in with whatever company he's keeping.*

When trying to impress Dawn, he was the greasy-haired, rock and roller, with flashy clothes and an ersatz Elvis sneer. At home he was the cardigan-wearing swot, guaranteed to make his mother think he was a good boy, and that butter wouldn't melt in his mouth. They'd picked him up today, direct from college, and here was the student Danny, wearing college colours, a neat hairstyle and tidy clothes. Danny Hutchence, Jack decided, was desperate to fit in, somewhere.

"Hello, Danny," he said. "Thanks for coming in to see us."

"It wasn't by choice," Hutchence said morosely. "I come out of college and there's a bloody great police car waiting for me at the gates. That's going to take some explaining on Monday."

"Well, I hope it won't be too much of an inconvenience for you." Jack smiled. "If you can just tell us in your own words, when did you become aware that Dawn Peterson was dealing in drugs?"

The question seemed to rock him in his seat. A dozen emotions flashed across his face in as many seconds, as if he was unable to decide what his reaction should be.

"I wasn't," he said, his face seeming to settle on a look of innocence.

Fuller sat forward in his seat, making Hutchence flinch. "Now, Danny, just tell us the truth. We know you were well aware of what she was doing."

Danny sagged in his seat, as all bravado deserted him. "Okay, okay. I knew what she'd got herself mixed up in. I realised earlier this year, when I first saw her with Dougie Marshall. The wrestler was bad enough…"

"Tommy Apollo?"

"Yeah, him, but I didn't think too much of it, because wrestling was just another one of her fantasies. Dougie Marshall was different. He was very bad news."

"What did you know about him?" Jack said.

"I knew he took drugs, and was a thoroughly nasty piece of work, but, in a way, that was typical for Dawn. She liked the dangerous ones."

"Would you care to elaborate on that?"

"Could I have a drink of water?"

Fuller left the room, and returned a minute later, handing Hutchence a glass. The boy took a long swallow.

"Even when we were kids she had some wild ideas. We'd play games where I would be some kind of outlaw, or a Gestapo officer, and she was the innocent damsel in distress. I would have to capture her, and tie her up and torture her – not really, only pretend – and she would get hysterical, but I knew she was enjoying it really, because she always wanted to play it. I think she liked being the victim, being dominated by some rough, dangerous type of bloke. Then, as we got older, her tastes got wilder and, I'm afraid I just wasn't able to keep up with her."

He took another sip of water, and set the glass down on the table.

"She started drawing on herself – making fake tattoos on her arms in Biro. Boy's names mostly, inside elaborate hearts. At first it was just random names, characters she'd seen on the telly, rough types, criminals in gangster films. But then she started watching the wrestling when they started showing that on TV, and suddenly she had some real bad guys she could fantasise about. The fake tattoos became more elaborate, and she even started using colours. I thought she would grow out of it eventually…but she never did, especially when she started working and earning money. Suddenly she could afford to go to the wrestling shows, and see the men she fancied in person. She started hanging around stage doors to collect autographs, and sometimes the wrestlers would invite her inside, and into their dressing rooms."

"And after that," Fuller said, "I suppose you never got a look in."

Hutchence gave a bitter laugh. "Look at me," he said. "Do I look like I could compare with a fourteen stone tattooed hunk?"

Fuller shook his head. "No, I suppose not."

"No, she started drifting away from me, and I was seeing her less and less. I'd see her at home sometimes, because we only lived up the street from each other, and she was at home a lot during the days, but the evenings were different. She was either working, or going to the wrestling."

"So, when were you first aware that she was involved with drugs?" Jack said, trying to bring the interview back to the original question.

"Probably about a year ago, when Marshall first started appearing at the house during the day. She wasn't going out with him or anything, because at that time she was in some kind of relationship with that Apollo bloke, but Marshall was at the house two or three times a week."

"Did you ever ask her what was going on with him?" Fuller said.

Hutchence nodded.

"And?"

"She laughed in my face. She said that Marshall was like all of them. That they wanted something that only she could provide."

"And you took that to be drugs?"

"No, I thought she was talking about sex. It was only later, when I saw her handing Marshall a small bag containing something, and him giving her money in return, that I realised."

"What was in the bag, Danny?" Jack said.

"Well, it wasn't bloody bulls-eyes, or pear-drops that's for sure."

"But how could you be sure it was drugs?"

"Because when I confronted her on it she told me it was something she got from work, and that I'd better mind my own business or Spider would do for me."

"Pardon?" Jack said.

"She said that Spider would do for me."

"Who was Spider?"

"Search me. Someone else she was involved with I suppose."

"Someone she worked with?"

Danny shook his head. "I don't know. I know she was scared of him though, and I thought, 'well done, Dawnie, you finally found your dangerous man. I hope you're happy.'"

Jack got to his feet. "Okay, Danny. That's all we need," he said.

Hutchence looked up at him. "That's it? I can go now?"

"Yes," Jack said. "Unless you can tell me who Spider is."

Hutchence shook his head. "Sorry."

"Just one more thing before you go" Jack said. "When you, as you say, confronted Dawn, and she made the threat about Spider, did you just leave it there, or did you make threats of your own?"

"What do you mean?"

"Did you threaten to expose her, report what she was doing, to the police perhaps?"

Hutchence gave a rueful smile. "Yeah," he said. "I did tell her that."

"What was her response?"

"She laughed at me again, and told me that she'd fix it so that the police would never believe me in a hundred years."

Jack nodded. "Okay, Danny. I'll get a car to take you home. I don't think we'll need to bother you again."

"She really was a calculating little bitch, wasn't she?" Fuller said once Hutchence had left the room.

"Yes, Eddie. I'm afraid she was," Jack said.

30 SATURDAY October 22ND 1960

"Myra, what have you managed to dig up on the Fallowell Institute?" Jack said, as he entered the squad room.

Myra pulled a manila folder from the back of the desk, and flipped it open. "Right, sir. I certainly opened up a can of worms when I started looking into that place," she said.

"Tell us what you have."

"It was opened in 1948 as a sanatorium, offering private treatment for people suffering from certain issues, mostly drug and alcohol dependence, but they also took in extreme cases of shell shock, and other mental issues."

"Who was behind it?"

"Two American brothers, sir. Samuel and Orville Fallowell. They came to Britain in '47, just after the American authorities closed down the facility they were running in California: the *Fallowell Sanatarium*."

"Sana*ta*rium, sana*to*rium?" Fuller said. "What's the difference?"

"None, apart from the fact that one's an American term, the other's English, but they mean the same. It's a place where you can go to convalesce after a chronic illness, or a place your family can send you if you're showing signs of mental disturbance."

"A nut house, in other words" Frank Lesser said.

"To put it bluntly, yes," Myra said. "But an expensive one. You have to be very wealthy to go there."

"But how did they get the licence to operate over here if the Yanks had shut them down?" Jack said.

Myra checked her notes. "It wasn't without some controversy, sir. Questions were asked in the House of Commons, and one MP put forward a bill to try to stop them, but certain members of the House of Lords managed to quash it, and the Fallowells were given leave to open it up. As I said, a can of worms."

"A nest of vipers more like, if politicians were involved," Fuller said. "Are the American brothers still running the show?"

"No. Orville died in '53 and his brother, Samuel a year later."

"So who runs it now?" Jack said.

"Ah," Myra said. "This is where it gets a little murky. A board of governors was set up after the first brother passed away, in case anything happened to Samuel, so that the *Institute* – as they rechristened it – would continue. They installed someone to run the place, Dr Oliver Cooper, but the governors continue to oversee the operation."

"Do we know who sits on the board?"

Myra shook her head. "I can't track them down, sir."

"But their names must be available somewhere, surely in some government or civil service file," Jack said.

"I did say, sir, that the objections to the place were quashed by members of the House of Lords. Powerful people, sir."

"But not above the law."

"No, but the Fallowell governors anonymity is protected by a mesh of misdirection, evasion and downright lies. I just can't penetrate it, and believe me, I've tried."

"We believe you, Myra."

"So it's one rule for the rich," Fuller said, "and another for everyone else."

"Tell me a time when it was different," Jack said.

"So what do we do next?" Fuller said. "If we believe that the Institute could be a possible source of the drugs, how do we go about proving it?"

"Well, that's where our case comes crashing down around our ears," Jack said. "We were looking at Fallowell because we knew Elise Gerard spent some time there, so it seemed possible that she had a contact there who was supplying her with the *Mogadon* she was using to drug the residents of Boswell House. We've since learned that Miss Gerard was also a customer of Dawn Peterson, so Elise could have been buying the *Mogadon* from her."

There was a thoughtful silence in the squad room broken by the appearance of Andy Brewer who entered the room, whistling chirpily.

"The report from Stevenage lab, sir," he said, handing a large brown envelope to Jack.

"Well, let's see what this tells us," he said, tearing open the envelope and pulling out several closely typed pages.

"*Purple Hearts, Disulfiram,* which, it says here, is a treatment for chronic alcoholism, as well as various amphetamines and barbiturates. Quite the pharmacy," Jack said.

"But no *Mogadon*?" Myra said.

"Not amongst the pills we found at Dawn's."

"Maybe Elise Gerard wasn't getting the pills from Dawn."

"Well, she was buying *something* from her." Jack said. "I suppose it could be the *Disulfiram*, if she was serious about giving up the booze," He shook his head. "No, that doesn't work. It says here that the drug induces copious vomiting. She was knocking back the scotch yesterday, and didn't retch once."

"Perhaps her supply had run out, and Dawn was killed before she could get it replenished," Myra said

"That's a possibility," Jack said. "So, by yesterday she knew she could jump off the wagon without throwing up all over us. Is that what you're suggesting?"

"Just a thought," Myra said.

"I think we should pay a visit to the Fallowell Institute, and have a word with this Doctor Cooper, don't you, Inspector?"

"I'll get my coat," Fuller said.

Jack phoned through to the front desk. "Andy, can you get Bob Meadows to meet us out the front. He's taking us to Cambridge."

"Yes, sir."

"And make sure he brings a map. Saturday in Cambridge can be a nightmare on the roads. Bloody bikes everywhere."

"Yes, sir."

Myra appeared at his desk. "Sir, could I come with you? Having looked into the place, I'd like the opportunity to actually see it."

"Of course," Jack said. "It never hurts to have another set of eyes. Meet us downstairs."

He picked up the phone and called Annie. "I could be home a little late this afternoon," he said.

"Not too late, I hope."

"Well, you have your lunch. Don't wait on me. I've got to go to Cambridge, so I might not be home until mid-afternoon."

"Not a problem," Annie said lightly. "I might pop into town and check out the new shoe shop that opened in Leys Avenue last week. I could do with another pair for the winter."

"Good idea."

"Oh, and just so you know, Rosie and Paul are dropping in later this afternoon."

"Twice in one week. We must be back in favour."

"She called a little while ago, and sounded a bit giddy. She said she had some news to tell us."

"Why didn't she tell you over the phone?"

"She said she wants to tell us both together."

"That sounds ominous."

Annie laughed. "No, she says it's *good* news. I think it could be something to do with that record."

"Let's hope that's all it is."

"Jack," she said warningly.

It was his turn to laugh. "Relax. I'm just pulling your leg."

"Ooh, you. Right, for that I'm going to buy two pairs of shoes. I'll see you later."

"See you, pet."

He grabbed his coat and hat, and went down to meet the others at the front of the station.

The Fallowell Institute stood in two or three acres of its own grounds in east Cambridge. From the imposing twin, wrought iron gates, they could look over the acreage, from the large kitchen garden off to the left, to the hard surface tennis courts out to the right, caged in by high chain link fences. Beyond the courts was a small wooded area, mostly conifers and poplars.

The house was large, and sheathed in ugly iron scaffolding that reached up to the roof, and was populated by a small team of men in overalls, engaged in some kind of building or renovation work, accompanied by the monotonous rumble of a bright yellow cement mixer, its large drum revolving, noisily mixing sand, cement and aggregate to feed the workers' almost insatiable needs.

As they walked through the large double doors, and let them swing shut behind them, the aural relief was palpable, the heavy doors blocking out the sounds of construction almost completely.

It was as if they had entered a high-class hotel. The foyer was spacious, with several low couches adjacent to smart coffee tables, their surfaces half-covered by neat piles of high-class glossy magazines, each table with its own sparkling cut glass ashtray.

The reception desk was polished oak, and ran the length of one wall, bare except for two latest-model cream-coloured telephones, and a green leather blotter. An electric bell push was mounted next to the blotter.

On the opposite wall was a framed colour photograph measuring four feet by two, above it a rectangular plaque bearing the legend in gold script, *The Fallowell Institute – helping you to help yourself.*

The photograph was of twenty of thirty people standing outside in the Institute's grounds, with the imposing building rising behind them, free of the scaffold cladding, revealing its impressive Victorian architecture rendered in yellow brick, with stern black-painted windows. The people in the photograph appeared to be gathered around a tall, good-looking man with swept back straight brown hair, and a neatly trimmed beard. He wore silver-framed glasses and he, like the others in the photo, was smiling broadly.

Jack walked across to the desk and pressed the button. Somewhere a bell chimed unobtrusively, and a door behind the desk opened.

The woman who stepped through the door looked to be in her twenties, neatly dressed in a grey suit, over a crisp white blouse, open at the throat to reveal a string of pearls that matched the earrings she wore. Her hair was brown and glossy, and secured neatly in a French pleat.

"Hello," she said, regarding each of them individually. "How may I help you?"

Jack introduced them, and said, "We would like to see Dr Cooper if that's possible."

The woman smiled. "Let me just ring through, and see if he's available to see you." She picked up one of the telephones, dialled a single number and waited.

"Hello, Ollie. It's Louise on the front desk. We have a delegation from Welwyn and Hatfield Police to see you. Are you free to receive them?" She waited again to get the answer, and then turned to Jack. "He'll be right out."

"Thank you," Jack said.

Louise smiled broadly, turned and disappeared into the back room.

Myra wandered across to the photograph. After a moment she looked back to Jack and Fuller, and beckoned them over.

"Isn't that the nurse from Boswell House?" she said, pointing to a jolly-looking girl in a nurse's uniform, sitting cross-legged at the front of the group.

"Sara Clay? I think you're right," Jack said, and scanned the faces in the photograph. "And that's Rodney Barton, the male nurse, standing at the back."

"And surely that's Veronica, Duncan Farlowe's secretary," Myra said, pointing to an attractive young woman, standing very close to the bearded man in the centre.

"Yes," a voice sounded behind them. "That's Veronica. Veronica Cooper, my daughter. Duncan poached her away from me last year, the old rogue, but then he could always spot talent. That was a staff photo taken eighteen months ago. A few of the faces have changed since then. My daughter for example."

31 SATURDAY

They all turned to see the tall, bearded man, smiling again, this time at them. He was leaning heavily on a black Malacca cane, but he extended a hand towards Jack. "Oliver Cooper, at your service," he said, a slight transatlantic twang to his voice.

"Chief Inspector Callum," Jack said, taking his hand. "And these are Detective Inspector Fuller, and Detective Constable Banks. You're American," he added.

"Indeed I am American, but I don't think it's considered a crime in your country these days."

Jack smiled. "No, no it's not."

"So why have the police come to visit me in such numbers?" Cooper said, still smiling.

"We're leading a team looking into two brutal slayings in our area, and we're hoping you may be able to help us in our inquiries."

"Great Heavens. Two killings you say? But that's terrible. I'm not sure how you think I can help, but I'll certainly do my best. Please come along to my office." He led the way, walking with a pronounced limp, and leaning heavily on his cane. At the desk he paused, and called out, "Lou, it looks like I'm going to be tied up for a while. Field my phone calls, will you?"

"Yes, Ollie. I'll see you're not disturbed," Louise's voice floated out from the room behind the desk.

"Thanks, Lou."

Cooper noticed the curious looks he was getting from Eddie Fuller and Myra. "We don't go in for a lot of formality

235

here at the Institute," he said. "All that stuffiness gets in the way of our work."

Oliver Cooper's office was large. but simply furnished. with a desk, a single filing cabinet, a red-velvet covered chaise longue, and three chrome-plated tubular chairs with black vinyl seats. The view from the large window was partially obscured by scaffolding, but beyond it they had a view of the tennis courts. and the two couples playing a game of mixed doubles.

"Please take a seat," Cooper said, settling in behind the desk.

When they were all seated, he said, "I won't be crass enough to ask who was killed, because you probably can't tell me, and it will save you the embarrassment of having to refuse."

"Thank you," Jack said. "Very thoughtful of you."

"I pride myself on being able to read situations," Cooper said. "I'm a doctor of psychology."

"So not a real medical doctor," Fuller said. He was beginning to find Cooper's bonhomie grating.

"Sorry to disappoint you," Cooper said to Fuller. "I'm that as well. The psychology doctorate came later."

"You said that your daughter is now working for Duncan Farlowe. Was that with your approval?" Myra asked.

"Oh, one hundred per cent," Cooper said. "Duncan's a great guy. I was kinda relieved when he offered Ronnie a job, miss her though I do, but I wanted her to experience different jobs and different working environments, rather than just the Institute. Not that's it's not a great place to work, but seeing your old man every day, as well as having to do his bidding, well…" He grimaced. "Not my idea of fun, I assure you."

"Nor hers, evidently," Myra said. "So, what *is* your relationship with Duncan Farlowe?"

"Duncan and the lovely Elise Gerard, his singing partner, are great friends of the Institute. You know, last year, just after that photo you saw in the foyer was taken, they hosted a charity gala event at the *Dominion Theatre* in your Tottenham Court Road, and the Institute was the beneficiary. It raised thousands, hence the scaffolding and workmen, and the very necessary repairs to the structure of the old building. It certainly saved us from having to track down new premises. That would have been a royal pain in the ass. Because this place is ideally suited to our needs."

"You say that Mr Farlowe and Miss Gerard hosted it?" Jack said.

"They did, and they brought in so many of their show business friends to help out. The place was packed to the rafters. One helluva show."

"I'm sorry I missed it," Jack said. "I understand that Elise Gerard was once a patient here."

For the first time since meeting him, the smile faltered on Cooper's lips. "Naughty, Chief Inspector," he said. "I think you've been reading the rumours printed in your awful tabloid newspapers."

"So there's no truth in them?"

Cooper smiled, but said nothing.

Jack decided to switch tack. "Are *Drinamyl* and *Disulfiram* some of the drugs you prescribe here?"

"*Drinamyl*...oh, you mean *Dexamyl* – that's what we call it back home – the *Purple Heart*, a very useful drug. Yes, we've used it on occasion, but it's not something I rely heavily on."

"It's problematic?"

Cooper nodded. "Two of your prime ministers took it," he said. "Anthony Eden is pretty common knowledge, but the great Winston Churchill started taking it after his first stroke in '53, so it used to be quite acceptable, but it's fallen out of favour recently, so no, I don't rely heavily on prescribing it."

"What about *Disulfiram*?"

"A sledgehammer to crack a nut, as you Brits say. That stuff can kill you. I prefer a more psychological approach to tackle alcoholism, though we have been known to try both but, as a general rule, I prefer not to use drugs if another form of treatment is practicable."

"But I assume you still keep them on the premises."

"Of course. It would be pretty damned stupid not to. Science has come a long way in the past twenty years. It would be a dereliction of my duty of care not to make the whole raft of treatments available to our guests."

"So, was Elise Gerard ever prescribed *Disulfiram* to tackle her alcohol problems?"

"Only briefly…dammit!" Cooper smiled. "Nicely played, Chief Inspector. Fifteen love, I think."

"This isn't a game, Dr Cooper. Two people suffered horrible deaths. One of them a young woman, not much older than twenty-one, and a young man not yet in his thirties, so I would appreciate it if you could be as candid with us as possible."

Cooper stared at his fingernails. "It's a matter of ethics," he said at last. "I am bound by doctor patient confidentiality."

"I appreciate that, but see if you can appreciate this. The young woman I mentioned had a cache of the drugs I just mentioned, as well as a few others, secreted in a shoe box in her bedroom wardrobe, and I know for a fact that she was selling on them for profit."

"Okay, I understand your problem, but I fail to understand how this involves the Fallowell Institute."

"Because our investigations have traced several different paths the girl could have taken to obtain the drugs she was selling, and unfortunately a number of them have led us here."

Shock registered on Cooper's face as a slight tightening of the laughter lines around his eyes. "Frankly, I'm surprised," he said, "and you think Elise Gerard was a signpost on one of those paths?"

"I'm afraid so," Jack said.

"Hell!"

"So, you have a dispensary here," Fuller said. "Somewhere that can be kept under lock and key. Only you've told us you don't go in for much formality here."

The smile had vanished completely now and Cooper glowered at Fuller. "You're taking my words, and twisting them to suit your own purposes," he said.

"But it would be nice to know, sir," Myra said, "that the dangerous drugs you have on the premises, can't fall into the wrong hands."

"Right!" Cooper snapped, using his cane to push himself to his feet. "Come along with me." He moved out from behind the desk. "You can see for yourselves." He hobbled quickly to the door, threw it open and looked back at the three of them still sitting at the desk. "Well? Come on then. You obviously won't be satisfied until I prove it to you."

He led them out of his office, across the foyer, and through another door that led to a short flight of steps. "Down there," he said, standing back to let them descend. "I'll follow, or I'll be slowing you up."

They found themselves at the foot of the stairs, facing a blank metal door that looked like it would be more at home in a bank. There was a combination lock, and a metal wheel about six inches across. Cooper reached them a minute later, and went immediately to the combination lock, turning it forwards and backwards with familiar ease, and then he spun the wheel and the door opened inwards.

"Who, apart for yourself, has the combination?" Jack said, as he stepped into the room beyond.

"Only people I trust implicitly. Senior members of staff, and a few of our governors."

"I'd like a list of names, sir." Jack said.

"Yes, and I'd like Sophia Loren to tuck me into bed every night, so it looks like we're both going to be disappointed."

"You're saying you won't give us the names of people who know the combination, sir?" Fuller said.

"Not exactly," Cooper said. "I'll write you a list of the staff members who have access to the dispensary, but as for the governors, I'm afraid my hands are tied. When I signed the contract to take this position I also had to sign a confidentiality clause. The governors will only make themselves known at a time of their choosing, and at the moment they choose to remain anonymous."

"Don't you think that's a little odd, sir?" Fuller said.

"No, Inspector, I think it's *very* odd, but I am only a humble employee, and grateful to be able to act with almost total autonomy. If the boat's running smoothly, you don't rock it."

They looked about the room. To Fuller it looked very much like the dispensary at Boswell House, but larger and much better stocked.

There were three banks of shelves, and two large metal cabinets containing about twenty long narrow drawers, each one clearly labelled and arranged alphabetically. Jack found the drawer marked *Dexamyl* and turned to Cooper. "May I?"

"Be my guest."

He slid open the drawer, and inside were row after row of short, squat bottles with black plastic caps. He took one out. It was filled with the now familiar blue triangular tablets.

"Each drawer holds one hundred bottles. Each bottle, fifty pills," Cooper said.

"So if you had the inclination," Myra said, "you could take two pills from each bottle and have yourself quite a haul, and no one would really be any the wiser."

"Your constable has a devious mind, Chief Inspector," Cooper said.

"But she has a point," Fuller said. "Doesn't she?"

"I suppose she does," Cooper conceded. "Though why anyone would…"

"Could I put it to the test," Myra said.

Cooper looked at her with undisguised hostility. "Sure thing." There was a small stainless-steel table standing against the wall. The table had rubber casters, and it moved silently as Cooper pulled it over. "Be my guest," he said, handing her a pair of tweezers from his pocket.

Myra unscrewed a bottle, tipped the contents out onto the table, and began to count.

"...forty-six, forty-seven." She stopped counting. "May I try another bottle?"

Cooper remained tight lipped, but gestured resignedly at the drawer.

Myra repeated the process. "...forty-five, forty-six." She laid the tweezers down next to the pills.

"Perhaps you'll let me have that list, sir, of all those with the combination for this room," Jack said.

The colour had drained from Cooper's face. "Yes, very well," he said. "You'd better come back to my office."

"Before we leave here, sir," Jack said. "I don't see a drawer for *Mogadon*."

"*Nitrazipam* is not a drug we use here," Cooper said. "There are far more effective hypnotics that don't carry the risk of addiction."

Jack nodded. "I understand. Your office then."

"There are two names not on here," Jack said. "Sara Clay and Rodney Barton, yet they both appear in the photo outside."

"Clay and Barton both left us this year."

"To go and work at Boswell House."

"Yes, that's right," Cooper said.

"Between them, Farlowe and Gerard are pinching a lot of your staff," Fuller said.

"You have a suspicious mind, Inspector," Cooper said sourly.

"I'm paid to have a suspicious mind, sir. Did any of them know the combination to the dispensary?"

"You're all here chasing shadows," Cooper said. "Chasing shadows and casting aspersions, and in the case of my daughter, I find that highly offensive."

"I'm sure Inspector Fuller meant no offence, but, with respect, you haven't answered his question," Jack said.

"My daughter was employed here in an administrative capacity only, and Clay and Barton moved to Boswell House simply because it's closer to where they live, so there's no great conspiracy, and no, none of them knew the combination to the dispensary. Satisfied?"

"For now," Jack said. "For now."

32 SATURDAY

"The proper channels, Chief Inspector," Watkins said. "The proper channels!"

"But Henry Lane would have…"

"Chief Superintendent Lane is no longer with us, but I don't think even he would have sanctioned you taking your team on what was little more than a fishing expedition, and onto another constabulary's manor."

"But the evidence is compelling."

Watkins shook his head. "The evidence is circumstantial at best, and you know it."

They stood toe to toe in Chief Superintendent Watkins' office, the atmosphere icy.

"What chance is there of you forwarding my request for a court order to uncover the identities of the Fallowell governors?"

Watkins folded his arms. "On the evidence you've provided me with so far, I would say there's very little chance."

"You're not making my life easy," Jack said.

"It's not my lot in life to make my junior officers' lives easy, Chief Inspector. If you think you have the beginnings of a case, then make it."

"I thought I had."

"Then make a better one. Because if you want me to recommend to Chief Constable Cox, that he apply for what is little more than a snooping order, I'll need to take him more than what you're offering me. Am I clear?"

"Perfectly, sir," Jack said. "Is there anything else?"

Watkins looked at his watch. "No, that will be all. It's past lunchtime. I suggest you go home, and spend the remainder of the weekend working out a better way to approach this investigation. I will go home to ponder whether your actions today should result in disciplinary measures for both you and your team. Good day, Callum."

"I told you Watkins was a shit, sir," Frank Lesser said, as Jack got back to the squad room, and told the others the upshot of his meeting with the chief superintendent.

"It's like working with one hand tied behind your back," Myra said.

"Think of it as a challenge, Myra," Fuller said.

"Life's never easy," she said.

"Especially when you've got idiots like Watkins working against you," Lesser said.

"All right, that's enough. I share your disappointment, but we made great strides today, no matter what anyone says." Jack pulled on his overcoat. "I'm going home," he said. "If any of you have any ideas on what to try next, then bring them in with you on Monday. We'll start again then."

Paul Bolton's large, red Pontiac Silver Streak sat in the street outside the Callum's home. Jack pulled onto the drive, and switched off the engine. On the way home from the station he'd tried to lift his mood, but Watkins's obstinacy had soured his day. He took a couple of deep breaths before getting out of the car.

Annie met him at the door. "They're here," she said, her eyes glittering with excitement. "Eric and Gerry are in there too."

"And Joanie?"

"She's on her way. Avril's driving her, so they should be here any minute."

"She should have lessons, and take her test. She can't always rely on Avril being there as her taxi service."

Annie ignored him. "We'll have quite a houseful by the time we're finished," she said, "so I have a lamb hotpot in the oven, and there should be plenty to go round."

"Just as well." He kissed her briefly on the cheek, took off his coat, and hat, and hung them on the hallstand.

"In here," Annie said, urging him towards the front room door. "Go on in. I'll pour you a *Mackeson*."

The room was buzzing with conversation and music. Both Eric and Gerry were sitting on hard chairs, each with one foot perched on a small pile of books, classical guitars resting on their raised knees, as they played a simple, but tuneful duet. Rosie and Paul were occupying the settee, listening attentively. Rosie glanced up at him, and sketched a wave as he entered the room. She'd had her black hair cut short, close to her scalp since he saw her last, and he was alarmed at how much older it made her appear. His little girl had grown up in a blink of an eye, and it seemed that he'd missed it happening.

"Is that all I get?" he said to her during a pause in the music. "A wave?"

Rosie leapt from the settee, and scooted across to him, throwing her arms around his waist. "Sorry, dad. I was just captivated by the music. Eric is getting *so* good." She turned to Gerry. "No offence, Gerry, but we all know *you're* a musical genius, so you being good comes as no surprise. But you, Eric...You've come such a long way since the Vikings."

There was no malice in Rosie's tone, and Gerry took the remark in good faith. Jack was glad to see that whatever differences there had once been between the two girls seemed to be a thing of the past.

"The Vikings are still around," Eric said. "But we're moving on from skiffle and rock and roll. Gerry and I are writing our own songs now."

"Well, perhaps you can write one for me one day. I'm going to need them." Rosie disengaged herself from Jack, and went back to the settee.

"Here you are, pet," Annie said, handing Jack a foaming glass of stout.

"You're a lifesaver" he said, sipping it gratefully, and went to sit down on the settee. "Come on, you two, budge up. Hello, Paul, by the way."

"Jack." Paul inclined his head.

"You too, Gerry," Jack said. "The piece you were playing was beautiful."

Gerry Turner blushed. "Thank you. It's called *Malaguena*. I think it's Cuban," she said.

"Very pretty. So, Rosie, I'll bet you're bursting to tell us your news."

"Yes," Rosie began.

"Hey, wait for me," Joan said, as she burst through the door into the room, followed more slowly by Avril Kendall, her friend and boss.

"Lovely haircut, Rosie," Avril said.

"Vidal Sassoon," Rosie said, colouring slightly. "I'm sorry, Av. I should have come to you, but Arnie wanted me to have something special for my meeting with Decca, so he paid Bond Street prices, and took me there."

"Worth every penny," Joan said. "It looks sensational."

"But did Decca approve?" Jack said.

Rosie nodded her head, her face glowing pink. "They've offered me a contract."

Her announcement was met by momentary silence, and then the room exploded into a cacophony of shouted questions, yelled responses and excited chatter.

As the noise reached a crescendo, a shrill whistle blast silenced the hubbub.

Every face turned towards Jack, who was standing at the fireplace, his arm resting casually on the mantelpiece, his silver police whistle clenched between his teeth. When he had everyone's attention, he removed the whistle, and dropped it back into his pocket. "Right," he said. "If the rest of you don't mind, I'd like to hear what my youngest daughter has to say." He looked to Rosie. "Go ahead, love," he said.

*

"...so the deal is, I make five singles for them, with the option to make a long player if the songs are reasonably successful."

"And we keep the publishing rights," Paul said. "Which is almost unheard of in the music business."

"Who negotiated that for you?" Jack said.

It was Paul's turn to blush. "I did."

"Well done," Jack said.

"Is the publishing important?" Annie said.

"If you design something and patent it," Jack said, "the rights to the design belong to you, therefore you get paid if someone wants to make a copy of it. I think song publishing works pretty much the same way. Am I right, Paul?"

"Pretty much. If someone records a song that Rosie's written, she'll get a percentage."

"I say again, well done," Jack said. "May I see the contract?"

Paul fished in the pocket of his jacket, and produced a long manila envelope. He handed it to Jack. "It just needs you to counter-sign and then it's all systems go."

He opened the flap of the envelope, and extracted the contents – three pages of closely typed legalese, with room for signatures and not much else. He scanned the pages quickly before deciding that he was totally out of his depth. "I think I said to you I want this approved by a lawyer who specialises in contract law before I sign anything."

"Totally understand," Paul said.

"How long will that take, dad? Decca want me in the studio as soon as possible."

Jack smiled at her. "Give me a moment. I just have to make a phone call." He left the room, still clutching the contract, and went out to the hall. Seconds later they heard him dialling a number. "Percy, it's Jack Callum." They heard no more as Jack reached back, and pulled the door closed.

When he came into the front room a few minutes later, every head turned towards him expectantly.

"Well?" Annie said, looking anxiously from Jack to Rosie and back again.

"Percy Phillips has offered to look it over for us," he said.

"That's great, dad, but when?" Rosie said, unable to keep the anxiety from her voice.

"In about five minutes, I should think," he said. "Percy's a friend from my gardening club. He only lives two streets away." There was a ring at the doorbell. "And I expect that's him now." He turned, left the room, and went to answer the door.

"So it's all in order?" Jack said to the well-built man with the ruddy face and dirt under his fingernails. Dressed in scruffy clothes, and even scruffier shoes, Percy Phillips couldn't look less like an important solicitor, but couldn't look more, like a weekend gardener, if he tried.

"Yes, all in order. On balance a very fair contract compared to some I've seen. You were fortunate to hang onto the publishing. That's usually the first thing these companies want to get their hands on."

"That's thanks to young Paul here," Jack said.

"You represent Rosie?" Phillips asked.

"Informally, yes," Paul said.

Phillips pulled a face and shuddered. "That's a word I loathe. I've seen more court cases brought about by informal agreements than I can shake a stick at. I'd suggest that to protect both of you, you make it formal PDQ. If you like I can draft out a rough contract for your inspection by Monday."

"I can't pay you very much," Paul said. "I'm afraid I've sunk most of my money into Rosie's singing lessons and suchlike."

"Whoa!" Jack said. "You've been bankrolling Rosie?"

"She's been helping out with the money she earns at the record shop and her session work."

"Well, that stops now," Jack said.

"Sorry, what does that mean, dad." Rosie said fearfully.

"What it means is that from now on I'm giving you an allowance. I'll pay for your singing lessons, your clothes, even your haircuts – not that I'm paying Sassoon's exorbitant prices. You can go to Avril, or even Joanie, for a trim when you need one – and I'll meet Percy's costs, if that's all right with you, Percy?"

"As long as you don't try to pay me in begonia cuttings," Phillips said with a smile.

Rosie shook her head. "I'm sorry, dad, I can't let you do that. This is *my* dream, *my* ambition. I can't ask you and mum to go without just because I want to sing."

Jack looked at his daughter sternly. "Now, listen here, young lady, the case I'm currently investigating involves a singer, Elise Gerard, and singing was all she ever wanted to do, but due to circumstances, some of her own making, some not, she's turned her back on a successful career as a soprano, leaving it all behind her, and a more miserable, tragic character you wouldn't wish to meet. I'm not going to let you go down that road, so I'll help you achieve your dream in any way that I can, understand?"

Rosie's eyes were brimming with tears. "Yes, dad. Thank you," she said in a shaky voice.

"Then come and give your old man a hug."

"I think I'd better go before I start blubbing," Percy Phillips said.

"I'll see you out," Annie said, leading him from the room.

"You want to watch that husband of yours," Phillips said as they reached the front door. "I'm a hard-bitten contract lawyer with ice in his veins, and even I was beginning to thaw out in there. He's very persuasive."

"Oh, I know, Mr Phillips, I know."

"Well, I'll be off. Make sure you give that young man, Paul, my details and I'll sort him and your daughter out with a contract to protect both of them." Phillips opened the door and stepped out onto the front step. "If Jack is really in contact with Elise Gerard, can you ask him if he could get her autograph for me? I used to have quite a crush on her before the war – pictures on my wall, her records on the gramophone, the full nine yards. I'd really appreciate it."

Annie smiled. "I'll certainly mention it to him," she said.

"Thank you," he said. "You're a lucky woman, Mrs Callum. You've got a lovely family."

"I know that," she said. "But thank you anyway. It's nice to hear it from someone else occasionally. Sometimes you can lose sight of what's sitting right there under your nose."

"Amen to that," Phillips said, and trotted off down the path, whistling.

"Right," Jack said. "Let's get this contract signed." He spread it out on the coffee table, and produced a fountain pen from his pocket. He handed it to Rosie. "You first," he said.

Smiling, Rosie took the pen, and wrote her signature across the stamp half way down the third page. She replaced the cap and handed it back. "Your turn," she said.

Jack made a performance of unscrewing the pen cap, and bending over the contract with an elaborate bow.

He signed.

There was a loud pop, and something went flying through the air and bounced off the ceiling. They all turned.

Annie stood in the doorway, a bottle of champagne in her hand, vapour pouring from its uncorked neck like steam. "There are glasses in the cabinet behind you, Paul," she said.

"My pleasure, Annie."

33 MONDAY October 24TH 1960

"Did you have a good weekend, Myra?" Jack asked.

"It depends what you call good, sir," Myra said. "I went to church."

"You?" Eddie Fuller said in astonishment.

"Do you think I'm that much of a heathen, Inspector?" Myra said.

"I don't think you're that, Myra, but I never saw you as a God botherer either."

"Don't worry, sir, I won't be preaching sermons from my desk."

"You went to St Stephens to check out Duncan Farlowe's alibi," Jack said.

"I stuck my head around the door of that ecclesiastical establishment, yes, sir."

"And?"

"It was as you said, sir. Duncan Farlowe likes an audience."

"So, the vicar remembers him?"

"Not in the church so much as outside, after the service, when Farlowe was standing in the churchyard, signing autographs for his adoring fans, of which there were at least two. A pair of old biddies who couldn't get enough of him."

"You're kidding," Fuller said.

"I wish I was," Myra said. "And I dare say the vicar shares the sentiment. He was very sniffy about Farlowe's contribution to his weekly service. He made comments to the effect that his singing drowns out the rest of the congregation. He used words like raucous and foghorn. I didn't press him further."

Jack laughed. "Nice work, Myra. I appreciate you sacrificing your Sunday afternoon. I think we can safely cross Duncan Farlowe's name off the list. What about the rest of you? Any thoughts?"

"Maggie Linden said she heard a motorbike roaring away from Dougie Marshall's caravan," Fuller said. "Do either of the two nurses at Boswell House ride a motorbike?"

"I've met both of them," Jack said, "and neither of them strikes me as ton-up kids. Saying that, we need to speak to Sara Clay and Rodney Barton to see if either of them took the phone call from Dawn last Sunday, and we can ask them at the same time if either of them ride motorbikes."

"Another trip to Boswell House?" Myra said. "Elise Gerard is going to love us."

"After her last performance, I don't give a damn what Elise Gerard thinks one way or the other. I've decided that when we've caught the killer, we're going after her for drugging the residents, so Inspector, telephone Boswell House and ask to speak to Clay and Barton, and if they're not there today because they're working the night shift, pry their addresses out of Elise Gerard, pay them a visit at their homes and question them in situ. It's time we put more pressure on. I'm tired of everyone giving us the run-around."

"And you, guv?" Fuller said.

"I'm going to pay a visit to the doctor."

"Are you feeling poorly?" Myra said.

Jack shook his head. "I've arranged to see Barry Fenwick this morning. I want to see if he can shed any light on this whole drug supply problem."

"It's strange," Fuller said. "I've only ever met Fenwick in his capacity as the police doctor, looking at corpses and signing death certificates. I can't imagine going to see him with an ingrowing toenail."

"I understand he has quite a thriving practice in Buntingford," Jack said. "But I know what you mean. I can only imagine his bedside manner as being funereal. I'll let you know how it goes."

Barry Fenwick operated his practice from a four bedroomed detached house on Compton Avenue, a tree-lined road in the centre of Buntingford.

The house was double fronted, with bay windows flanking a neat red brick porch. Suspended in the centre of the porch was a white globe with the word, SURGERY, written across it. Jack pushed the front door and went inside.

The entrance hall had three doors leading from it. The area at the end of the hall was walled off, the wall half-glazed with frosted glass. There was an open hatch in the centre, through which Jack could see a vivacious middle-aged woman wearing a white lab coat, sitting at a desk surrounded by filing cabinets. She turned as he entered and flashed a welcoming smile.

"Hello," she said. "Do you have an appointment with Dr Fenwick?"

"Yes," he said. "Jack Callum. Ten thirty."

"Ah, you're the famous Jack Callum," the woman said, suddenly disappearing from view, only to appear a second later as she opened the nearest door and stuck her head out. "Elizabeth Fenwick. I'm Barry's wife, receptionist, chief cook and bottle washer. I've heard so much about you. It's a real pleasure to finally put a face to the name."

"The pleasure's mine," Jack said, extending a hand.

She took it, and shook it warmly. "Come through. Barry's upstairs. He's just taking a break before he goes out on his rounds."

Jack went through the door, and found himself in a short corridor that ended in a flight of carpeted stairs.

"Go on up," Elizabeth urged. "First right at the top of the stairs. He's expecting you."

"Thank you," Jack said, and climbed the stairs to meet Fenwick.

"Jack, good to see you," Fenwick said, rising from his armchair. "Did Lizzie offer you a cup of tea?"

"I'm fine, Barry. It's good of you to slot me into your busy day. I know you've got your rounds coming up."

Fenwick glanced at his watch. "I've got half an hour yet, and I don't think Gladys Crompton's constipation will be much affected if I'm a few minutes late. Grab a seat," He gestured to an armchair. "You were asking on the phone about how easy it would be to get hold of certain drugs. I take it this relates to the two most recent killings."

"I certainly does. I must admit this is relatively new to me. It's my first case where drugs have played a significant part in the investigation. Just how easy is to get your hands on such things as *Purple Hearts* and *Mogadon*?"

Fenwick settled back into his armchair. "Are those the major drugs involved here?"

"They seem to be. There are others, but those are the two the case seems to revolve around."

Fenwick frowned. "Then I'm sorry, Jack, I'm going to have to disappoint you. The answer is that they're both pretty easy to get your hands on."

"Why is that?"

"Because they are very successful, and the drug companies are manufacturing them in their millions for worldwide distribution, so if a thousand, or even a hundred thousand go missing from the supply line, their absence is rarely noticed."

"That's appalling," Jack said.

"But a reality, I'm afraid. These companies are huge, multi-million dollar organizations, and they employ a small army of staff, hundreds of people, so it's impossible to check every one of them for their honesty and scruples, and, yes, hundreds of pills go missing every day, and the companies just write them off as natural wastage, and do nothing about it."

"No wonder our jobs are so difficult sometimes," Jack said.

"Come off it, Jack. It's the incompetence of others, and their moral shortcomings that keeps us in work. No one said it had to be easy." Fenwick crossed his legs. "Are you sure I can't get Lizzie to rustle up some refreshments?""

"Okay then, thanks. As long as I'm not holding you up."

"Mrs Crompton's constipation. Need I say more?" Fenwick said, jumped up from his chair, and crossed to the door. "Lizzie? Can we have some tea up here?" he called down the stairs.

"Chief cook and bottle washer, and tea-lady now, is it?" Elizabeth Fenwick called back.

"She loves me really," Fenwick said, grinning as he came and sat down again.

"Where would I go, if I wanted to get my hands on these drugs?" Jack said.

"That I couldn't tell you. Not specifically anyway, but there is a thriving black market out there, and it's been there for generations. If you know the right people, you can get your hands on just about anything, and remember, we're talking about the genuine article here. We haven't even touched on the counterfeit drugs, of which, believe me, there are thousands more."

"Counterfeit drugs?"

"Oh yes, there are some unscrupulous so and so's out there who buy up stocks of these drugs in their raw unprocessed state, and mix them with all manner of things to make then go further, thus increasing their profits tenfold."

"What kind of things do they mix them with?"

"Chalk is used a lot – common or garden calcium carbonate. Plaster of Paris is another, and those are the safer additives they use, but I've heard of heroin and cocaine being cut with strychnine and other nasties to make stocks go further."

Jack shook his head.

"Some of these black marketers even have their own factories set up in places like garages or garden sheds, and have even got access machines to make actual tablets. You looked shocked, Jack."

"I wasn't aware it was such big business."

"It's vast, and global. The demand for common prescription drugs like penicillin in countries like Africa is huge, and when that level of commerce is involved there are always those who will ride the wave, and make a tidy profit for themselves in whatever unscrupulous way they can."

"But I'm talking about a handful of *Purple Hearts* and *Mogadon* in Hertfordshire, not bloody Africa."

"It's the same business, Jack, just on a smaller scale."

The door opened, and Elizabeth came in carrying a tray. "Don't forget you're due to visit Gladys Crompton at eleven," she said to her husband.

"How could I forget such an exciting prospect, my sweet," Fenwick said.

"Do you know of any black-marketers around here?" Jack said, when they were alone.

"I could give you a couple of names," Fenwick said. "But it would be a pretty pointless exercise. Once they realise it's the police sniffing around they'll either scatter, never to be seen again, until they start up their next operation, or they'll close ranks and you won't get a peep out of them."

"Any suggestions?"

"I'm not going to tell you how to do your job, Jack, but I would go back to the people involved – the purchasers – and lean on them heavily until they give up their sources."

Jack nodded. "Yes, you're right, Barry. I was just hoping to save some time, but thanks, you've given me some fascinating insights, and made me realise just what we're up against."

"You're welcome. Drink your tea before it gets cold." He picked up his cup. "Spurs had a good result last week."

"Yes, four nil against Forest. I couldn't go. I went to the wrestling at Stevenage Astoria instead."

Fenwick laughed. "I'm sure you had your reasons."

"Oh, I did, Barry, don't worry. Given the choice I would have driven to Nottingham, and watched Spurs give the Forest a pasting, instead of watching two grown men dancing around a wrestling ring, pretending to hurt each other. The sacrifices I make for this job."

"You love it. You know you do."

Jack smiled and drank his tea.

He climbed into his Morris Oxford, and started the engine. The meeting with Fenwick had left him disappointed. Although the background information had opened his eyes to the problem of the drug trade, it brought him no further forward in discovering who might be behind the local distribution set up.

He sighed, and looked at his watch. It had just turned eleven. He would be back in time to do what he needed to get done today. A small detour on his way back to the station was not too difficult to justify to himself.

He started the car and set off towards Walkern. He would pay Dr Maitland a call and see if he would be more forthcoming than Fenwick, and at least point him in the right direction.

34 MONDAY

Rodney Barton lived in the top flat above the *Wimpy Bar* in the middle of Stevenage.

Fuller climbed the four flights of stone stairs, his appetite growing, and his patience eroding with each flight. His stomach growled.

"Are you hungry, guv?" Brian Peck said, bringing up the rear.

"It's my own fault," Fuller said. "I was running late this morning, so I skipped breakfast. The smell of hamburgers is making my mouth water."

"At this time of the morning?"

"'A hungry man will eat anything', my old man used to say."

"But *hamburgers*? All that grease."

"I suppose you had your *Shredded Wheat* this morning, like a good boy."

"*Weetabix*, actually, but yes, I have eaten today."

"Well, bully for you," Fuller said sourly. "Here we are, number 26." He pressed the bell.

Rodney Barton answered the door promptly, and stood staring at them for a good ten seconds before saying, "Yes?"

"Inspector Fuller and Constable Peck. Welwyn and Hatfield CID," Fuller said, noticing that the young man had a floral apron tied around his waist.

Barton suddenly became aware of Fuller's attention, and quickly untied the strings and pulled the apron off, screwing it into a ball and hurling it behind him. "Sorry. You caught me in the middle of cleaning my shoes. Boot polish is the absolute devil to get off of your clothes."

Peck stared down at his own polished shoes, and Fuller smiled indulgently. "May we come in, sir? We have a few questions we'd like to ask you, and we don't want to ask them out here."

Recognition finally dawned in Barton's eyes. "You two were at Boswell House on Thursday."

"Indeed we were, sir. May we come in?"

Barton seemed to shake himself. "Yes, yes of course." He turned and walked back into the flat, kicking the discarded apron into the corner.

He led them into a compact living room, with a chintz covered three-piece suite, a television that stood in the corner of the room on spindly wooden legs, and very little else in the way of furniture. The walls were covered with flower-patterned wallpaper, that clashed alarmingly with the upholstery, and an electric fire was fixed to one wall, one of its three bars glowing red, making the temperature in the room quite oppressive.

"Please, take a seat," Barton said, indicating the chairs, and went to sit down on the sofa. "Now what would you like to ask me? Is it about Dawn?"

"Yes," Fuller said. "There's a record of Miss Peterson calling Boswell House at six forty Sunday evening. Do you remember the call?"

Barton shook his head. "No, but then at six forty on Sunday evening I would have been on my rounds, so I wouldn't have heard the telephone. Sara must have taken it. Funny, she didn't say anything to me about Dawn phoning, and you would have thought she'd tell me if she knew Dawn wasn't coming in, and she didn't, you know?"

"No, sir. I wasn't aware of that fact." Fuller said. "Did you get on well with Miss Peterson?"

"Oh, yes. Dawn was a treasure."

"So we've been hearing."

"Well, she was, and don't let anyone tell you otherwise. All of our guests loved her and…"

"Do you ride a motorbike, sir?" Peck asked, cutting Barton off mid-gush.

"A motorbike?" Barton looked almost affronted. "What on earth would I do with a motorbike?"

"Ride it, sir?" Peck said. "To work?'"

"But I get the bus to work," Barton said.

"The eighty-three, sir? Only Miss Peterson used to take that one, and it only runs once on a Sunday evening, so you would have noticed if she wasn't on it," Peck said.

"I most certainly would have but, alas, I take the thirty-five. It's more direct, and doesn't pass through Graveley. I think that's where she lived."

"So," Fuller said. "You didn't take the phone call, you don't ride a motorbike, and you think Dawn Peterson was a treasure." Fuller looked at Peck. "I think we're finished here, Constable." He got to his feet. "Thank you, sir. That will be all for now."

"Are we finished?" Barton said, standing up and looking at his watch.

"For now," Fuller said.

"Right then," Barton said, walking out to the hallway, and scooping up his apron. "I'll get on with polishing my shoes then. Good day." He opened the door to let them out.

"Do you think he was a poof, sir," Peck asked, as they walked down the stairs.

"Whatever gave you that idea, Constable?"

"Well, the apron, the…" Peck caught Fuller's eye and stopped mid-sentence.

"Do you know, Brian, we'll make a detective out of you yet," Fuller said. "Come on, let's see if the *Wimpy's* serving yet. My stomach thinks my throat's been cut."

Peck winced.

"Sorry. Bad taste, in the circumstances."

The woman who opened the door to Myra and Helen looked like an older version of Sara Clay, although her blunt cut, pageboy hairstyle was a sandy grey instead of brown.

"Mrs Clay," Myra said. "We're here to see Sara."

Mrs Clay smiled benignly. "Oh, how lovely. Are you friends from work? Only she's not long been in, and she's taking a shower.

"Actually, no, Mrs Clay. We're with the police, and we'd like to ask Sara some questions."

The smile faltered. "The police, you say? Is it about that awful business with Dawn?"

"Your daughter, Mrs Clay?" Helen said.

"I told you. She's taking a shower." She glanced at the staircase.

"Do you think you could call up, and tell her we're here?" Myra said.

"It *is* about Dawn, isn't it? Well, what else could it be about?"

Helen started to tap her foot impatiently.

"If you could just give her a call," Myra said.

"I suppose I can see if she's out of the shower or not. Can't stand showers myself. I never feel clean after them. I prefer a good old-fashioned bath."

"Give me strength," Helen muttered, her teeth clenched.

"Mrs Clay?"

"Oh, yes. Come in. You can wait here for her to come down." She walked to the bottom of the stairs and called up. "Sara! People to see you! Police!"

Sara Clay appeared at the top of the stairs wrapped in a towel, her hair tied in a turban. "Did you say police?"

"Hello, Miss Clay," Myra said. "Myra Banks and Helen Carter, Welwyn and Hatfield Police."

"Here? To see me?"

"Just a few questions you may be able to help us with."

Sara's plump features moulded themselves into an expression of disbelief. "I doubt it," she said.

"You won't know unless you come down here to let us ask them."

"All right then. If I must."

"Thank you," Myra said, but the girl had disappeared.

A minute or so later she walked barefoot down the stairs, drying her hair with a hand towel. She was wearing a white Terrycloth robe, tied at the waist. It did nothing to flatter her, and Helen was put in mind of a walking, talking suet pudding.

"Come into the front room," Sara said. "Mum? Cup of tea, please."

"Yes, dear," Mrs Clay said, and scurried out to the kitchen.

The room was comfortably furnished with a modern blue-tiled fireplace, and a green velour settee.

"Make yourselves comfortable," Sara said, and went back to the doorway, poking her head out into the hall, calling, "and biscuits, Mum. Don't forget the biscuits."

She came back into the room and sat down on a hard chair, facing them. "Well, what do you want to ask me?" she said, her tone just shy of belligerent.

Helen took out her notebook, and rested it on her knees, her pencil poised over the open page.

"A telephone call was made to Boswell House early on Sunday evening," Myra said. "The call was from Dawn Peterson. Did you take the call?"

"Yes," Sara said. "Is that it?"

Myra smiled. "Not quite. What was the nature of the call?"

"Just Dawn saying that she wouldn't be coming in."

"Is that all?"

"Well, there wasn't much to say after that. She'd let us down again. More work for Roddy and me."

"Roddy? Would that be Rodney Barton, the staff-nurse at Boswell House?" Helen said.

"That's right."

"How did Dawn seem?" Myra said. "Did she sound distressed, upset in any way?"

"She just sounded like Dawn, ringing in on the skive."

"You're saying you didn't believe her?" Helen said.

"No, *you're* saying I didn't believe her. Don't put words in my mouth." Sara was glaring at her hotly.

"If we can just calm down," Myra said. "Sara, what did you mean when you said that Dawn was ringing in *on the skive?*"

"Well, that was just Dawn. We were used to her putting everything else before the job. It just wasn't that important to her."

Mrs Clay bustled into the room clutching a tea tray, and a plate of bourbon cream biscuits. "Sorry, pet," she said to her daughter. "I couldn't help but overhear. But what you just told them is not what you told me she said."

"Mum," Sara said warningly.

Mrs Clay shook her head. "Well it wasn't, and I'll not having you telling fibs to the police."

Sara glared at her mother furiously.

"What did Dawn say, exactly?" Myra said.

"She said she'd missed the bus, and she couldn't get in, and could we cover for her if Miss Gerard asked where she was," Sara said, still glaring at her mother.

"Is that all?"

"Yes," Sara said sulkily.

"There you go again," Mrs Clay said. "What on earth's the matter with you today? That wasn't all she said. You haven't told them about the doctor."

"Mum! That's enough!"

"The doctor?" Myra said. "What doctor?"

"Why that lovely Dr Maitland, of course," Mrs Clay said. "They were all sweet on him, Sara, Dawn, even Rodney. I think they were all carrying a torch for him."

"Is your mum telling us the truth, Sara?"

Sara shook her head. "I didn't fancy him. He's old enough to be my dad."

"But Dawn did? Is that what you're saying?" Myra said.

"She liked his tattoos," Sara said. "She really had a thing about tattoos."

"What tattoos does Dr Maitland have, Sara?"

Sara shrugged. "I don't know. I never saw them. All I know is that he got them during the war, when he was a soldier."

"You still haven't told the officers what Dawn wanted you to do," Mrs Clay said.

"Well, Sara?"

"She wanted me to phone him, and ask him to pick her up. She said she was stranded out by the old printing works."

"Couldn't she phone him herself?" Helen said.

"She didn't have any more pennies. She'd used her emergency coins up phoning me."

"Why didn't she just phone him directly? Why call Boswell House?"

"She thought he'd be there. They used to meet there often, when she was on duty. They had a room. A private room."

"Okay, Sara. Dawn asked you to phone Dr Maitland, and to tell him she was stranded out by the old printing works. Did you?"

Sara nodded. "Dawn was a mate," she said.

35 MONDAY

Myra climbed into the squad car, picked up the radio, and called Dispatch. "Can you put me through to Chief Inspector Callum?"

"I'm sorry, Myra. Mr Callum's not in the station at the moment."

"Isn't he seeing Dr Fenwick this morning?" Helen said.

"Damn! Yes, he is, and he's driving his own car."

"So? Get Elaine to patch you through."

"He doesn't have a radio in his own car, but we need to speak to him." She thought for a moment. "Elaine," she said into the radio, "Mr Callum might be at Dr Fenwick's house. Can you see if you can reach him there?"

"I'll try, Myra. Stay on the line."

Myra drummed her fingers on the steering wheel as she waited. After a few minute's Elaine's voice crackled out of the speaker. "Sorry, he left there about five minutes ago."

"Damn! Damn! Damn!" Myra said. "Sorry, Elaine. Can you put me through to Inspector Fuller?"

Again, she waited, chewing her lip.

"Sorry, Myra. It's not your day today. He's not picking up."

"Jesus! I don't believe this," Myra said. She started the car.

"Where are we going?" Helen said.

"Walkern, to Maitland's house. We'll just have to deal with this ourselves."

Helen looked at Myra doubtfully.

"Don't look at me like that. We don't have a choice." She let in the clutch and pulled out into the traffic.

Eddie Fuller popped the last piece of burger into his mouth, and washed it down with a swig of coffee. "That's better," he said.

Brian Peck picked up a chip from his plate and bit off the end. His burger lay on his plate unappetizingly, half eaten and almost cold. "I'm done," he said. "Shouldn't we be getting back?"

"There's no rush," Fuller said, eyeing the half-eaten burger. "Are you going to finish that?"

"I've had enough."

"Waste not, want not," Fuller said and pulled Beck's plate towards him.

Jack drove down the lane towards Maitland's cottage, and pulled up outside. An old man was standing in the front garden, a pair of shears in his hands, attacking the hawthorn hedge that ran along one side of the path that snaked around to the back of the cottage.

"Hello," Jack called to him. "Is the doctor in?"

The old man stopped snipping, and laid down the shears on the grass, as if welcoming the interruption. "I saw him earlier," he said.

"Thanks." Jack approached the door, and pulled the bell.

"Terry won't hear that, and Doris is out shopping," the old man said. "Anyway, the door is unlocked. It just needs a push."

"Oh," Jack said, and made to push the door open.

The old man stretched out his hand. "Albert Cavendish," he said. "Doris is my sister. She's his housekeeper, and I come in from time to time to help with the odd jobs, and to do a spot of garden maintenance – like trimming this sodding thing."

"Will the doctor be back soon?"

"He hasn't gone out," Cavendish said. "I just said he won't hear the bell. Never does when he's out the back."

"Can I get around to the back using the path?"

"Aye...but he won't thank you for it. Hates being disturbed when he's working out there. Are you a friend of his?"

"Just an acquaintance."

"He's a good lad is Terry. One of the best."

"I'm sure," Jack said. "I'll take a chance and go round."

Albert Cavendish showed no sign of moving out his way to let him pass. "He's very popular in the village, being the doctor," he said. "He's a bit of a local hero."

"Really?"

"I could tell you stories."

Jack tried again to get past.

"A mate of mine served with him during the war, in the SOE. That's the Special Operations Executive."

"I know," Jack said, growing impatient.

"He told me he saw Terry take out three German guards one night, outside a research establishment, one by one, silently, without a sound. Crawling over the top of the building with those long limbs of his, dropping down behind them one at a time, a loop of cheese wire over their heads, and whoosh!" He mimed the action, clenching his fists and pulling them apart. "Never knew what hit them. That's what my mate said anyway. He said you never messed with Spider Maitland. He could take your head clean off with that garrotte of his."

"Excuse me," Jack said, pushing the old man out of the way, and racing around the path to the back of the house.

The garden was empty. There was no sign of Maitland, but on its stand, in the middle of a threadbare lawn, stood a gleaming BSA motorbike.

The back door hung open.

Cautiously, Jack approached, and peered inside. There was no sign of Maitland. He moved through the kitchen, beyond him was the living room, but there was no sign of the man in there either. He walked back out into the hall, and was about to climb the stairs, when there was a whisper of a breeze on the nape of his neck, and something heavy cracked against the back of his skull. There was a brief explosion of light in his brain, and then it was extinguished, and he pitched forward, as blackness swallowed him.

Fuller and Peck climbed into the Wolseley. Fuller reached for the radio to check for messages when Elaine Simmons' voice crackled out of the loud speaker. "Dispatch to Inspector Fuller. Come in Inspector Fuller."

He pressed the button on the radio. "Fuller here. Hello, Elaine."

"Patching you through," Elaine said, foregoing the pleasantries.

"Hello?" Helen Carter said.

"It's Inspector Fuller."

"Where have you *been*? We've been trying to get hold of you for ages."

"I don't have to account for my whereabouts to you, Constable Carter. You'd do well to remember…"

Myra came on the radio. "Shut up, Eddie and listen. It's Maitland. He's the killer."

"How do you know?"

"There's no time to explain," she said. "I'm driving over to Walkern now to confront him."

"Myra! Not without back up." He stared at the radio as she disconnected. "Damn!" he said. "Walkern, Brian. As quick as you like." As he reached out to switch on the bell, Peck stomped on the accelerator, and the car shot forward, throwing Fuller back in his seat, his hand pawing at empty air. "Damn it, Peck. Turn on the bell!"

Something was batting his cheek. Jack's eyelids opened to find himself staring into the cold blue eyes of Terence Maitland.

Maitland tapped him on the cheek again, and Jack made to lunge forward, but his wrists were tied to the arms of an antique oak carver, his ankles secured firmly to the legs. He was going nowhere.

"Ah, you're awake," Maitland said pleasantly. "Good."

"I know you killed them, Maitland," Jack said.

"Well I assumed as much when I heard you out the front talking to that old fool, Cavendish. Still he won't be gossiping so much now." He stood to one side to allow Jack a view of the front garden, where Albert Cavendish lay, sprawled on the ground, his garden shears buried up to their handles in his chest. "I won't pretend this has been an easy venture, Mr Callum, juggling, and trying to keep all the balls in the air."

"My heart bleeds for you," Jack said.

Maitland ignored him, and continued.

"I thought that having to deal with that quack Cooper and my fellow trustees on the Fallowell board, always sticking their idiot noses into my business was bad enough, but then to have that old fool, Albert Cavendish, giving away my wartime secrets to all and sundry, Dawn Peterson telling that unedifying lump, Sara Clay about our business venture – her loss, by the way. She had to start *paying* the blob, just to stop her opening her mouth and blabbing, and then there was that moron, Marshall." He rolled his eyes. "But that was my fault. Once I'd dispensed with Dawn's services, I thought I'd give him a chance to prove himself. He'd impressed Dawn with tales of his nefarious adventures, dealing in drugs, and making the police look stupid – it was either his stories or the tattoos. I tended to think it was the latter. That girl had a really strange attraction towards tattoos – a bit disturbing, I thought – but the sight of mine used to drive her wild in bed, so, lucky me."

Jack was watching him carefully. Maitland had torn the flex from a table-lamp, and was winding the ends around his fists and pulling the flex tight.

Maitland saw him watching. "I have to apologise. This won't be nearly as quick as the others, thanks to Marshall's bloody dog. It grabbed my garrotte from me when I was trying to clean it, and then the damned thing wouldn't let me take it back, and started barking loud enough to wake the dead. Not loud enough for its master though, unfortunately. Dougie Marshall was way beyond help. He was drugged up to the eyeballs when I got there. He was a junkie, so it was easy enough to get him to inject the magnesium sulphate into his arm and, boy, did that stuff make the hula girl dance. I only garrotted him as a safeguard, but in reality he was dead the first time Dawn met him. After that it was only a matter of time until I realised I'd have to kill him. Fat Sara is next. I'll do her once I've finished here."

Moving swiftly, he circled around and looped the flex over Jack's head, uncrossing his arms, and pulling it tight around his throat.

Jack jerked in his seat, but he was powerless to stop Maitland as he strained every muscle and every sinew to apply pressure, and for the second time that day, Jack saw lights before his eyes, but, gradually, one by one, they went out, and he lost consciousness.

36 MONDAY

"There's Mr Callum's car," Myra said, as they pulled up outside Maitland's cottage.

They were barely out of the car before they saw the grisly remains of Albert Cavendish. "Jesus H Christ!" Helen said, but Myra was already running at the door, and forcing it open.

She crashed through the door, and ran straight into Maitland's fist.

"Oh!" she gasped, as it thumped into her face, and she went down as if she'd been poleaxed.

Helen followed her, running into the cottage and pulling back her fist to take a wild swing at Maitland. He caught her wrist easily, twisting it up and back, snapping it like a dry twig. As her arm fell, to hang uselessly at her side, Maitland closed his hands around her throat, squeezing and lifting her until her feet left the floor.

In the lane outside came the sound of a police bell, jangling as it approached. Maitland glanced at Helen, then tossed her aside like a rag doll, and ran to the back door. He mounted the motorbike, pushed it off its stand, and kick-started it into life. He twisted the throttle, and roared down the path at the side of the house. He paused for a second, but couldn't ascertain from which direction the ringing was coming. Taking a chance, he turned left, and sped off along the lane.

He knew the blind bend in the road well, and knew he could make the turn without slowing down, so he twisted the throttle harder to increase his speed, took the turn, and crashed head-on with Fuller's Wolseley. The impact lifted him into the air, and he landed on the car's bonnet, sliding the length of it, to smash face-first through the windscreen.

Eddie Fuller slammed on the brakes, leapt from the car, and ran towards the cottage.

When he burst through the door, he couldn't appreciate what he was seeing. Jack was sitting in the centre of the room, tied to a chair, his eyes open but blinking rapidly, trying to focus. Myra was picking herself up slowly from the floor, blood dribbling from her smashed mouth. Helen was lying on her back in the middle of the hearthrug, her eyes staring glassily into space.

Numbly, Fuller walked across to where Helen was lying, crouched down beside her, and lifted her uninjured wrist, feeling for a pulse. He shook his head, refusing to believe it when he couldn't find one.

Myra untied Jack from the chair.

Brian Peck ran into the room. "Maitland's dead. Broken neck," he said, and was sick on the carpet.

Fuller still had hold of Helen's arm, and was tapping her wrist with his fingers. "Come on, Helen. Come on!"

Jack laid a hand on his shoulder. "Leave her, Eddie. You can't help her now."

Fuller shrugged him off violently. "No!" he shouted, tapping her wrist with his fingers again and again. "Come on. Helen! Come on!"

"Leave her, lad," Jack said sternly. "She's gone." He turned to Myra, grabbing her arm for support. "Let's get out of here," he said, and moved slowly from the cottage into the miserable October afternoon.

A fine drizzle was falling from the sky.

It matched his mood.

37 SATURDAY December 17TH 1960

"Coffee and two slices of toast please, Yvonne," Jack said.

Yvonne Morrison smiled. "We don't usually see you in the canteen this early in the day, Mr Callum. What have we done to deserve such an honour?"

"I came in to listen to the radio," he said.

"What's on?"

"*Saturday Club*. Can you turn it up?"

Yvonne reached up to the radio on the shelf, and twisted the knob.

"Hello, my name is Brian Matthew, and welcome to *Saturday Club*. An early Christmas present dropped onto my doormat this week. It's a beautiful new record by someone you may not be familiar with. Recently signed to the Decca label, and with a great future in front of her, this is Little Rosie Callum with a song she penned herself, *Try, Don't Say Goodbye*."

The introduction he was so familiar with flowed gently from the radio, and then Rosie's heart-breaking vocal refrain glided out over the music.

He looked up as Yvonne set his coffee up down on the Formica-topped table in front of him. "That's *your* girl, isn't it, Mr Callum?"

He swallowed a mouthful of coffee to dislodge the lump in his throat. "It certainly is."

"What a set of pipes. *And she wrote it?* You must be so very proud of her. Your girl, on national radio, on the BBC no less, can you imagine?"

"Yes, I am proud of her, Yvonne," Jack said, wiping a tear from his eye with the cuff of his jacket. "Very proud of her indeed."

If you enjoyed this book tell me, tell your friends and, if you have time, please leave a review on the site where you bought it

To purchase this and other titles by Len Maynard, as well other books written in collaboration with Michael Sims please visit Amazon.co.uk or Amazon.com and search for Maynard-Sims

Other DCI Jack Callum Mysteries

Three Monkeys
A Dangerous Life
Appetite for Evil
Deadly Ambitions
Sins of the Fathers

GLOSSARY

Words, phrases and slang terms used throughout the DCI
Jack Callum Mystery series

A

Addles your brain -	Messes with your head
All hands to the pumps -	Lots of help needed
Arse -	Ass

B

Babycham -	Cheap alternative to Champagne – perry made from pears.
Bakelite -	The first plastic made from phrenol and formaldehyde
Balloon's gone up -	There is an emergency situation
Balls up -	An error, a mistake
Banana boat -	Derogatory term for immigrants' transport to UK

Beat bobby -	Uniformed police officer who patrols the streets
Bells and whistles -	Top specifications
Bells ringing -	Equivalent of police sirens today
Belter -	It was a fantastic goal
Beverley Sisters -	English singing group loosely based on the Andrews Sisters
Billy Cotton's Bandshow -	A Saturday evening BBC variety television show
Billy Fury -	Popular rock and roll singer
Biscuits -	Cookies
Black Maria -	A police van
Bod -	Derogatory term – anonymous person
Brained himself -	Hit his own head against a wall or some other hard object
Bread and butter work -	Routine work
Brilliantine -	Highly scented men's hair oil

C

Calling in the cavalry -   Asking for reinforcements

Car park -   Parking lot

Castrol Oil -   Brand of engine oil lubricant

CID -   Criminal Investigation
                                  Division

Chris Barber -   Trombonist and band leader
                                  specializing in Traditional or
                                  Trad New Orleans jazz

Clobbered -   Hit hard

Copper -   Slang for policeman

Council Estate -   Social housing - projects

Crazy-paving -   Patio or path made from
                                  concrete slabs in an irregular
                                  pattern

Cuppa -   Cup of tea

Cut along to -   Go along to

D

Doormat -   Meek and submissive

Dressing down -   A telling off

E

Emergency police box -	Telephone box for police use
Excuse my French -	Sorry I cursed/swore

G

George Formby -	Toothy Lancashire comedian and banjolele player popular in the 1930's, 40's and 50's
Get you a brew -	Get you a cup of tea
Get your skates on -	Hurry up
Greenhouse -	Glazed building for raising plants and flowers
Go to the dogs -	Go to rack and ruin – be destroyed
Good collars -	Good arrests
Guv'nor -	The boss
Gymkhana -	Horse riding event
Gymslips -	Girls school uniform of bib and skirt design

H

Half of bitter -	Half pint of beer
Harold MacMillan -	British Prime Minister
Haversack -	Back pack, rucksack

Hendon -	North London based Police training school
Henry Cooper -	British Heavyweight boxing champion
His beat -	The area he patrols
Huge chip on her shoulder -	Resentful

I

I'm spitting nails -	Very angry
I-Spy -	Childs identification game

K

Keep it under your hat -	Keep it a secret
Keep mum about it -	Keep it a secret
Kip -	My bed, sleeping place
Knighted -	Awarded a British honour
Knock down Ginger	Childs prank of knocking on doors and running away
Knock his block off -	Punch him hard – block = head

L

Larry Parnes -	Music impresario
Late birds -	Go to bed at a late hour

Lavatory -	Restroom
Loo -	Toilet - John
Little hussy -	Girl of loose morals
Lonnie Donegan -	Scottish singer and guitarist – an early exponent of Skiffle
LSE -	London School of Economics – a London college

M

Mackeson -	A dark brown "stout" beer
Mantelpiece -	Shelf above a fireplace
Marmite or Bovril -	Savory yeast and beef sandwich spreads
Milkman -	Person who delivers milk to the house
Mosquito -	British fighter airplane used in WWII
Mooning over a boy -	Girl infatuated with someone

N

New Musical Express -	A weekly music newspaper

O

Off his chump -	Mad - crazy
Old toffee -	Lies
Off-license -	Shop selling alcohol
On the game -	Prostitution
Ovaltine -	A warm malted-milk beverage

P

Palais-	Dance hall
Pathé News and Pearl and Dean -	Short news film and advertising film shown before the main feature
Playing cards close to her chest -	Being coy with the truth
Polo mints -	Known elsewhere as Lifesavers
Pounding the beat -	Working as a uniformed offer on the streets
Pretty good going-over-	A thorough investigation
Prick -	Slang for penis

R

Rexine -	Faux-leather upholstery material
Rozzers -	Slang for policeman
Ructions -	Disagreements and arguments

S

S.P. -	Staring Price = the truth about what is being said
School Friend -	British comic-book aimed at young teenage girls
Settee -	Couch
Sissy -	Derogatory term for effeminacy
Sixpence -	English currency – one fortieth of a pound
Skiffle -	Style music popular in 1950's Britain
Slacks -	UK trousers, US pants
Sobranie	Black or pastel-coloured Russian cigarettes
Snapshots -	Photograph

Stick of rock -	A long thin candy often sold at the seaside
Sticking plaster -	Band Aid
Stitching me up -	"framing me"
Swot -	Nerd or geek

T

Tabard -	Apron worn for some work
Tart -	Woman with loose morals
Tart's boudoir -	A hooker's bedroom
Teddy boys -	Juvenile delinquents with a particular 'Faux Recency' dress code
Ten bob -	Ten shillings in English money pre-1971
Tizer -	Carbonated fruit-flavoured drink
Toc H -	An international Christian movement
Tommy Steele -	1950's and 60's pop singer and actor
Tugging my forelock - manner	Acting in a submissive

Tuppenny tart-	A cheap hooker
Two peas in a pod -	Two people very similar to each other
Two-way family favourites -	Popular BBC radio request program

V

Very snarled up -	Gridlocked traffic
Victor Sylvester -	1950's popular dancer and band-leader

W

Winkle-picker shoe -	Pointed male shoe
Woodbine -	A cheap brand of cigarettes made by W.D & H. O Wills
Workers Playtime -	Popular BBC radio variety show aimed at factory workers

Y

Yobs -	Thugs

For more details about Len Maynard and DCI Jack Callum visit

www.lenmaynard.co.uk
www.jackcallum.co.uk

or you can find me on Facebook

Photography by Kate Potton